D0807551

WHERE WATERS RUN NORTH

A Kent Stephenson Thriller

FRANK
MARTORANA

$\mathcal{V_v}$

VinChaRo Ventures

VinChaRo Ventures
3300 Judd Road
Cazenovia, NY 13035

vincharo.ventures@gmail.com

This book is a work of fiction. Names, characters, places, and incidents either are the products of the author's imagination or are used fictitiously, and any resemblance to actual events or persons, living or dead, is entirely coincidental.

ISBN: 978-0-99893-266-8 (print)
Library of Congress Control Number: 2022907924
ISBN: 978-0-99893-267-5 (ebook)

Cover designed and illustrated by Amanda and
Sebastian Martorana
Sebastianworks.com

Author photo by Rosemary Martorana

Printed in the United States of America

In memory of
James F. Seamon

ACKNOWLEDGMENTS

Countless friends and acquaintances, close and casual, have contributed to this book when, often unbeknownst to them, I picked their brains. I can't name them all without embarrassing errors of omission, but I do thank them deeply. There are some members of the team I just have to acknowledge because they contributed so much. If they had not, this book would never have been written, much less published. Marlene Westcott, you are truly the Word Wizard, to say nothing of a merciless critic. Sebastian and Amanda Martorana, the covers your design are works of art in themselves. Celia Johnson, your eye as an editor is amazing and I thank you for taking this book from rough to refined. Anajanette Lecher, thank you for providing me with insight into Iroquois life and customs so that, hopefully, this book is in no way disrespectful to Native Americans. Julie and Jeff Rubenstein and Ken Frehm, once again you did a stellar job critiquing and helping to polish the manuscript. Rosemary Martorana, you get special thanks for always smiling and showing great patience while solving my many logistics issues. Last, but never least, there is my wife, Ann Marie, who makes it possible for me to write.

PROLOGUE

IT MAKES A BIG DIFFERENCE WHERE RAINDROPS fall in Jefferson, New York. A few feet one way or the other determines whether they flow to the Atlantic Ocean by the northern route or the southern route. That is because Jefferson sits exactly at the peak of a geological ridge known as the Onondaga Escarpment. This natural wonder was formed millions of years ago by shifts in the earth's crust and, later, erosion of it. Once a craggy cliff with huge rock outcroppings, it's now a northerly slope, some places steep and some places gentle, running east and west and dividing New York State into two watersheds. Water flows either south through a series of creeks to the Susquehanna River then out to the Chesapeake Bay into the Atlantic, or north to the Chittenango River, Lake Ontario, then out the St. Lawrence River to the Atlantic.

When droplets land on Albany Street in Jefferson, they hesitate for just a fraction of a second deciding which way to flow—south or north— then off they go. Those that eventually travel north are the lucky ones. Their journey is unique; rivers that run north are far less common than those that run south.

The Iroquois, who inhabited the region since the beginning of time, recognized that the river was special for that reason. They named it Chittenango—*where waters run north*. The village of Jefferson lies along the shore of Heron Lake which is where the Chittenango originates as a small creek that is the outflow of Heron Lake. It gathers water through several tributaries on its journey north and is a sizeable river by the time it enters the Great Lake, Ontario.

For eons before Europeans arrived, the Chittenango River provided sustenance for the Iroquois in the form of Atlantic salmon. Every fall huge runs, millions of fish, swam upstream to spawn in shallow water where they were easily harvested by the Iroquois—an annual gift from The Creator.

Nowadays, most of the Indian land has been swallowed up by the westward progress of white men. So much damage was done to the river by pollution, dams, and commercial fishing that the Atlantic salmon have all died out. Today there are salmon in the Chittenango, yes, but they are *stockers*—Pacific salmon, a whole different species, introduced for the sport fishermen after it was too late for the native Atlantics.

The few Iroquois who remain live on a handful of small reservations throughout the state. The Owahgena, a tiny offshoot of the Onondaga Iroquois nation, live on a mostly forgotten postage stamp-size piece of land along the western shore of the Chittenango River as it descends the escarpment headed north out of Jefferson. To this day, they adhere to the traditional ways to a greater degree than their more progressive brethren. The Owahgena are to the Iroquois as the Amish are to mainstream America. For the Owahgena, the Chittenango River is sacred.

CHAPTER 1

Spring 1999

IT WAS A PERFECT MORNING. LUTE CRIMSHAW lumbered like an ol' bear in knee-deep water a few feet from shore. The current was light, so he turned to let the first rays of sunshine warm his broad shoulders. Moments like these reminded him of why the Owahgena considered the Chittenango River sacred. *To the east the sun was on the horizon sending an explosion of red and gold into the sky. The air held the scent of a promising day.* Lute had three nice brown trout in his creel. He needed four, two for himself and two for Otsi, his blue tick hound.

Lute heard a splash and an Indian curse. He turned just in time to see Jimmy Silverheel regain his balance, narrowly avoiding a cold dip.

Lute's features were coarse and worn from a lifetime of work in the weather. His jaw jutted like a bronze anvil. And even though his eyes were surrounded by deep creases, the humor in them was still there. He chuckled. "Keep your feet under you, buddy."

"The bottom is slippery through here, is all."

"Like you never waded this river before. How many have you got?"

"I'm moving over to the sandbar. Two."

"Good, because I have three and the one that just rose over there behind that rock is going to be number four."

Lute and Jimmy were Owahgena, born and raised on the reservation. They were in their forties now, best of friends, and had fished the Chittenango River their whole lives. They knew it like the back of their hands.

"Uh-huh," Jimmy said, without much faith.

Lute stripped line off his reel, preparing for a long cast. "I'm telling you."

Jimmy scowled and mumbled something like, "Big talker."

Lute lifted the tip of his fly rod and began a series of smooth, rhythmic casts. His line glistened as it sailed back and forth making S-curves over his head.

When Lute let the fly settle into a pool below a rock the size of a bushel basket, its touch-down was natural enough to fool any trout. There it sat, bobbing on the surface.

"I don't see much happening," Jimmy said, making a point.

"Keep watching."

Lute let the fly sit for one or two more heartbeats then he flipped his rod tip just enough to make the fly twitch. The water below it exploded as a brown trout rose for its last meal.

On shore, Otsi, who had been gnawing happily on a knucklebone that Lute had given him to keep him busy, lifted his head when he heard his master whoop.

"Here comes breakfast," Lute yelled over his shoulder to his dog.

Jimmy groused, "Total bull crap."

Both men laughed the way they had a hundred times before.

Lute played the fish, exaggerating his effort and telling Jimmy to watch how the fish was bending the rod tip. "This one's a fighter!"

When he had the fish close enough, he hooked his finger under a gill and lifted it for Jimmy to see.

"Two pounds, I'd say. Nice eating size. What do you think?"

"I've seen better."

"Come on," Lute said, trying to draw out a compliment.

"Forget it. Bragger."

Lute waded to the bank and held the trout down to Otsi's level. The black and white speckled hound brought his nose up and gave it a sniff, then wagged his tail.

"See there, Jimmy?" he teased his friend. "Otsi thinks it's a good fish."

Jimmy was a full fifty pounds smaller than Lute, and wiry. He cut through the water like a knife as he waded to shore. "One lies and the other swears to it. I'll clean the fish."

"Darn right, you will. That's the rule; he who catches the fewest fish, cleans them."

"Oh, right. It's been so long since you beat me. I forgot."

"Uh-huh. I'll start the fire."

Lute retrieved a thermos of coffee and a bag of corn muffins from his pickup and, within a half hour, the two men and Otsi were enjoying a riverside breakfast.

Lute knelt on the ground and picked through Otsi's fish removing as many bones as he could. "Better than that ol' knucklebone, right buddy? Chew carefully," he told the dog, fully aware that he was wasting his breath. "I may have missed a few of the bones."

As expected, Otsi ignored Lute's instructions and dove in.

Jimmy sat on his favorite stump. He let his eyes drift over the scene—blue morning light, mist on the water blurring the bridge in the distance. The only sounds were those of nature. He took in a deep breath then exhaled a contented sigh. "How long have we been doing this?"

"You've perched your ass on that stump off and on ever since we were old enough to fish. How long is that?"

"Longer than I want to think about." Jimmy went silent for another second, then said, "You can't beat it."

Lute brushed a blackfly off his ear. "I guess The Creator knew what He was doing."

Jimmy's eyes went to the opposite bank and his expression darkened. "The Euros wouldn't let anybody build a strip joint next door to one of their churches, right? So how come they can build that monstrosity next to our river? I mean, just look at their sign, for Chrisake. The fish on it makes me want to puke."

Lute smothered a laugh at his friend's analogy. He knew without looking that Jimmy was staring at the construction site on the far bank, the future Northern Lights Resort. And he knew Jimmy was serious. "Yeah, you're right."

"How are we going to stop them?"

"Pegger will figure something out," Lute said, his voice confident. Less so, he added, "I hope."

"He's your nephew, and I mean no disrespect. I think the world of Pegger, you know that. But he's one Indian against that whole pack of bean-counting white bastards. And he's running out of time."

"He's up to it."

Jimmy smacked a blackfly on his neck then flicked it off his fingertips. "Damn flies are nasty today." He stood and stretched, rolling his shoulders under his plaid flannel shirt. "I guess I'll head back," he said without much enthusiasm. "I've got things to do."

Lute nodded. He was pretty sure Jimmy didn't have much going on, but he didn't argue. "Otsi and I are right behind you. I'll catch up with you later at…"

Lute's words were cut off by the sound of a rifle. Then Jimmy's head exploded like a pumpkin at a target range. His body held upright for a second, then wilted to the ground.

The impossibility of the event paralyzed Lute. Confused, he stared at his friend for a long second, then he went into panic mode. He scrambled to cover behind the stump. Two more shots fired. One made a whistling sound as it flew over his head. He did not know where the other one went—until he heard Otsi cry out.

CHAPTER 2

IT WAS A PERFECT MORNING. KENT STEPHENSON'S daughter, Emily, and her riding instructor, Chris Mayer, were in the outdoor ring at Orchard Hill Farm. Spring weather in Central New York could be like a rain forest. That, combined with the brutal winters, made every nice day a gift not to be wasted indoors. *To the east the sun was on the horizon sending an explosion of red and gold into the sky. The air held the scent of a promising day.*

Emily was a tall, slender high schooler with blue eyes and freckles across the bridge of her nose. Her blonde hair was in a braid, as usual, to make it more manageable in a riding cap. She was as silly as any teen but, at the same time, she could be mature beyond her years, no doubt the consequence of having survived a crippling birth defect and a gunshot wound.

Chris was short and sinewy. Her skin had the healthy, leather-smoothness of one who has spent decades outdoors. Rarely was she seen in anything but riding breeches and boots.

This morning it was business as usual. Chris, on foot in the center of the ring, weaved through a maze of verticals, walls, oxers, and other jumps, watching Emily's every move and shouting instructions as Emily rode around the perimeter.

Emily was on Simpatico's Gift, son of the great racing Thoroughbred, Simpatico. He was the horse that everyone knew would carry Emily on her dream to ride in the Olympics. Emily and Sim were a team, the quintessential *two bodies, one mind.*

"Left lead, Emily," Chris said, in a voice that automatically projected after years of instructing in open spaces. "You're still too late. You need to get him onto his left lead a solid two strides sooner."

Emily, cantering Sim on the rail, gave Chris the slightest nod, her brow creased with determination. She was leaning forward to make the correction when a gunshot rang out. It came from the direction of the river and close enough that Sim jumped out of his skin. He landed six feet from the rail with Emily half out of the saddle and clinging to his neck like a monkey on its mother.

There were two more shots.

"What the. . .," Chris said. "Are you all right?"

Emily collected the reins and straightened her helmet. "I'm fine. Frickin' poachers! It's summer, for Pete's sake. Hunting season is not open."

"Yeah, well. Welcome to Upstate New York, where hunting season is always open. Until you get caught."

"We need more game wardens."

"We need fewer idiots." Chris skipped a beat of conversation, then said, "But there's a little bright side. It's good training for Sim. Getting startled like that will help him learn to keep calm around crazy fans and photographers. And…" Chris smiled broadly and pointed a finger directly at Emily, drawing the next words out of her. Emily joined in, laughing in anticipation of the last line. "…that's why you wear a helmet," they recited in unison. Chris had preached that mantra to Emily and a hundred other students each time there was a mishap.

"Let's try it again," Chris said. Emily and Sim re-took the rail and resumed their lesson.

Within seconds, Chris shouted, "Hold up!" And there was concern in her voice.

Emily knew why Chris had given the order, and she suddenly felt sick. She could feel what Chris had seen. Sim was limping on his front leg. She slid to the ground. "Hey, man, are you all right?"

Emily ran her hand down Sim's leg, from shoulder to leg wrap, like she had seen her father do a thousand times. *You can tell as much with your hands as your eyes,* he often told her.

"Nothing too obvious," she said.

Chris took the reins from Emily. "Undo his wrap. Let's take a closer look."

Emily pulled the Velcro tab on the rundown bandage then unwound six feet of wrap and a sheet of cotton. She drew in air through pursed lips when she saw the cut.

"There it is." She pointed to Sim's foot.

There was a patch of bloody hair on the horse's pastern. When Emily touched it, he winced and pulled his foot away.

"Sorry, boy," she apologized. "Looks like he clipped himself when he sidestepped." She squatted for a closer look. "The one unprotected spot right between his wrap and his bell boot. How's that for bad luck?"

Chris craned her neck over Emily's shoulder. "Actually, it could have been a lot worse. It doesn't look like it's into his coronary band."

"Thank goodness he was wearing bell boots." Emily knew that even a slight injury to the sensitive ring of tissue that generates the hoof could cause permanent problems for any horse.

Chris gave Sim a gentle rub on the forehead. "That's it for today, obviously. Let's get some ice on it and wrap it. Then we can call your dad and see what he thinks."

Emily took back the reins. "I'm on it."

For a moment they stood in silence, looking at Sim's leg. Both women wrestled with thoughts of the many obstacles that lay between them and the Olympics.

It was during that lull that they heard the sirens approaching.

CHAPTER 3

IT WAS A PERFECT MORNING. DAVE MUDGE LET IT in through his bedroom window without lifting his head off the pillow. *To the east the sun was on the horizon sending an explosion of red and gold into the sky. The air held the scent of a promising day.*

He rolled onto his elbow. His alarm said 5:28 so he punched it off. What was two minutes? No need to wake the wife. He sat up and stretched. He'd gotten up at 5:30 every workday for—*let's see now, 1964 to 1999*—for the last thirty-five years. He didn't even need an alarm clock, really. Still, every night he set it.

He blinked the sleep out of his eyes and focused on a picture sitting on his nightstand—his newest grandson. It made him smile. Another fishing buddy. That made four.

He let Misty, their golden retriever, out and then fed her. He looked for his usual Cheerios, couldn't find any, so he settled for a bowl of Teenage Mutant Ninja Turtles, left over from the grandkids, while he skimmed the newspaper.

By 6:30, Dave was out the door and into his new-for-him, four-year-old pickup, lunch pail at his side. He had lived in the village of Jefferson most of his life and still enjoyed the early morning drive through town. At that hour it was all quiet, things just waking up. He made his usual stop at the convenience store, got his travel mug filled with coffee, and headed north out of town along the Chittenango River.

Dave drove a bulldozer, and any guy who dug holes and pushed dirt around for a living was bound to develop at least a casual interest in geology. For Dave it was more than casual. Over the years he'd read books, attended lectures at the local college, and dug up enough dirt in Central New York to become quite an expert on its geology.

He took great pride in the fact that Jefferson, New York sat smack dab at the top of Onondaga Escarpment, the mega-cliff pushed up by the glaciers. "'And what,' you ask, 'is the significance of that?'" he would say to anyone willing to listen. "It is where the water changes direction."

Whaaaat?

"That's why our river is special." Sadly, most people didn't get it or didn't care.

He fumbled in the glove box, found the cassette tape he was after, and pushed it into the dashboard. For the next fifteen-minutes, he drove down Route 13 along the river, humming to Alan Jackson's latest hit, "Right on the Money." He fired up a cigarette, and generally enjoyed the peace and quiet. It would be the last serenity he would have for the next eight hours as he bounced and rolled to the roar of the big machine he operated.

His mind was a million miles away as he passed the bridge that crossed over the river to the reservation side. Just beyond that, he arrived at the Northern Lights construction site. He turned onto the temporary road, snaked his way through an assortment of colossal digging and earth-moving machines, and stopped in a makeshift parking area for the workers. It was empty. As usual, he was the first to arrive.

He scowled at the huge billboard that dominated the site. Across the center of it, a clownish, googly-eyed fish that looked more like a Disney cartoon character than a real fish jumped happily out of water that was too blue against a background that was too yellow. Bold letters shouted: COMING SOON, NORTHERN LIGHTS RESORT. MORE FISH, MORE FUN. Dave figured it would have served better as an ad for a Florida condo complex. Worst of all, the billboard blocked the view of the river. But, by nosing his truck into just the right spot, at just the right angle, he could still see a pretty good section of the water. He stared at it through the windshield, sipped his coffee, and watched the first rays of sun sparkle off the ripples as they drifted past. He thought a lot lately; with his retirement coming soon, would his knowledge of the history and geology of the area dry up in his brain like the rest of his body? He was pondering that when something happened that was not part of his daily routine.

Out of the corner of his eye, Dave saw a small child step out from the shadow of the billboard a few paces away—a little girl.

She just stared up at him.

Surprised, he swiveled his head around looking for the grown-up he assumed he must have missed. He didn't see a soul.

He looked back at the child who was still staring at him, not moving, but not showing any indication of distress.

"What the…" he mumbled and climbed out of his truck.

He moved slowly, not wanting to frighten the child, and squatted in front of her.She studied him for a brief moment, then broke into a broad smile. Her perfect row of tiny white teeth glowed in the early light.

He guessed her to be about two, maybe three, same age as his middle granddaughter. Her hair was jet black and straight, cut short, and her skin was light brown. Her eyes were darker brown but twinkled to match her smile. She had on a pink hooded sweatshirt, blue jeans, and tiny sneakers. To Dave, she was as cute as a kitten.

She was clinging to a tattered stuffed animal that he surmised might once have been a puppy. She didn't seem to be the least bit afraid.

Dave stood and scanned the lot again, expecting an adult to appear at any moment. Still nothing.

"Hey, there," he said to the child, in the friendliest tone he could muster.

She sent him back only the smile and a stare.

"What's your name?"

Nothing.

"Where's your Mommy?"

Blank.

He stood, hands on hips, perplexed. He looked around the work site for the third time, and this time, lit from the side by the low sun, he saw a woman, all alone, standing on the bridge.

That's got to be this kid's mother. He breathed a sigh of relief.

CHAPTER 4

IT WAS A PERFECT MORNING. KENT STEPHENSON was sitting on a wrought iron loveseat next to a grave in the Matson Cemetery. He was alone except for his redbone hound, Lucinda. *To the east the sun was on the horizon sending an explosion of red and gold into the sky. The air held the scent of a promising day.*

The cemetery was a small parcel, maybe two acres total, cut out of the rolling rural landscape. It was surrounded by a stone fence that needed work. It contained less than a hundred mossy stones that leaned in all directions. Some dated back to the Revolutionary War. A driveway that was not much more than two tire tracks, circled through it.

It had always been one of Kent's favorite places. He loved its serenity and the way it blended with nature. For years, when he was doing veterinary calls to nearby farms, he and Lucinda, and whoever else was riding with him at the time, would hide out there for a lunch break. Each person would climb out of the mobile unit and find a stone canted at the perfect angle for a back rest and surrounded by a bed of myrtle to sit on. They would eat their bag lunches and chatter with one another about the topic of the day even though they might be several stones apart. Back then, the cemetery was a place of peace and comfort. Not anymore.

The name engraved on the headstone where Kent was sitting now read AUBREY LEA FAIRBANKS. It seemed like yesterday that his soulmate died. At Thanksgiving she mentioned that she had a stomach bug. They didn't think much of it. She died two days before Christmas. A form of cancer, gastric carcinoma, had spread through her beautiful body by the time they found it. He, his daughter, Emily, and Aubrey's son, Barry, had watched her starve to death, helpless to do anything about it. Tears welled in his eyes as he remembered.

Since Aubrey's passing, it had become his routine to start each day at the cemetery watching the first rays of sunshine illuminate her headstone. He could feel those rays warming his shoulders, but no amount of sun could warm the cold he felt in his heart.

He watched a fat gray squirrel descend the gnarled trunk of an ancient maple tree. Lucinda saw it, too. Her ears perked up. In the past, she would have darted after it like a rocket—it was great sport. But now she knew Kent needed her. Devotion trumped fun, so she let the little guy search for his breakfast in peace.

Kent stayed for a few more minutes, stroking Lucinda and wondering when the pain would stop. Finally, he stood and dusted off the seat of his pants. He inhaled and released a cleansing breath.

"Come on, girl. We've got an animal hospital to run."

CHAPTER 5

IT WAS A PERFECT MORNING. JODI CYR LIKED TO walk each day at sunrise when it was quiet and the blackflies were not yet out. She lived with her older brother, Lute, in his cabin on the reservation. And the time she spent strolling along the bank of the Chittenango River with Max, her Chihuahua, was her favorite part of the day. *To the east the sun was on the horizon sending an explosion of red and gold into the sky. The air held the scent of a promising day.*

Her expression was sullen, as always. Dark makeup applied heavier than necessary and smeared from the night before, made it worse. Even so, her natural beauty shown through. She was tall and slender, gifted with Native American features—dark eyes, smooth light brown skin, and black hair that glistened in a braid down her back. When she smiled, dimples tried to bring cheer but lost the battle against her sadness. Her V-neck tee shirt was a size too small and clung tight. Her body was nicely toned in spite of the way she treated it.

She walked early even though she went to bed late because she didn't sleep well. Nights brought back terrible memories that buzzed in her head like flies around a carcass. That was also why, if she would admit it to herself, she drank too much and hung in the bars around town till closing time. And, yes, it was why she made bad choices in men. None as bad as the first one, thank God, but still bad. By now you'd think she'd be able to get it right. Or, maybe she should give it up all together.

She clicked off the Walkman that she wore constantly and removed the tiny earphones. She lived in a self-imposed world of hard rock music. Like the booze and the bars, the crashing, screeching songs kept away the memory flies. Only in the serenity of the woods did she allow herself the luxury of quiet, the freedom to listen to her surroundings. She relished the time. She walked slowly, listening to the birds and the sounds of the river. Max, all of ten pounds, and a mass of black and tan vitality, led the way pulling on his leash trying to speed her up.

From the cabin, each day she and Max followed the woods path to the river, and then walked along it to the bridge. Max ranged ahead as far as he could stretch his leash, alternately putting his nose to the ground to smell something interesting or snapping his head to prick-eared attention in response to a rustle in the bushes. He constantly glanced back to be sure Jodi was okay. His tail was always pointed to the sky.

Jodi knew Max would love to be off lead, but she didn't dare. The woods were home to too many wild creatures, stray dogs, and even some cats that were bigger than he was. And Max did not back down from anybody or anything. He was his own worst enemy when it came to danger, plowing in headlong without fear, even against a foe that could eat him in one gulp. She allowed him the longest leash she could manage to keep untangled from the brush. That was the best she could do.

Jodi paused to listen to a pair of wrens planning their day. Their duet was a mix of cascading, whistling notes and throaty, bubbling rattles. It brought tears to her eyes. She would give anything to have their love of life.

She scolded herself for her emotions and wiped the tears away with the back of her hand. She started walking again, and when they reached the bridge, Max automatically turned, pulling Jodi onto it. He knew the routine as well as she, and she was so infuriatingly slow.

The bridge was a flat-decked concrete structure spanning the Chittenango River and connecting the Owahgena Reservation with the rest of the world. Built in the 1930s, it was a row of pylons stabbing into the water like massive gray teeth and supporting a road two lanes wide for traffic.

As always, Jodi stopped Max in the middle of the bridge. There was no traffic this time of day. For that matter, not more than a few dozen cars crossed the bridge all day. Without thinking, she teased a crumpled pack of cigarettes from the hip pocket of her jeans, shook one out, and lit it. She took a long pull, then exhaled a plume of smoke into the breeze. She looked north—a clear view downstream. The sun was rising to her right, mist on the water. It was breathtaking—except for the recent addition of the Northern Lights construction site on the right bank.

For Jodi, like all Owahgena, the river was sacred, a source of comfort and strength, tradition, and security. But as she looked out at how the river divided poverty and paganism on the left from wealth and prosperity on the right, she wondered if the river had failed the Indians.

She drew a thin flask from her other hip pocket and took the first swallow of the day. She knew it wouldn't be her last.

Jodi noticed a man at the construction site, the same moment Dave saw her on the bridge.

He waved at her and got no reaction. *Huh, his wife and most other women he knew would be frantic if their kid was out of sight for even a second. Maybe she didn't see him.* He whistled through his fingers, loud, like he did when he needed to get the attention of a coworker while earth-moving machines were roaring.

Jodi screwed the cap back on her flask. Dave's shrill whistle silenced the birds and that irritated her. Immediately, her guard went up. She fumbled with her earphones and was about to shut him out of her world when he shouted. "Hey. Over here!"

In the morning stillness his voice was strangely loud. Who was this guy? She didn't recognize him. Why was he trying to get her attention?

Through gaps in the railing, Max also saw the stranger. He tucked his tail and let out a string of barks. Jodi reeled him in, still trying to figure out what the man wanted. He was wearing an orange hard hat, which, she reasoned, meant he must be one of the workers. But there was a child with him. That was odd, although the toddler seemed calm and happy enough from what she could tell.

She held for a long moment, then she butted her cigarette on the railing, and tucked its remains in her pocket. She would never desecrate the river by littering it with a cigarette butt. She held up her hand, signaling to Dave that she was coming his way.

As Jodi crossed the parking area toward Dave, he said, "Sorry. I didn't mean to startle you, but I think I have something that belongs to you." He smiled broadly and waited for the heartfelt reunion of a mother and her lost child that he fully expected. It didn't happen. Instead, Jodi scooped Max up in her arms. A wave of confusion blanketed her face.

The child flashed Jodi the same warm smile she had given Dave. Jodi let out a mournful sound that startled Dave.

"She's fine," he said, a little disappointed in the lackluster reunion. He pointed toward the billboard. "I found her over there. Amazing how fast kids wander off."

Jodi held Max close to her chest and placed a hand on his muzzle to stifle his protective growl. For a long moment, she stared at the child, ignoring Dave. She made the sound again, but this time it was more plaintive, like a doe signaling to her fawn. There was confusion behind her eyes.

"Happens to me all the time when I'm watching the grandkids," Dave said. "Scares the heck out of me, though."

Jodi ignored him. She crouched in front of the child, searching the little girl's face, looking deep into her eyes, as if assembling puzzle pieces in her own mind.

The child reached for Max and Jodi instinctively pulled the snappy little dog back worried for the girl's fingers. But, to her surprise, Max did not try to bite. Instead, he whined and stretched his nose toward the child, drawing in her scent.

Cautiously, Jodi brought Max closer to the girl, until she could pet his head. Max's tail began to wag, his eyes sparkled, just like the child's. Max didn't like strangers and Jodi was surprised by his quick acceptance of the child.

"What's her name?" Dave asked.

There was a silence that held so long Dave was starting to get uncomfortable. Jodi's brow creased. Finally, she turned to Dave and, as if she could not believe her own ears, said, "Wren."

Dave nodded approval. "Wren. Like the little bird. Nice name."

He stood there watching Wren coo and hug Max as the little dog nuzzled into her neck. After a moment, Jodi wrapped her free arm around her.

It was the sweet moment Dave had been hoping for. Man, he was getting sentimental in his old age.

After a while Jodi stood and took Wren by the hand. Her eyes flicked to Dave's for a brief second. In a soft voice, she said, "Thank you. I will always be in your debt."

"My pleasure."

Dave watched Jodi lead Wren at the little girl's pace toward the river trail. When they were out of sight, he turned to start his workday. That's when he noticed Wren's threadbare stuffed dog on the ground. He picked it up and was about to call to the woman, but when he looked, she, the little dog, and the girl had disappeared. He set the animal on a nearby post in plain sight. He was sure that when they realized it was missing, they would return for it. He had work to do. One good deed was enough for the day.

CHAPTER 6

BY THE TIME KENT PULLED HIS MOBILE VETERI-
nary unit into his space at the Compassion Veterinary Center, the
parking lot was almost full. His business was thriving, even if he wasn't.
Before Aubrey's death he was always the first to arrive. Nowadays, he let
things get underway without him. He felt sad and guilty about it, but at
the same time, he didn't care. The CVC had meant everything to him.
He had seen it emerge from a tiny one-doctor animal clinic to become
a state-of-the-art veterinary center with dozens of veterinarians and
technicians, and a huge ancillary staff. He had been so proud. Now it
didn't matter. He was glad the staff cut him slack.

He and Lucinda entered through the side door. Office hours were
in full swing, a ballet of medical chaos. Veterinarians and technicians
ducked in and out of exam rooms, the pharmacy, and the treatment
area. In quickstep they dodged each other and avoided entanglement in
leashes attached to canine patients. When gurneys passed, they pressed
themselves to the wall without breaking stride. Doctors barked terse
instructions to staffers who acknowledged them on the run. Through
it all, their faces flickered back and forth with cheerful expressions of a
crew proud of their work and determined to provide the best care for
their patients. All was as it should be. He thought of the military acro-
nym, SNAFU, *situation normal, all fouled up*, and something close to a

smile showed on his face for the first time that day. Lucinda stuck close to Kent's leg to avoid being trampled as they were swept up in the energy.

"There you are," came a familiar voice from behind him. It was Beverly, the hospital manger. "I just this minute got off the phone with Emily. She would like you to stop by and check Sim. He's got a small cut or something. Not urgent, just when you get a chance." She handed him a slip of paper with the note on it.

He thanked her, slipped the note in his pocket, and started down the hall. He thought about how Aubrey would have insisted that he drop everything and head over to check Sim that very moment. Her image appeared in his head and brought the day's second faint smile. She had been like a mother to Emily and she would do anything for her. For Aubrey, any injury to the stallion that she believed would take Emily to the Olympics, even a scratch, was a flat-out emergency.

He stopped short when an exam room door opened in front of him and a teenager's head popped out. It was Barry Fairbanks, Aubrey's son.

"A little help, please," he said to anyone within earshot.

Several nearby people recognized the distress in his voice and turned to lend him a hand.

Kent raised his palm. "I've got it."

Barry still had just his head sticking out of the door. It was obvious that he was trying to shield the conversation from whoever was inside. His face was flushed. "Doctor Homcox and I need some help with an ultrasound."

"Okay, easy enough," Kent said, with a quick shrug. "I can help you."

He stepped toward Barry, expecting him to back into the room. Instead, Barry held his ground. "It's Mrs. Flannigan."

"Oh, Jesus." Kent instantly understood why Barry was flustered. Nothing was ever easy when it came to Nora Flannigan, self-proclaimed expert on all things related to dog breeding.

"She won't let me hold the dog."

Kent nodded, understanding. "Let me talk to her. I'll see what I can do."

Barry withdrew into the exam room and Kent followed. As expected, on the table was the padded V-tray to position the patient on her back so that Dr. Homcox could place the ultrasound probe on her abdomen. Next to it, on a roll cart was an ultrasound machine the size of a small TV. Its screen was lit and ready to go. Lindi Homcox, in Kent's opinion the best ultrasonographer in New York State, was standing, probe in hand, waiting, frustration all over her face.

Kent gave a cheerful greeting to the massively buxom woman seated in the corner. "Good morning, Nora."

"Hi, Doctor Stephenson. I'm so glad you are here."

"Me, too. So, we're checking for pups today, eh? Well, first we need a patient."

"She's in there," Barry offered, delicately pointing at Nora's cleavage."

Kent glanced quickly at the woman's chest. Two mountains. He'd seen smaller udders on cows. "Where?"

Barry stepped closer and pointed a little more accurately. "Down in there."

Nora's eyes narrowed like a dog about to bite, and Barry withdrew his hand.

Kent noticed movement under Nora's knit shawl just as a tiny brown face poked out and gasped for fresh air. "There she is," Kent gushed and beamed a broad smile. But when he reached for the dog, Nora slapped his hands away and stuffed the dog back down into the abyss.

"No one is going to hold ChiChi but me. She's terrified. I can see it in her eyes."

"I think she's suffocating," Barry said.

Nora gave him a look. He took another step back.

Nora crossed her arms over ChiChi and pointed at the V-tray with her chin. "You're not putting her in that thing. I've seen you do it with my other dogs, and that's fine. But I know ChiChi and she's extra sensitive."

Kent pushed a finger into the tray's soft padding. "It's really quite comfortable. I have a larger version in my office. I use it for naps."

Barry and Dr. Homcox chuckled.

Nora's face remained frozen in a scowl. "No way."

Kent leaned back against the counter considering his options and letting things de-escalate. "Dr. Homcox, how about you watch the screen, and I will handle the probe? You can direct me."

Dr. Homcox gave him a dubious look. "Okay."

"Nora, are you willing to try that?"

"I'm not letting go of ChiChi."

"That's all right."

Nora stared down into her cleavage and whined, "Oh, ChiChi, I'm so sorry."

"Okay. Here we go," Kent said. He leaned toward Nora, probe extended. "Just let me slip this under here…good."

After a moment, Dr. Homcox said, "There. Hold it. I see something."

Kent breathed a sigh of relief. ChiChi whined. Nora drew her eyebrows even further together.

"What have you got?" Kent asked Dr. Homcox, his impatience surfacing.

"Move the probe an inch or so down and to the left," she instructed him.

"Better?"

"I think so, maybe," she said, in a slow cadence as she studied the screen. "It looks odd for an abdomen." She squinted at the screen for a moment longer. Then, before she could cover her mouth to hold back her words, she blurted, "That's a mammary gland!"

Kent yanked the probe back. Red faced, he pleaded, "Nora, help me out here!"

"I wasn't sure how to tell you, Dr. Stephenson."

Barry made a choking sound as he struggled to contain his laughter and ducked out of the room.

Kent drew a calming breath. "Okay, we are going to try this one more time. That's it. So, you can still hold ChiChi, but I want to see her with my own eyes."

For an infinitely long five minutes, Kent scanned ChiChi's belly while Dr. Homcox watched the screen and guided him.

Finally, Dr. Homcox said, "She's pregnant. I see four healthy pups."

Nora lavished praise on her little dog.

Kent's relief was palpable.

When Nora exited the exam room for the reception desk, Barry stuck his head back in. "Did you find any lumps, Doc?"

Kent made an exaggerated lunge for his neck then pulled up and laughed.

He was thinking how Aubrey would be proud of her son. That was just the kind of wisecrack *she* would have made, when he saw a big man in a dark blue police uniform coming his way. It was the Chief—and he didn't look happy.

CHAPTER 7

BESIDES BEING JEFFERSON'S CHIEF OF POLICE, Merrill Stephenson was Kent's brother. Kent could read him like a book, which at times was more than a little scary. Today, as he stood in the CVC watching Merrill approach, he saw a mix of anger and frustration.

"You don't look so good," Kent said.

"Did you hear about Jimmy Silverheel?"

"Nope." He was sure Merrill was about to tell him that their friend wrecked his truck, sliced his foot with an ax, or some similar catastrophe. "What's up with ol' Jimmy?"

"He's dead."

"Whaaat?"

"Got shot early this morning. On the river."

The news was like a physical blow. Kent grimaced and braced himself against a counter. "Jesus! How? What happened?"

"I don't know all the details yet. I wasn't the one who took the call and stuff is still trickling in. But what I can tell you is he and Lute were fishing over by the bridge and he got shot. Bullet hit him in the head. Killed him instantly."

Barry walked by, leading an Irish Setter that had the area around the base of its tail shaved. Around the dog's neck was a huge plastic collar that slapped against Barry's leg with each step.

"Hey, Chief. How are you doing?" he asked, oblivious to the fact that he was interrupting an important conversation.

"Hi, Barry. I could be better."

Barry stopped for half a step. "Doc, that fiasco we just had in there with ChiChi got me thinking. Maybe we should breed Lucinda?"

"We're not doing that," Kent said, still focused on Merrill's news about Jimmy Silverheel.

"Why not?" Barry persisted. "I bet she'd make nice pups. We could breed her to Otsi and make *Bluebones.*"

At that moment, Kent was in no mood to get wrapped around the axel of another one of Barry's crazy schemes, but the comment was too much to ignore. "Bluebones? What are you talking about?"

"Bluebones," Barry repeated, as if it were obvious. "Half blue tick hound and half redbone hound."

Kent just shook his head. "Jesus, Barry. Can we talk about that later?"

Barry steered the Setter down the hall. "Sure," he said over his shoulder, still oblivious to the moment. "But keep an open mind."

Kent turned back to Merrill. "Was it an accident?"

"So far, that's our working theory. It looks like bad luck. He got in the way of a stray bullet from some fool who wasn't paying attention to where he was shooting."

"Lute was with him?"

"Just the two of them. Out by the sandbar."

Kent went quiet, trying to get his head around the fact that he would never see Jimmy again. After a minute, before Merrill could see them, he used the back of his hand to wipe away tears that were welling up in his eyes. It seemed like he cried all the time these days and he hated it. He sniffed in deeply and told himself to get a grip. "Is Lute all right?"

"He didn't get shot, if that's what you mean. I haven't spoken to him yet, but I'm sure he's a wreck otherwise. He and Jimmy were really close, as you know. Plus, Otsi got shot."

Kent looked at Merrill, eyes narrowed. "Are you kidding me? How bad?"

"He's still alive, but bad. Lute took him to his cabin."

"Dammit! I wish he'd have brought him here so I could take a look at him."

"Not likely. You know how he is. Anything white-man medicine can do, Indian medicine can do better."

"I know. I know. We've had that difference of opinion since I went to vet school and he followed traditional Owahgena medicine ways."

The two brothers went quiet again, watching the activity around them. Then Kent said, "Man, I would *not* want to be the person who did the shooting if Lute gets hold of 'em. Accident or not, Lute will kill him."

Lute and Jimmy grew up on the reservation, but they had attended the same public school as Kent and Merrill. They were in the same classes. They played on the same baseball and lacrosse teams. But, truth be told, it was their love of hunting, fishing, and all things outdoors that really bonded the four of them.

"Nobody would shoot Jimmy on purpose. He didn't have an enemy in the world." The words floated out on Kent's breath. He couldn't believe he was talking about his friend in the past tense.

Merrill squirmed so slightly that Kent almost missed it. "I agree. But, the first words out of Lute's mouth were that Northern Lights was behind it. Just his gut feeling, of course. He's got nothing to go on."

"That's crazy. Way over the top. They are tough businesspeople, for sure, but they wouldn't kill anybody."

"He's worried they might go after Pegger next."

"See? Right there. That counters Lute's bet that they killed Jimmy. Pegger is heading up the Owahgena side of the fight against Northern Lights. Pegger is *the guy*. The powers that be at Northern Lights know that. They constantly call him an agitator, troublemaker, whatever. *He's* the thorn in their side. If they wanted to go after someone, it would be Pegger. There's no reason for them to kill a simple guy like Jimmy."

"He is…was…an Indian."

"A harmless one. Besides, it's just a frickin' river. Why do they get so damn hot over it?" He was venting. He knew the answer to that question before Merrill spoke.

"It's more than just a river to them. It's the focus of their lives."

For over a year, the building project on the shore of the river had consumed the Jefferson local news. A group of investors, the Northern Lights Corporation, purchased land along the Chittenango across from the reservation. They did it quietly, cozy and cooperative with anyone involved with the sale. They said the right things, promised to be good neighbors, and managed to stay under the radar. When they were sure they had control of the chunk of the riverbank they wanted, they did the chameleon thing. They went from secretive to high profile. They announced plans to build a complex that would become the fisherman's mecca. Northern Lights Resort—a grand hotel, a gigantic sporting goods outlet, guided fishing trips, fly casting classes, an RV park—the works. There was even a rumor that they would have a casino. They promised "Jobs! Jobs! Jobs!" And tourist dollars to boot. It would be a godsend for Upstate New York's economic vacuum. The politicians went into a frenzy. They couldn't get on board fast enough. Everyone else was full steam ahead, too. That is except for one group, the folks on the *other* side of the river, on the reservation—the Owahgena.

In their eyes the river was a gift from The Creator. For eons, it had provided an abundance of salmon and trout to feed their people. While the Owahgena did truly enjoy fishing, they did it for a purpose—their survival—and they took no more fish than they needed. They would never insult the gods by misusing their gift. To allow careless, thought-less outsiders to abuse the river for profit—it was unthinkable. Sport fishing, catch-and-release, was wasteful, cruel, and contrary to nature. Meddling in the lives of other creatures for entertainment, for fun—it was an abomination.

"This whole thing has gotten way out of hand," Kent said.

"I agree. Northern Lights thought once they had the whites on board, they would just roll over the Indians."

"They didn't figure on Pegger."

Percival Cyr, aka Pegger, was Jodi's son. As kids, Kent, Merrill, and the rest of the gang hadn't given Jodi a second glance. She was just Lute's scrawny little sister. She grew up rebellious, the family malcontent. She was sixteen when, in spite of the family's best effort to prevent it, she fell for Dewey Cyr, a big-talking, little-doing drunk out of Canada. He lured her away from the reservation with wild tales of the white man. She bought it, lock, stock, and barrel, and went away with him. To no one's surprise, after a few years she was disillusioned and tired of the beatings and bullshit. When Dewey disappeared, never to be heard from again, no one gave a good goddamn. Jodi came home to the reservation to live with Lute—Baby Percival in hand. How they got *Pegger* out of *Percival*, no one really remembered.

Pegger was a quiet boy, bookish, and a good student. He enjoyed academics, and Jodi encouraged him to learn and make something of himself. She was quietly proud that he inherited her rebellious nature, and she stoked it by instilling in him her distrust of Euros, which was her label for people of European decent—white men. "If they call us Native Americans, we should call them European Americans," she would say. "White men like being called white men. It makes them feel superior. Don't give them that edge. Level the field—call them Euros." Then she would smile with her mouth but not with her eyes. To Pegger, white men were always Euros.

When Pegger came back with Jodi to live on the reservation, Lute took him under his wing. He taught Pegger the traditional ways of the Owahgena. To Lute's delight, Pegger embraced Indian life, too. He was as eager to learn about his ancestral ways as he was to stick his nose in a math book. Pegger became the son Lute never had. Even though Pegger maintained a liberal bent and Lute a traditional one, there was love and mutual respect between them.

Pegger got a scholarship to Syracuse University and left the reservation. For a few years, they pretty much lost track of him. Then one day, seven years later, he came home with a PhD in environmental science—and a reputation as an outspoken advocate for Native Americans.

Kent recalled a night soon after Pegger returned when the gang—Kent, Merrill, Lute, Pegger, and Jimmy—went coon hunting. They were giving the dogs a break, sitting on a rock pile eating sandwiches in the dark. They started quizzing Pegger about what it was like to be scientist. It was their usual banter. Pegger was familiar with it. He knew the conversation would be at his expense, but he didn't mind.

"Potamologist," Merrill said, out of the blue.

"Here it comes," Pegger chuckled, shaking his head in resignation.

The conversation stopped. The others confused, waited for more. Only silence.

"What?" Kent asked, when the silence had gone long enough.

"Potamologist," Merrill repeated, as if everyone should know the word.

"What are you talking about?"

"Do you know what that is?"

"No, but I'm sure you are going to tell us."

Merrill took on a teacherly tone. "A potamologist is one who studies rivers."

Pegger groaned and made a big show of sticking his fingers in his ears.

"So Pegger is a potamologist?" Kent deadpanned.

All eyes went to Pegger searching for his aura.

"Correct," Merrill said, and gave Pegger a slap on the back.

The others mumbled approval.

Kent turned to Lute. "There you go, Lute. Be proud of your nephew! You have a potamologist in the family."

"See? That's what I'm talking about!" Lute said, the frustration in his voice dampening the mood. "Euros use big words and make things complicated. Then they miss the point. Pegger knows to respect the river. *I* taught him about the river long before he went away to college and became a pota…whatever."

Merrill straightened and stared down his nose at Lute as if looking over spectacles. "Potamologist."

"Pota Pegger," Jimmy said, sensing that Lute was getting too serious.

Merrill and Jimmy laughed until Lute pushed them both off the rocks and into the mud.

Kent was shocked back to the present by Merrill's voice. For a moment the hectic activity of the CVC disoriented him.

"Well, I got to be going," Merrill said. "I wanted to tell you about Jimmy. I'll give you a shout if I hear anything."

"Thanks," he said, but it didn't sound like enough. Another shudder of sadness spread through his body. His mind flashed to Aubrey. The list of people he missed terribly was growing.

CHAPTER 8

IT WAS MIDAFTERNOON BY THE TIME KENT AND Lucinda headed to Orchard Hill Farm to check Sim. Kent rolled down his window and let the wind flow over his face as they drove through Jefferson. Everything he passed, the village green, the Presbyterian church, the Red Horse Inn, all brought memories of Aubrey. His depression wafted up like the stench of a sewage pipe. Lucinda whined and he glanced over. She was studying him with a worried look on her face. *That* made him smile. His therapy dog. He fondled her ears and felt better. So did she.

They picked up Route 13 north and Kent glanced over at some of the best fishing water in the state as the road wound along the river. It was a beautiful drive and usually one of his favorites. But today, when he got to the bridge, thoughts of Jimmy Silverheel rolled in like thunderheads. Jimmy loved to fish by the bridge. Kent wondered if he'd ever be able to get out on the river again without thinking of Jimmy.

He shook that thought from his head only to have it replaced by an even more dismal memory. Whenever he and Aubrey happened to drive near the bridge, even if they were behind schedule, she would ask that he stop in the middle of it. If he protested, she would remind him that it only took a moment, and she was right. She would roll down her window, fill her lungs with fresh air, and slowly scan the vista. Then she would close her eyes and drift to only she knew where. A minute or two would pass without a break in the silence until finally she would say, "Okay, let's go," and they would continue on their way. Now, looking back, he cursed himself for being impatient with her. His heart ached to have those moments again. He reached for Lucinda's ears.

He forced himself to concentrate on Emily. He was so proud of her. He wanted her to achieve her goal of riding in the Olympics as much as she did. She deserved it. She had survived a spinal birth defect—which compromised her legs—*and* a gunshot wound. What kid did that? Not to mention the divorce of her parents. If it hadn't been for Aubrey, he didn't know what he would have done. She inspired Emily. She taught her to ride, and that, Kent honestly believed, saved his daughter's life. She had recognized Emily's talent and her all-important drive to succeed. The clincher came when Elizabeth St. Pierre, a Jefferson aristocrat, his client, and most importantly, his friend, gave Emily a Thoroughbred stallion that any world-class rider would kill to have. As Emily's skill level progressed, Kent and Aubrey had agreed that she needed to have instruction at the next level. That was Orchard Hill.

Orchard Hill Farm was the de facto stepping-stone to the US Equestrian Team in the Northeast mainly because Chris Mayer was the head instructor. She had spent her whole thirty-plus-year career in the world of fine hunters and jumpers. Injuries had robbed her of her chance to bring home the gold, but she had parlayed her experience and infinite patience with young elite riders into a successful equine academy. To be accepted as a student by Chris Mayer was in itself a testimony to the student's ability and future prospects as an equestrian.

Kent turned into the parking lot, admired the professionally groomed landscaping as he always did, then parked in front of an indoor riding ring that was the size of a college fieldhouse. To his left, the main barn was joined to the ring by a breezeway. It had stalls for sixty horses and all that went with them, like tack and feed rooms, wash stalls, and a farrier station. Attached to the end of the barn was the office—*no muck boots permitted!* Beyond the three buildings, encircled in a crisp white fence, was the outdoor ring. Riders there were treated to a spectacular view of the Chittenango River while they trained.

Kent told Lucinda to keep an eye on the truck, grabbed his black case, and entered the barn. He paused for a moment just inside. He loved that first breath of a horse barn—leather and neatsfoot oil, sawdust, and hay—yes, even the manure. He let his eyes adjust to the soft light and earth tones, then approached a young man with a handsome Trakehner cross-tied in the alleyway.

"Hi, Doc," the man said. "You here to check out Sim?"

Once again, Kent was amazed just how fast news travelled on the horse-world grapevine. "I am." He nodded at the horse. "Riesling is looking good."

The man stopped braiding Riesling's mane and stood back admiring his horse. "Thanks to you. That pneumonia really kicked his butt. But his cough is totally gone now. I upped his feed like you said and he's gained back most of the weight he lost."

"I'm glad we got ahead of it. Hey, have you seen Em?"

"I just saw her. She's got Sim in the far wash stall."

Kent headed that way. Over his shoulder he said, "Hang in there, Riesling ol' buddy."

Riesling snorted a "will do" that got a laugh out of the young man.

Kent made his way along a dozen stalls, the horses in them drawing inquisitive sniffs as he passed. Further along, he found Simpatico's Gift standing cross-tied in the wash stall. Its floor was covered with a black rubber mat and there was a drain in the center. On the walls were several shelves holding assorted buckets, sponges, soap, and grooming supplies. Emily was seated on an overturned pail next to Sim's left front leg. In her hand was a hose and she was running cold water over Sim's foot.

"What you got there?" Kent asked, being careful not to startle either Emily or Sim.

Emily stood as she twisted the nozzle, shutting off the water. She gave her dad a peck on the cheek. "Thanks for coming."

"No problem." He bent to take a look. He could see a small skin wound and soft swelling an inch above Sim's coronary band. He slid his hand down the leg and gently touched the area. Sim pulled his foot away.

"It's tender. How lame is he?"

"Not bad. He's fine at the walk, but Chris and I both noticed just a little head nod when he trots."

Kent straightened. Eyes still on Sim's wound, he said, "How did it happen?"

"Did the Chief tell you about all the excitement on the river this morning?"

Instantly, Kent wanted to redirect the conversation but knew it wouldn't work. "Yeah, he stopped by the hospital. He told me Jimmy Silverheel was shot and killed." He nodded toward Sim's leg. "Does that have something to do with this?"

Emily's face creased. "Oh my God! I heard someone was shot but I didn't know it was Jimmy. That's awful! Dad, I'm so sorry."

"Me, too. He was a good friend."

"You know more than I do. What happened? How did he get shot?"

"The Chief didn't have a lot of details. He said Jimmy and Lute were fishing over by the sandbar. They think Jimmy got hit by a stray bullet."

"That's sick." She thought about it for a beat. "But there were *three* shots. I heard them."

"It happens. Some guy fires at a deer or whatever never thinking that if he misses, the bullet can travel up to a mile. By bad luck, once in a while someone is in the line of fire."

"I can't believe it! Jimmy was such a nice person. He was always friendly to me."

"We'll all miss him."

"Damn poachers! It's not even hunting season."

"People are always firing guns for one reason or another. Whoever it was could have been shooting at a coyote that's been killing their chickens. Who knows?"

"I don't care. It's not right."

"Your uncle's on it. The Chief will figure it out."

"That won't bring Jimmy back."

"No. No, it won't."

They were silent for a moment as they remembered the good times with Jimmy. Emily was first to break the silence. "But as far as Sim is concerned, early this morning Chris and I were working in the outdoor ring. Everything was going fine till, all of the sudden, we heard the gunshots from down by the river." Emily gave a weak laugh. "Sim jumped a mile. He almost went right out from under me." Her voice went serious again. "He sidestepped and, presto, he was hurt. I think he stepped on himself; he's got new shoes, and they're sharp. I iced it and put some nitrofurazone ointment on it, then I wrapped it. I called Beverly right after that."

"Did *you* get hurt?"

"No, I'm fine."

"You had your helmet on, right?"

"Jeez, yes," Emily answered in a teenager drone. "You and Chris."

"Yep, me and Chris. And everyone else who cares about you."

"Whatever."

Kent gave her his "I'm not kidding" look.

"I know. I get it."

He turned back to Sim's leg. "Well, it doesn't look too bad. You did the right thing with the ice and ointment. I think I'll throw a couple of sutures in it just to be on the safe side, and I'll leave you some Banamine to make him more comfortable. Say, for three days."

"Sounds good. I'm glad it's nothing worse."

Over the next half hour Kent clipped the wound, then scrubbed it with disinfectant. He numbed it with lidocaine and sutured the skin.

Through it all, Emily stroked Sim's muzzle, stared at the back of Kent's head, and worried, not so much for Sim as for her dad. Since Aubrey's death he had become fragile in a way Emily would never have imagined. Now Jimmy Silverheel, a big part of his unofficial male support group, was gone. What was that going to do?

Kent stood up and inspected the bandage he had applied, never suspecting his daughter's concern for him. "That should do it. Like I said, it doesn't look too bad. Rest him. Change the bandage every day with the nitrofurazone ointment. And the Banamine in his feed for three days. He should be fine. I'll swing by in a week to take the stitches out. If you think anything is not right before that, call me."

"Thanks, Doc. You are the best." She kissed her dad on the cheek and wrapped him in the kind of hugs fathers love.

As she helped him load his equipment back into the mobile unit, she said, "I know how close you and Jimmy were. If there is anything I can do to help, tell me."

"I'll keep you posted."

His flat tone gave her no clue as to his condition. She gave him one last peck on the cheek and thanked him again. Hands on her hips, she watched him drive away.

CHAPTER 9

IT FELT ODD TO KENT TO BE DRIVING SOMETHING
other than his vet truck. He headed to the river in his Cherokee because,
today, he needed his canoe. It was lashed to the roof. Barry was on the
seat next to him, quiet, still working the sleep out of his head. Lucinda
was in the back, raring to go. He had promised the crew that, this time,
he'd be there to fish. In the past, before Aubrey's death, when his life
centered around the stresses of running a huge animal hospital, he
could hardly wait for these Sunday morning escapes onto the river. But
these last few months he'd made excuse after excuse to avoid joining
in, opting instead to visit Aubrey's grave. Now, with Jimmy's death, the
pendulum was swinging the other way. He felt a need to be with his
friends. They were missing Jimmy too.

He turned off Route 13 into a cut through the trees that was not
much more than a deer path. Most people wouldn't even notice it, but
Kent had found it in the pre-dawn darkness a hundred times before.
It led through the woods, down to the river, and ended at their secret
launch site.

He stopped on a patch of reedy grass just large enough for three
vehicles, if they squeezed in tight. His headlights settled on Lute's
battered pickup truck. Kent remembered fondly how excited Lute had
been when he bought it secondhand a few years ago. He raved about
it being such a great deal—a 1984 F-150, low mileage, hardly any rust.

Now, in 1999, that old beater was fifteen years old and still Lute's pride and joy.

Lute came around into the light and nodded *hello.*

"You're here early," Kent whispered, not wanting to upset the tranquility.

Lute was wearing a flannel shirt and jeans, as always, but he looked tired, bent and his shoulders didn't fill his Carhartt vest the way they usually did.

"You okay?"

Lute shrugged. "I didn't sleep well. I just can't get my head around Jimmy being gone."

"Me neither."

"It won't be the same."

Lute Crimshaw was one of the most stoic men Kent knew and it was unsettling to see him so down. Silence lingered. Finally, Kent asked, "How's Otsi?"

"Fair. The bastard got him in the hind leg. Ripped up his thigh pretty good. Jodi and I have been double-teaming him."

Kent envisioned Lute and Jodi working day and night applying poultices and coaxing Otsi to lap various herbal teas.

"She's been a huge help," Lute said. "She made herself a bed right next to him."

For Lute to mention his sister was odd. He was always quick to talk about Pegger, but he rarely mentioned Jodi. Of course, Jefferson's omnipresent rumor mill was more than willing to take that role. They called her a barfly and said that she slept around. Never anything good. Kent liked hearing something nice about her.

"I don't think I'm going to do much fishing today," Lute said, "but Otsi needs the river."

Kent was about to ask Lute to explain that when Barry called for help unloading the canoe off the top of the Cherokee. They each took an end and carried the Grumman that Kent had fished in since he was a boy to the river. They slid it in next to Lute's. They were climbing back up the bank when another set of headlights eased toward them through the dark. It was Merrill in his police cruiser moving slowly to keep from scraping his muffler.

Merrill greeted Kent as he got out, then turned to Lute. "How are you doing?"

Lute raised and lowered his shoulders the same way he had to Kent.

"It's going to be weird without Jimmy."

"Do you have anything yet?" Kent asked his brother.

"Not much. The ballistic guys figured the shooter was on the Rez side of the river. They weren't able to find an exact location. It could have come from the Rez, but not necessarily. Bullets travel a long way."

"Did they recover a bullet?"

"The medical examiner gave us the fragments he got out of Jimmy, but they are useless."

Lute hissed out a breath. "Kent, we're talking about a poor Indian here. Don't expect anything to happen fast, if at all."

Merrill bristled. "Wait a minute, dammit. Where do you get off saying that, Lute? It's a homicide and we are giving it top priority. Our whole department has dropped everything else. The State Police are on it, too. Besides the fact that Jimmy was my friend, just as much as yours."

Lute rose up to his full height. His eyes clashed with Merrill's. "What I'm saying is…"

Kent breathed a sigh of relief when they were interrupted by the sound of Lucinda barking and scratching on the door of Lute's old truck. All three men turned to her.

Kent gave Lute a questioning look. "What have you got in there?"

"I brought Otsi."

"Here. This morning? You're kidding me. He needs to be in CVC, if you ask me, not out here."

"He needs to be on the river! You don't understand, Kent."

Kent paused to get the tone of his voice under control.

Lute stared down at his boots for a long second doing the same thing.

"Can I at least look him over?"

Lute shook his head. "No, thanks. Just the river today."

The door hinges of Lute's truck made a groaning sound as he pulled it open. Otsi, was lying on the seat. There was a collective moan from the others when they saw him. For Otsi to be so lifeless was shocking, so much in contrast to his usual crazy high energy level. He did not even lift his head. He lay on his side in a thick blanket, eyes squinted shut.

Kent reeled. What terrible wound was that blanket hiding that would cause Otsi to be so near death? "It's just his thigh?"

"Left one."

Lute gave Otsi a gentle pat on the head to prepare him, then slipped both arms under the dog. When he lifted, Otsi let out a cry and Lute set him back down.

In an instant, Barry was there to help. Each of them took two corners of the blanket.

"He's heavy," Lute warned. "Ninety-five pounds, the last time I weighed him, the fat old hound. Let's take him down to my canoe."

Within minutes Barry and Lute had Otsi situated on the floor of the canoe.

Kent watched, thinking. *Out on the river is no place for a dog that sick. Otsi should be in the ICU at his hospital.* He kept his thoughts to himself.

"Who's riding with who?" Merrill asked, hoping to refocus the group on to a less divisive topic.

Before anyone else could make a suggestion, Barry said, "Me and Lute, you and Doc?"

They grabbed their rods, loaded in, and pushed out into the river.

When Barry and Lute approached the Turtle Log, a notorious hangout of big fish, Barry picked up his rod and began to strip out line. He glanced back at Lute, expecting him to be doing the same thing and was surprised to see him with his paddle across his knees staring at Otsi.

"Aren't you going to fish?"

"I'll let you catch them today. I don't feel much like fishing. I just need to be on the river. Otsi, too."

"Okay," Barry said, a little confused, and began casting. He let his gaze drift to the bridge in the distance then back to his fly. "You think the river will help Otsi?"

"It does what it wants, but I'm hoping."

"I get how the Owahgena consider the river sacred because it provides food. The medicine part? Not so much."

"Typical Euro," Lute said. He sounded defeated.

"I can't help what I am."

"No, but you can watch, and learn. And believe."

"I try to keep an open mind, but I work at the CVC with Doc. That's the medicine I believe in."

Lute spoke slowly, choosing his words carefully. "Kent is my friend, and a good doctor, but he doesn't understand the river either. He respects it. I'll give him that. But he doesn't understand its power."

"You really think it has supernatural powers?"

"Yes, I do. The river is alive. Most Euros don't get it at all. They disrespect it. They poison it with chemicals. They build dams that block the salmon from running. They catch fish for money. For a thousand years this river was plenty for all of us. Now the river is near death. Most of the salmon are gone." In a hollow voice he added, "I would not blame the river if it said, 'To hell with you all.'"

"There are still salmon in the river."

"Pacific salmon, not the ones The Creator put in our river. The Euros put them in after they killed off all the Atlantic salmon, and even *they* can't survive. They have to keep stocking a new supply from the hatchery every season. All salmon may be the same to Euros, but not to the Owahgena."

Barry rolled Lute's words around in his head. "At least nowadays it's mostly catch-and-release. That's a step in the right direction."

"Catch-and-release." Lute spit the words.

"What?" Barry said, surprised. "Is that a problem? At least they aren't taking all the fish out."

"There is a special place in hell for catch-and-release fishermen. Right between the ivory hunters and the whalers."

"Wait a minute," Barry said. He took a deep breath to argue but stopped when he felt the canoe rock. He turned to see that Lute had shifted off his seat. He was on his knees leaning over Otsi. Barry twisted for a better look.

Lute withdrew a worn leather pouch from his creel. It was dyed red, the color of dried blood, and on the front, in faded white, was a symbol that Barry couldn't identify. Attached to it were two long black feathers, tattered from age and wear. It had a tie-string closure which Lute opened with his teeth then set next to Otsi. He began a soft, mournful chant. His voice rose and fell as he looked up to the sky and then down at Otsi.

Barry, no longer interested in fishing, reeled in his line. The canoe drifted slowly with the current. Lute took a pinch of brownish powder from the pouch and sprinkled it on Otsi's head. He pulled out a thin braid of corn stalk and whipped Otsi lightly with it several times. He repeated the powder and whipping three times. Through it all, Otsi never moved.

Lute searched in his pouch and retrieved a section of deer antler that had been hollowed and fashioned into a cup the size of a shot glass. He scooped water from the river and poured it first on Otsi's injured leg, then his head, and lastly, into his mouth. Otsi barely had the strength to swallow it.

When he was done, he sat back on his heels and folded into deep meditation for several minutes. Barry watched it all, fascinated. Finally, Lute slid back up onto his seat and spoke in a voice that resonated with the crushing weight on his mind, "Now it is up to The Creator."

Barry wasn't sure how long they drifted after Lute presented his case for Otsi to the gods. He was afraid to break the silence and relieved when Kent and Merrill paddled over. Lucinda was sitting high in the middle of their canoe like a queen. Her eyes searched for Otsi. Her nostrils flared as she tried to breathe in news of his condition. The four of them watched her waft the air above him. When she drew her head back and whined, they let her be alone with her thoughts.

"Any luck?" Kent asked to lighten the mood.

"Nothing yet," Barry said, covering for Lute, who was rubbing his face, working his way out of his trance. "How about you guys?"

Merrill held up his creel and tipped it toward them. There were several nice brown trout in it. "We have a good start on breakfast."

"Nice."

"I'm surprised you didn't pick up one at the Turtle log."

Lute stabbed his paddle into the water. "We are going over to Sunday School Bay. That's where they are."

"The blackflies are going to eat you alive over there."

"Now you sound like Jimmy."

Lute's words gushed up thoughts of their friend.

"I used to tell him that the flies are part of fishing. Plus, they keep you white guys away."

"Whatever."

It was a short paddle to Sunday School Bay. Barry's mind drifted with the current. "Lute, what does the name Otsi mean?"

"Bird Brain."

Barry chuckled. "Seriously?"

"He was dumber than a box of rocks as a pup."

"So, he finally got some sense?"

"A little." Lute gave Otsi a loving look.

"Did you ever think of using Otsi for stud?"

"He runs free."

"Do you know if he sired any pups?"

"There are a few dogs running around on the Rez that could be his. I don't know for sure."

Barry touched his fingers to the water and watched the tiny wake that trailed from them. "Otsi and Lucinda would make nice pups, don't you think?"

"First we have to keep him alive."

"Of course. But pups with Lucinda would be cool, right? I bet they'd be awesome coon hunters."

"Lucinda never comes into heat."

"I know. That's the problem."

"If the spirits don't want her to have pups, best to let it be."

"But their pups would be awesome."

"We're here. Get ready, we need fish."

Lute guided the canoe into Sunday School Bay. The water was dark, the air heavy and still. The willows wept into the water—and the blackflies attacked with a vengeance.

They both started slapping flies and waving their hats. Barry pulled a small squeeze bottle out of his pocket and showed it to Lute. "DEET."

"Skippy, put that poison away."

"It's the only thing that works."

"Bullshit." Lute pulled an ointment tin from his breast pocket and tossed it to Barry. "Use this. You shouldn't have that stuff anywhere near the river."

Barry opened the tin and whiffed it. "Smells pretty good."

"And it won't give you cancer."

"Where did you get it?"

"I make it."

"Does it work?"

Lute gave Barry a "what kind of question is that?" look. "Yes, it works, Skippy." He took back the tin and applied it on his own skin. "Now let's get us some breakfast."

Lute and Barry both had to paddle hard against the current to get back to the landing, but knowing they had four fish made it easier. Kent met them at the shoreline as Lute nosed the canoe in. "Any luck?"

Barry held his creel for Kent to inspect. "We're all set."

They laid out a bed in the shade for Otsi, then worked together cleaning the fish.

Merrill threw a handful of green leaves on the fire and a thick cloud of smoke billowed up. The blackflies scattered. Eddies of smoke swirled above their heads as they enjoyed a riverside breakfast—the quiet sounds of nature as the day awakened, the comfort of one another's company, and memories of past times with Jimmy.

They were jarred out of the moment by the roar of diesel engines cranking up. Across the river, Northern Lights was starting its day and taking the peacefulness with it.

Lute growled. "What is it about white men and noise? Why can't they stand silence? They don't get it—the river needs silence."

Barry took a mouthful of fish and cornbread, then let his eyes settle across the river to the worksite. The googly-eyed fish billboard stood out on the shore. He pointed at it with his fork. "That fish is so ridiculous."

The other men turned and squinted at it through the smoke.

Lute tossed the dredges of his coffee into the fire. "It's as if they are *trying* to insult the river." He waved his fork at Barry. "You know, you and I were talking about DEET earlier? You watch, they'll use airplanes to spray the whole place with chemicals that make DEET seem like baby's milk. There won't be a bug around anywhere. What will the fish eat then?"

Kent scraped his plate into the fire. "There's no way those people should be allowed to waltz in here and disrupt something that's been so important to the Owahgena for centuries."

"Then how are we going to stop them?" Barry asked.

"Pegger is our best bet. Lately he's been in Albany trying to get the attorney general to step in. He's been lobbying the politicians like hell. He might..."

Lute cut him off. "If it were up to me, we wouldn't be as diplomatic as Pegger."

Merrill perked up. "Ah, an Indian uprising!"

A smile crossed Lute's face and Kent noticed it. His chest tightened, and it wasn't from the smoke that was swirling around him.

CHAPTER 10

AS USUAL, KENT STARTED HIS DAY AT AUBREY'S grave. He updated her on Sim, things around home, and the CVC—all relatively unchanged. Then things sort of caught up with him. He slid off the bench and down to the grave. With his arm around Lucinda and his forehead pressed against her headstone, he let it all out. He told Aubrey, really, things were a mess. Their fishing trip had been a disaster. It wasn't the same without Jimmy. Lute was a wreck over Otsi getting shot, to say nothing of Jimmy, and even though he hadn't admitted it, Kent was pretty sure Lute figured Northern Lights was behind it. The cops didn't have any leads yet, and Merrill and Lute almost had a fight over that. To top it off, Lute made a comment that came out like a veiled threat against the resort. When he was done, he sat back, surprised and a little ashamed of himself for venting. "I've got to get a grip." He was sure he felt Aubrey's hand on his shoulder. Lucinda leaned into him, whined, and waited. He ruffled her ears. "Thanks for listening, both of you."

When Kent found a break in the action at the CVC, he escaped to his office and called Merrill. With his feet on his desk, he leaned back and toyed with the phone cord.

"Got anything yet?"

"Still not much. Like I told you before, the bullet fragments from Jimmy weren't in good enough shape to tell much."

"Did you get *anything* from them?"

"Only that it was fired from a rifle, not a handgun."

"Which we pretty much knew anyway."

"Right. The crime-scene guys found a fragment of one bullet. They couldn't get much from it either. They were able to pin down that the shots came from the Rez side, but they couldn't find an exact location. No tracks or shell casings along the river. They've had guys canvassing a two-mile radius talking to people and checking things out. The usual suspects. We pretty much know who the poachers are." He paused. "You know, it doesn't have to be a poacher. It could be just a tragic accident. Some guy way off looks up and sees the hawk that's been getting his chickens sitting at the top of a tree, so he fires off three quick ones. He never gives it a thought that maybe he just killed somebody miles away."

"There's a whole lot of rifles in your two-mile radius."

"That's for sure."

Kent dropped his feet to the floor and shifted the receiver to the other ear. "Have you checked in on Lute?"

"Yesterday. I stopped by his cabin to ask him a few more questions."

"How is he?"

"Terrible. As you might expect. Jodi is keeping an eye on him. She's worried."

"I'd bet. How's Otsi?"

"He's terrible, too. Lute seems to think he's getting better. To me, he looked just as bad if not worse than when we were at the river. Really weak. Not eating. Jodi's with him constantly. She's worried about him, too. You know, that woman's had a lot of problems, but I have to give her credit. Her heart is in the right spot."

"She's sure loyal to Lute and Pegger."

"Right." Merrill laughed into the phone. "And she's got this little land shark of a dog. He can't weigh more than ten pounds, but he wouldn't let me out of the damn car."

"I remember back when they were growing up, Lute would take her hunting once in a while. I think she got a deer or two."

"Yeah, I remember that."

"I wish Lute would let me have a look at Otsi."

"Lute is Lute. He'll do it his way."

"I know. I just hope it works out. If Otsi dies, Lute will go crazy."

"True." Merrill's mind shifted. "Speaking of injured animals, how's Sim doing?"

"How'd you hear about that?"

"I'm a cop. I am all-knowing."

"He's okay. He just dinged his ankle."

"I'm glad that's all it is. We're all counting on him making Em famous. He needs four good wheels to do that."

There was a silence on the line as both brothers considered all that was happening.

Finally, Merrill asked, "What about you? How are you holding up?"

"I'm okay." No way was he going to mention his minor breakdown at the cemetery that morning.

"Are you sleeping?"

"Fair."

"Did you talk to the doctor about getting something?"

"That stuff makes me feel like crap."

"Still having dreams?"

"Can we talk about something else?"

"Are you?"

Kent huffed a sigh into the phone that he was sure Merrill would hear. "They are so damn vivid. It's like she's right there."

There was another stretch of silence.

Merrill broke it again. "It takes time. It hasn't been that long."

"Uh-huh. About every third person I talk to tells me that."

"It's true."

"Like you are an expert."

"I'm not. But I'm here for you. Count on it."

"I'm good."

Kent made Merrill promise to keep him up to date on the case and ended the call.

The receiver wasn't on the hook for ten seconds when the phone rang. It was Barry. "I'm restocking your truck. I've got the list, but I wanted to check with you, make sure there isn't anything else."

Before Barry could say more, Kent said, "I'll be right down to give you a hand."

He stood and stretched. To Lucinda, he said, "Saved by the bell. I've got to get out of here. Let's go help Barry."

Lucinda stood and stretched, too. Then she shook herself, setting off a wave that whipped her ears then jingled her collar tags and washed its way back off the tip of her tail. She smiled up at Kent. *I bet you can't do that.*

On the way to the large animal pharmacy, it dawned on Kent just how good an assistant Barry had become. When he first showed up in Jefferson a few years ago with Aubrey, it had been obvious to Kent that he was bright. He quickly won over everyone he met with his goofball sense of humor. But back then, he was fatherless, directionless, and pretty much adrift. Aubrey did her best to mother him, but she had a lot on her plate, too. Kent and Barry had bonded quickly. He became a role model for the boy. Now Barry was focused on becoming a veterinarian and Kent held a fatherly pride in that. He knew Aubrey would be proud of him, too.

When he arrived at the pharmacy, Kent saw that Barry had backed the mobile unit into one of three bays.

He scanned the list of what needed to be restocked. "What's left?"

"I've got most of it. Anything that's not checked off."

"You're getting pretty good at this."

"Practice makes perfect."

Kent headed into the pharmacy and returned with a cart of calcium, dextrose, oxytocin, and assorted hormones.

Barry was loading equine vaccines. With his head still in the unit's refrigerator, he said, "Doc, have you had a chance to consider what I mentioned the other day?"

Kent was blank. "What was that?"

"About breeding Lucinda."

"Not really."

"I think we should breed her to Otsi."

"You're dreaming."

"Why do you say that?"

"Because she has not come into heat in her whole life."

"Why is that?"

Kent took the last item off his cart and stowed it in the mobile unit. "I don't know. Back when I first noticed that she didn't cycle I tried to figure out why and couldn't. So, I took her to Cornell and had her checked by the experts at the vet school. She's had X-rays, ultrasounds, endoscopy, cultures, bloodwork, hormone assays, you name it, the whole works— all normal."

"How come you didn't go ahead and spay her if she couldn't have pups?"

Kent let the question hang for a moment, then said, "Well, I guess I hoped one day she would come into heat."

Barry's optimism surfaced. "You never know. Maybe someday she will."

"At this point, I wouldn't bet on it."

They were just closing up the mobile unit when Kent's pager chirped. He pulled it from his belt and read the message: *Luther Crimshaw in the ER. We need you there. Now.*

CHAPTER 11

KENT PUSHED THROUGH THE DOUBLE DOORS
into the emergency room with Barry and Lucinda on his heels. His
heart sank as he saw Lute in the center of the room. Otsi, wrapped
in a blanket, sagged in his arms like a bundle of laundry. Lute was
protecting him, spinning first one direction then the other, like an elk
surrounded by wolves, trying to ward off the half-dozen or so technicians and assistants who were trying to get close enough to help Otsi.
He was shouting, "I want Doc to check him! No one else. Just Doc!"

They made eye contact, and Lute froze. The whole staff turned
to Kent. Each face showed relief but asked the question: *What do you
want us to do?*

Lute didn't wait for an answer. He held Otsi out toward Kent like
an offering. "I think it's too late." He choked on the words.

Kent moved to Lute and signaled for the others to step back. He
grabbed Lute's shoulder and gave it a reassuring squeeze. "I've got this,"
he said loud enough for his staff to hear.

He wanted to thank Lute for bringing Otsi to him, and for having
confidence in him. He knew how hard it was for Lute to admit that
Kent's medicine could do things his couldn't. But instead, he was going
to have to tell his friend that it was too late. Too late for *anyone* to save
Otsi. Kent recognized the limpness of death. He'd seen it hundreds of
times in hundreds of animals throughout his career, and now he saw it

in Otsi. Kent kicked himself for not being more insistent when Lute had Otsi at the river. River magic, praying to spirits—precious time wasted.

He shifted the blankets so that he could inspect Otsi, going through the motions for Lute's benefit. Without taking his eyes off the dog, he reached out behind and waggled his fingers. "Stethoscope."

Instantly several appeared and one was slapped into his hand. The room locked into a nervous quiet as he listened to Otsi's chest.

After an eternity, Kent's face folded into disbelief, and he looked up at Lute. In a voice that sounded like he had witnessed a miracle, he said, "There's a heartbeat. Not much of one, but it's there."

A murmur wove through the staff.

Lute's eyes shone with the conflict that thrashed inside him. It was as if he couldn't believe the blasphemy in his next words. "I don't want the spirits to take him."

Kent's expression was anything but optimistic. "Then we will see what we can do." He reached for Otsi. Automatically, Lute pulled back.

"It's okay, Lute. I promise you I will stay with him. Barry, too."

Lute glanced at Barry, who was a few steps away, hanging on every word. Barry nodded vigorously.

Slowly Lute released Otsi into Kent's arms. Kent set him on the gurney that had appeared and signaled for his ER staff to get going. He turned back to Lute. "It's going to take a while. Do you want to wait here, or do you want me to call you?"

"I'll wait," Lute answered without hesitation. He cast a look around the room, then took a seat in the farthest corner, his back against the wall. Kent had seen that posture before. Lute had the stamina and stubbornness to hold it for hours.

"I'll be back as soon as I know something," Kent said, and headed in the direction they rolled Otsi. When he looked back, Lute's eyes were closed. In his hands he was manipulating a string of tiny shells as if it were a rosary. His lips moved in a silent prayer. *Owahgena or Catholic, not much difference in a pinch.*

Barry met Kent in back. Still walking, he said, "They've got a tube in and an IV line already. Shock meds going in. And oxygen, of course. His temp is ninety-seven."

"I was afraid of that; he's really cold."

"They're heating him up, too."

When Kent reached Otsi, he surveyed the IV bag with its crystalline line dangling to Otsi's front leg. A latex tube an inch in diameter protruded from his mouth. It was connected to a hissing machine that heaved rhythmically, inflating and deflating like a bellows stoking a fire. EKG, pulse ox, and other monitors were accumulating around his bed by the minute. He was thankful that Lute didn't have to see it all.

"What's the wound look like?"

A young doctor lowered her stethoscope. "We haven't gotten that far. We are still trying to keep him alive." She lifted the blanket and gestured toward a thick cloth bandage covering Otsi's leg from hip to hock. His swollen toes protruded out of the bottom like ripe plums. It was clean, probably recently changed. The sweet smell of wild herbs wafted up in an odd mix with the stench of fetid tissue. "Let's cut that poultice off and take a look."

She gave Kent a dubious look. "That's going to be a project."

"Yep, it's going to be a gooey mess," Kent agreed. He lifted Otsi's lip; his membranes were the same color as his toes. "We don't have much time. You keep him alive. I'll do the leg."

Kent stepped to a glove dispenser, pulled out a pair of latex gloves, and snapped them on. He grabbed a pair of bandage scissors, and as the team worked to keep Otsi alive, Kent cut away the poultice.

Barry watched Kent struggling. "It's like cutting through a mattress."

"Yep. A wet, smelly one."

Kent kept cutting, unwinding, and teasing at the poultice. When it finally fell free, everyone in the room moaned.

The smell of the rotten wound overpowered the exhaust fans. Team members made gagging sounds as they scrambled for face masks. A slough of dead skin and nastiness the size of a man's hand came away with the bandage as Kent lifted it. He dropped the whole thing into a stainless-steel kick bucket. It landed with a wet thud.

At the bottom of the crater-like wound that remained, Kent could see Otsi's femur stewing in pus and corruption.

"What a mess," Barry said.

"That's about as bad as it gets," the young vet said. "There is no saving that leg."

Kent bit his lip and nodded agreement. Lute would be heartsick to have Otsi with only three legs. But at least, maybe, this way he'd have his dog.

A sad silence crept in and lingered. Kent stared down into the hole for several slow breaths. Gradually his brow furrowed. He shook his head almost imperceptibly at first, then more forcefully. "No. No. No!"

Barry and the rest of the team looked at him.

If it had been any owner but Lute, any patient other that Otsi, Kent might have resigned himself to an amputation. No, he needed to save this leg, that was for sure, but there was more at stake than that. A lot more. He needed to justify his medicine to Lute.

He stuck his fingers into the wound, exploring through the slime. "I feel a pulse in the femoral artery."

No one responded.

He scratched the surface of an exposed muscle with a scalpel. "Look. It's bleeding."

He felt Otsi's foot. Even through the gloves he felt heat. "His toes are still warm."

He arched his brow into a defiant look and scanned his team members. "The leg still has circulation. Let's see if we can save it."

The silence that followed dripped with skepticism.

"Come on, guys, this is what we went to school for! Anybody can do the easy ones. We do the tough ones."

Heads nodded slowly at first then more confidently. Gradually, smiles broke onto masked faces, until finally, a surgical team version of a rallying cry rattled through the group. They returned to their tasks with renewed energy.

Kent watched a tech push a bolus of antibiotics into Otsi's line. "You guys get him stable enough for anesthesia and we'll take him to surgery. See if we can fix this thing."

The looks from his crew were still cautious, but more positive now.

Another thought crossed his mind. "You know what? Somebody get the portable X-ray machine in here. I want pictures of the leg. I don't want to overlook a fracture."

Within minutes they had a series of X-rays taken at various angles. Barry grabbed the cassettes that held each film and headed for the dark room. He and Kent stood next to the processor, treading like kids that needed to pee, as they waited the infinitely long six minutes for the films to develop. When they emerged, Barry slid them onto a view box along one wall.

Before Kent had even turned for a look, Barry's voice came through the darkness. "Holy shit!"

"Language, young one," Kent said, like Obi-Wan Kenobi. "You must be professional at all times." He turned to look at the films for himself. "Sonofabitch!"

Barry gave him the side-eye.

Near the center of each film, a white mushroom glared back at him.

"That's a bullet, right? The bullet is still in his leg."

"Yep. That would be a bullet. It's tucked up behind his femur."

"That explains why Lute's treatments didn't work."

"Where it's lodged, he couldn't feel it. Hell, I couldn't feel it either."

They headed back to the ER.

"How's he doing?" Kent asked the clinician in charge.

"His vitals are better. Stronger pulse. His temp has come up a little, and his color is better."

Barry blurted, "There is a bullet in his leg."

The clinician looked at Barry, then Kent. "Wow, good call on the X-rays."

"It's medial to the femur. Midshaft."

"That's not exactly good news, but at least we have an explanation. And maybe something we can fix."

"My thoughts exactly. Barry, you stick with Otsi. I'm going to tell Lute."

When Kent found him in the waiting area, Lute's head was leaning back against the wall and his eyes were closed. He was still chanting softly and working his string of shells. Kent cleared his throat and Lute jumped. As his eyes opened, his face folded into fear. Fear of the news Kent was about to give him. Fear of losing another close friend. Kent had never seen fear like that in Lute. It shook him.

"He's a little more stable but he's not out of the woods."

Lute closed his eyes and said something in Owahgena.

"The bullet is still in his leg. That's why he hasn't responded to your treatment."

Lute's face showed shock. Then he said defensively, "I felt for one."

"It's behind the bone. I missed it too, until I saw the X-rays."

Lute went quiet, assimilating the news. "Can you get it out?"

"Maybe. Assuming we can get him through the anesthesia, yes, I can get the bullet out, but that doesn't mean we can save his leg."

"I don't want to lose Otsi."

"I will do my best."

"I know you will." Lute sat back down, closed his eyes, and resumed fingering his string of shells.

CHAPTER 12

IT TOOK THE ER STAFF A BIG CHUNK OF THE AFTER-
noon to bring Otsi around enough that he had at least a reasonable
chance of surviving anesthesia. It took Kent and a surgical team, with
Barry assisting, another two hours to extract the bullet, debride the
wound, and piece it together as best they could. Otsi still had his leg—at
least for now.

Kent was applying the last layer of bandage. His voice sounded
tired but registered the satisfaction of a job well done. "Barry, my young
friend, by the time this is over, you are going to be an expert at applying
a wet-to-dry dressing."

Barry pulled a thermometer from under Otsi's tail and held it at
arm's length for a clear view of the red column. "One oh one and a half.
I'll take it. Sorry, Doc, I missed what you just said."

Kent repeated himself. "It's a special bandage that actually cleans
the dead tissue out of a wound. It gets the rest of the stuff we couldn't
get with a scalpel during surgery. You start by covering the wound with
gauze that has been soaked in saline, then leave it on overnight to dry.
When you take it off the next morning, the rotten stuff comes off a little
at a time with the bandage. If you do it every day for a few days, and get
lucky, you end up with a clean wound."

"Sounds gross, but cool. I can handle that."

"We'll start that tomorrow. I'm sure the techs will be more than happy to show you the details."

"How come I get the gross jobs?"

The others in the room smiled slyly.

"Consider it an addition to your experience library."

That brought a few chuckles.

Barry mumbled something about having *sucker* written on his forehead, then eased Otsi into a recovery cage.

Kent gave the staff one last acknowledgment of what a great job they had done and how proud he was of each and every one of them. Then, he reminded them, needlessly, to keep a close eye on Otsi. He went to give Lute an update.

It looked like Lute had not moved a muscle in the hours since Kent left him. His head was still resting back against the waiting room wall. His eyes were closed, he was still working his string of shells and mouthing Owahgena prayers.

Kent sat down across from him. Lute's eyes opened and instantly the fear was back.

"Well, I'm happy to report that Otsi's still with us. He's resting quietly. He's still got his leg, but—it's iffy, to say the least. Time will tell."

Lute let out a long sigh. "Thanks, Doc. I had my doubts." He stood. "I want to see him."

"Of course. I'll take you back."

As they made their way down the hall, Kent filled him in. "We're going to have to keep him for at least a few days. You get that, right? He'll be on intravenous antibiotics, pain meds, and fluids until he's eating and drinking on his own."

Lute did not respond and that worried Kent.

"Are you okay with that?"

"Did you save the bullet?"

"I did."

"Good. I want it."

"Sorry, I had them call Merrill. He's sending a guy over to get it."

"It came out of my dog. It's mine."

"Actually, it's evidence in a homicide investigation."

"I don't care. I want it."

"Merrill gave strict instructions that no one is to touch it. Something about chain of custody."

"Bullshit."

"Sorry, that's the way it is, Lute. Why do you care about the damn bullet anyway?"

Lute hesitated. "You wouldn't understand."

"Try me."

In an exasperated tone, Lute said, "Offering the weapon of an enemy to the spirits is a sign of respect. They look favorably on that."

Kent nodded as the reason for Lute's insistence sank in. "Okay, I get that. At least, I sort of get it. But it's the law." There was an uncomfortable silence.

Kent took another tack. "You want to find out what happened to Jimmy, right?"

"I don't give a damn about the law, and as far as Jimmy is concerned, I don't hold out much hope of the cops figuring it out, with or without the bullet."

The silence that followed was downright scary as tensions rose. Lute's face darkened. Kent watched as he drew in a monstrous breath to blast words he knew they would both regret. Kent stopped him with a raised palm.

"Hold on, Lute. I have an idea. Give me five minutes." He backed out of the waiting area, keeping his eyes on Lute and gesturing for him to sit tight. When the door closed, he bolted to the nearest phone and almost ripped it off the wall. He punched in a number and ran his hand though his hair while he listened to several rings.

"Come on, Merrill. Pick up!"

To his relief, the Chief did on the next one.

"You send your guy yet?"

"I don't think he's out the door. What's your hurry?"

"Do you have the bullet fragments the ME got from Jimmy?"

"They're in the evidence locker."

Kent quickly explained that Lute was insisting that he have the bullet they just recovered from Otsi and why.

"Don't let him have it. I mean it, Kent. It's important that no one even touches it. I appreciate that Lute wants it for a ceremony or whatever, but he can't have it. Period. I'm sorry."

"I figured you were going to say that. The problem is that, at this very moment, Lute's in my waiting room and he's about to explode."

"Yep. That's a problem, I'll admit."

"So, I have an idea." He explained it to Merrill.

Merrill listened then thought for a moment. "What you are asking me to do is… let's just say… not kosher."

"I know that." He waited for his brother to decide. It was Merrill's reputation that would be on the line.

Another couple of heartbeats and Merrill's self-confident voice came over the line. "I'm willing to roll with it, seeing how we're talking about Lute Crimshaw. I'll be over. I'm not going to get any of my guys caught up in this."

When Kent and Lute entered the recovery room, Barry stepped back out of the way. He remembered Doc's rule that staff members were to be silent observers when a doctor was talking to a client.

Kent shifted an IV line that passed into Otsi's cage, then opened the door. Lute groaned at the site of his canine friend so near death. He ducked his head into the cage, pressed his forehead to Otsi's, and murmured something in Owahgena.

A long, uncomfortable silence blanketed the room. It was a familiar silence. Kent had experienced it many times over the years as owners came to terms with what he had just told them. He waited.

Finally, Lute backed out of the cage. He stood and squared his shoulders. In a tone that was respectful but left no room for discussion, he said, "I'm taking him home."

Kent gave an optimistic nod. "I hope so. In a few days."

"Now."

Barry's jaw dropped. A tech looked up from the medical record she was writing in.

Kent's lips thinned into a smile that was a mix of understanding and frustration. "I had a feeling you were going to say that."

Lute was like stone.

"That's a bad idea, Lute."

"I appreciate all you have done. You are a true friend." He hesitated. "And an excellent veterinarian."

Kent opened his mouth to reply, but Lute continued.

"I am in your debt. You got the bullet out. I could not have done that. But, I'm taking Otsi with me. And I want that bullet."

Kent felt the temperature in the room rise. *Shit. Where was Merrill?*

He got his answer and a wash of relief when the Chief pushed through into the room. He'd caught Lute's last words.

"You can't have it. It's evidence."

Lute and Merrill faced off like dogs over a bone.

Kent stepped between them and asked Merrill, "Did you bring them?"

"I'm not saying anything until you clear the room except for you, me, and Lute."

Kent waved his arm. "Everybody out."

Confused and curious, the staff shuffled out whispering.

Kent closed the door behind them and gestured to Merrill that he had the floor.

Merrill reached in his pocket, pulled out a zip-lock bag, and held it up for Lute to see. "The spirits are going to have to make do with these."

When Lute shook the bag into his palm, three bullet fragments fell out. "These from Jimmy?"

"Yep. They are too beat up for the forensic guys to get anything. I'm sticking my neck way out by giving them to you, buddy."

Lute studied the twisted slivers of lead for a long second. Then, with a grunt that sounded like he was making one of the all-time great trades between white men and Indians, he said, "They'll do."

Merrill cautioned, "Not a word of this to anyone, right? I could get into big trouble for evidence tampering."

Kent was beyond relieved. Problem solved. He opened the door and his staff filed back in. That's when Lute said, "I still want to take Otsi home."

Kent reminded himself that his friend was in a terrible turmoil. He forced his voice to stay in compassion mode. "Lute, no, you can't. Please, let us keep Otsi here. Just for a few days."

"No."

The terrible pain of losing a patient swept over Kent. He glanced around the room, trying to come up with a way to change Lute's mind.

"You and I have had this conversation before. We both learned the art of healing and we both know where the other one stands when it comes to the style of medicine we prefer and trust. We've always respected that in each other. But all of us who hope to be healers, regardless of the type of medicine we practice, know that there is no treatment that always works. And, if the one you are using isn't working, you have to try a different one. If you don't, you will watch your patient die before your eyes. Am I right? You know this."

Lute remained stone-faced.

Kent went on. "What you were doing for Otsi was not working. You saw that. That's why you brought him here. What we are doing—at least for the moment—seems to be working. Please let us continue."

Lute drew a breath so deep, it seemed to suck the air out of the room. He stood there biting his lip and studying Otsi. The silence made it even harder to breathe. Finally, his head gave a tiny shake that increased into a series of firm ones, indicating his decision. "No, he's better off at home."

Kent stared at the floor, teeth clenched to keep himself from protesting.

Lute pushed his shirtsleeves up and ducked into Otsi's cage. He slid his arms under his dog and lifted gently.

Otsi, who had not moved since they placed him in the cage, let out a scream of pain that rattled the room.

The chests of the onlookers went hollow.

Lute pulled back. He stroked Otsi's head while the dog whimpered a few times then lapsed back into drug-induced sleep. Lute's shoulders started quaking. He whispered an Owahgena apology. It was the first time in all their years of friendship, that Kent had seen Lute cry.

Kent held up a hand, silently signaling his crew not to move. They waited.

Finally, Lute pushed himself back out of the cage. Still kneeling, he folded his arms across his chest and became motionless for what had to be a full minute. Finally, he stood. His eyes shifted from Otsi to Kent and held for another moment.

In a voice laden with fear that the decision he was making was wrong, he said, "Call me when he is ready to come home," and walked out of the ER without looking back.

CHAPTER 13

TO AUBREY'S HEADSTONE, KENT SAID, "YEAH, Hon, today is shaping up to be one hell of a day. For starters, the Northern Lights folks are throwing more gasoline on the fire by having their official groundbreaking ceremony today. Don't want to miss that. Assholes. From what I understand, they haven't even gotten full approval from the town, or state, or whoever and they just keep plowing right ahead—literally. If truth be told, they broke ground weeks ago anyway." He let out a growl. "They are so damn confident that it's all going to fall in place for them that they are not bothering to wait. I guess that's the whole reason for the ceremony, to show the public how confident they are. Man, I wish Pegger had as many lawyers working with him as they do." He seethed for a moment. "Jimmy's funeral across the river on the Rez caps off the afternoon. That makes for an exciting day, wouldn't you say?"

He paused, half expecting her to reply. When she did not, he said, "There's going to be a lot of angry people around Jefferson today."

He watched Lucinda sniff around headstones for a few moments. "When I talked to Em the other night, she said Sim is sort of in a holding pattern. No worse, but not a lot better. She's wishing his cut would heal faster than it is. I can't blame her for that. And before you have a fit, don't worry, I have him scheduled for a recheck. The good news is

Otsi seems to be on the mend. I'll see Lute today. A few days without his dog, he's probably going crazy."

He waved away the blackflies and tried to think of something more to say but couldn't. So he said, "I miss you more than you will ever know." He sat for a while longer. "I guess I'll see what's up at the office." He called Lucinda and headed to his truck.

● ● ●

Kent's morning at the CVC was packed. By the time he finally crossed paths with Barry, they were running late for the groundbreaking ceremony. "Have you got Otsi ready?"

"Yep."

"Good. I've got one quick discharge to do. I'll meet you at the truck."

"Want me to see if one of the other docs will do it for you?"

"No, I've got it."

The truth was that Kent had been watching and admiring the patient he was about to see since the first time he saw it as a ten-week-old. The pup was a perfect example of a redbone hound, as far as Kent could tell. Each time he did a follow-up, he wished that Lucinda could have a litter like that.

He ducked into an exam room.

"Okay, Roscoe," he said in an ominous voice to the now eleven-month-old dog. He waved a plastic bag. "This is strike two. You know how it works, right?"

Roscoe gave Kent an adoring smile—tongue lolling, tail wagging—totally oblivious to the scolding.

"Don't try to butter me up with your good looks. I'm onto you."

"He doesn't get it. At least last time he eventually passed all four socks. This time he needed surgery," the middle-aged woman holding Roscoe's leash said.

Kent opened the plastic bag. Using two fingers, he teased out a slimy length of brownish-green cloth and held it up for her to see. "The techs are guessing it's a bikini top."

Jen leaned away, studying it at arm's length. "My daughter's. She's missing one."

"You think she wants it back?"

"Eww, no!"

Kent dropped it into a nearby garbage can. "You and your family are going to have to keep everything picked up and," Kent patted Roscoe's head, "watch this handsome guy like a hawk."

"Believe me, we've already had a family discussion about that. We love him to death, but he's getting way too expensive."

"Okay, then. The techs will walk you through the meds and follow-up. Roscoe, I'll see you in about ten days to get your stitches out."

"Great, Doc. Thank you."

As he opened the door to leave, he said, "One more thing. Roscoe's diarrhea has pretty much stopped, but I wouldn't let him in on the expensive oriental rugs for a few more days."

"Thankfully, we don't have any of those."

"Good thing. He'd probably chew the corners off of them anyway."

It was a fun moment, another reminder of how much he had enjoyed veterinary medicine before he lost Aubrey. He wanted that feeling back.

Kent met Barry at the mobile unit and off they went along the Chittenango River toward Northern Lights. He reached over and gave Lucinda a pat. She was enjoying her chance to be in the front seat. "You guys okay back there?"

Kent glanced at his watch as they turned on the driveway into the site. "We're definitely late. This shindig started at eleven."

He noticed that they had spruced up the place since his last visit, at least as much as one can spruce up a construction site. There was fresh gravel on the road. The heavy machinery had been hosed off and now was squared away in a neat row like yellow army tanks so arriving guests would be impressed by it. The billboard was still there but was now decorated with streamers. A banner that read WELCOME CENTRAL NEW YORK was festooned across it. They had done nothing to improve the googly-eyed fish's ridiculousness.

The parking area was maxed out. Cars were tucked in haphazardly around the edge of it and along the shoulder of the road.

"Almost like a music festival," Barry said, peaking up from the back seat.

Ahead, they could make out a stage elevated on construction scaffolding. There was a crowd around it. They could hear the muffled drone of someone making a speech over a PA system.

Kent's eye was drawn to a car that stood out from the rest. It was a sleek, fire-engine red Mustang convertible.

Barry saw it, too. "Looks like Pegger's here."

"Go figure."

He wedged his truck into a shady spot next to it.

"I'm leaving all the windows down. Are you sure the two of you are going to be okay until I get back?"

"We're good. It's cool enough with the breeze and the shade. I brought some water, too."

"Good. We'll be back soon." As he got out of the truck, he patted his thigh. "Lucinda, you stay close to me." He turned and headed toward the crowd.

Lucinda hesitated, looking back and forth between the truck and her master, deciding. She followed Kent.

Kent perused the crowd. Even though he was looking at the backs of their heads, he recognized many of the people. There were the local merchants, the politicians that didn't make the cut to be on stage, farmers, and the usual squad of retirees that attended everything just for something to do.

Several dignitaries, men in dark suits and women in prim dresses, were seated in a row across the back of the stage in folding chairs. Each of them was wearing a bright smile and an even brighter new orange hard hat. Kent was immediately reminded of the googly-eyed fish.

A sixtyish man with a girth approximately equal to his height, and a smile broader than all the others, was at the podium leaning into the microphone. He was playing the crowd and enjoying every minute of it. Kent recognized him as J. Benjamin Balt, Northern Lights' exalted leader.

He used the word *jobs* in almost every sentence and the crowd cheered each time. "By this time next year, on this very spot where we are standing, there will be a hotel, The Caddisfly, a four-star beauty, the Trout Fishing Hall of Fame that tourists won't be able to resist, and a sporting goods store that will make Bass Pro and Cabela's look like mom-and-pop stores. On top of that, we will have a fly fishing school, guided fishing trips, and"—he lowered his voice as if letting the crowd in on a secret—"I probably shouldn't tell you this yet because it's not official," he teased, "but we're currently working with tournament officials to become a stop on the national trout fishing tournament circuit. Northern Lights Resort will be the fisherman's mecca."

The crowd roared. Balt leaned back, both hands on the podium, letting the approval wash over him.

There was that *mecca* thing again, but really it was all about jobs.

"What about a casino?" someone shouted over the cheers of the crowd.

Balt paused for effect and flashed a devious smile. "I'm not at liberty to talk about that—yet." He winked.

More cheers.

"There they are," slipped from Kent's lips when he picked up the Owahgena at the far side of the crowd. They were seated together, a dozen or so. The men looked like typical suburbanites in khakis and sport shirts; the women looked just as casual. Nothing out of the ordinary until you noticed the glistening black braids streaming down their backs. In the middle of the group was a scholarly-looking small man in his early twenties. His eyes burned with conviction through wire-rim glasses. Today he looked more like *Percival* than *Pegger,* and he had a thousand-knife stare aimed at Balt.

Lute and Jodi were sitting on either side of him. Lute's arms were folded defiantly across his chest. Jodi's face was framed by the cords from her earphones dangling down to her Walkman. She was staring straight ahead and looked worried. Kent hoped that the two of them would be able to restrain Pegger if things got crazy.

At that moment, a deep growl rolled up Lucinda's throat. The sound pulled Kent away from his crowd searching. He reached for Lucinda's collar and turned to follow her stare. She was watching a rough-looking woodsman and an alarmingly large dog approach them from behind.

The man was Feron Munn. The dog was Lip-Lip.

"Shit!" He hadn't figured on The Ferret.

CHAPTER 14

FERON MUNN WAS WEARING A CUT-OFF SWEAT-shirt with the Browning deer logo on the front. The shirt allowed full view of the tattoos that curled down his shoulders to his wrists. The focal point of the body art was on his right upper arm—a magnificent buck deer with a huge rack, standing tall. Centered over the buck's heart was a set of crosshairs from the rifle scope of an anonymous hunter. The takeaway was that the proud animal did not know he was seconds from death.

Feron had a five-day beard. His camo cargo pants sagged off his hips down into his loosely tied hunting boots. He was stick-thin, with a sinewy fitness. His build fit his nickname—The Ferret.

It bothered Kent to see how far his old friend had declined.

Lucinda growled again, her eyes fixed on Lip-Lip. He was a monstrous husky mix, nearly twice the size of Lucinda. His coat was brown, long, and coarse. That, and his lumbering gait, made him appear as much like a bear as a dog. His head was wide and his jaw massive. He had a permanent limp on one front leg. The story was that he got caught in a bobcat trap years ago. He was drooling through the heavy leather muzzle Feron put on him whenever they were out in public.

When he was close enough, Feron reared back on the leash restraining Lip-Lip as he snarled at Lucinda. She stood her ground, but Kent was thankful for the muzzle.

"Morning, Doc," he drawled and squirted brown spit at the ground. "That was something about Jimmy."

Kent's antenna went up. "Yes, it was. Do you know anything about that?"

"No. But I figured you might. Merrill on it?"

"They don't have much. Yet."

Ropey muscles stood out on Feron's arm as he held Lip-Lip back. "Who would shoot Jimmy Silverheel? Easiest going guy in the world."

Kent knew Feron was well connected in the secretive circle of marginals that turned below Jefferson's idyllic small-town façade. "Have you heard anything?"

"I told you, I ain't got nothin'."

Both men held back their dogs as they let sobering thoughts of Jimmy pass. Then Feron shifted the subject. "Figures you'd be here at this dog and pony show today—meddling."

"Actually, I'm surprised to see you here."

Feron smiled slyly. "Two reasons. One is I'm looking for a girl, a youngster, that's wandered off. And second"— he waved his free hand proudly—"I'm here because I've got an interest in all this."

Kent ignored whatever the thing was with the girl—Feron's domestic life was a legendary mess. If he was caught up in some family squabble, that was his problem. But the idea of Feron having an interest in Northern Lights intrigued him.

"Is that right? Tell me how you fit into all this."

"It's my land. Well, it was, until these wackos bought it."

Kent looked dubious. "Wait, you owned this land? In all the years I've known you, how come I never heard that?"

Feron shrugged. "You think you know everything. Either you or your brother. But you don't. It belonged to my ol' man but just like everything else in his life, he didn't do nothing with it. I got it when he died."

"Hmm."

Lip-Lip's frustration was building. He lunged at Lucinda again.

"Keep him back," Kent ordered. "This is no place for a dog fight."

Feron hauled on the leash again. "It wouldn't be much of a fight. And Lip-Lip ain't a dog. I told you that before. And you ought to know anyway being an animal doctor and all."

Kent catered to Feron's insecurities. "Right, he's a wolf hybrid. I remember that now."

Feron picked up on the doubt in Kent's voice. "He is, I'm telling you. I got him special from a breeder in Canada."

"Whatever. Bring that creature to my office and I'll castrate him for free."

Feron snorted. "Not a chance. You ain't getting anywhere near this guy's nuts with a knife."

Feron grew up in a tough, backwoods family. His ancestry was vague, but since he lived on the reservation, it was assumed by the locals that he was at least part Owahgena. As a kid, he hung out with Lute, Jimmy, Kent, and Merrill. He went to school, played sports, hunted, and fished with them, too. But, somewhere along the line, Feron took a wrong turn.

Nowadays, as far as Kent knew, Feron split his time between hanging out at the bars or hunting, fishing, or trapping—regardless of the season. He also smuggled various contraband down from Canada, like cigarettes, weed, and hunting trophies of endangered species. The locals called his business "The Canadian Express" and pretty much looked the other way.

Lip-Lip growled at Lucinda again. "Stay!" Feron ordered. He yanked his dog back, and this time put his knee on Lip-Lip's rump using his body weight to make the dog sit.

"Like I was saying, I got this land from Pap, and a few rifles, when the ol' man died. But you know, I live on my boat most of the year and I got my trapper's cabin in winter. What did I need with this dirt? It was just sitting here building up back taxes."

"So you sold it to these idiots even though you knew what they intended to do."

Feron shrugged. "At the start, they lied about how big they were going to get. They made it sound like they were just going to put in a regular boat launch. After a while I figured out what they really were going to do. I didn't like it then, and I don't like it now, that's for sure." He gave a bigger shrug. "But their money was the greenest."

"You sold out your own people."

Feron's brow creased. "That's easy for you to say. Standing up for the lowly Indians and all. You and Merrill are both a couple of self-righteous pricks. You know that? You had everything handed to you on a silver platter."

Kent rolled his eyes. "Uh-huh."

"I'm telling you, Kent, not all of us got what you did." Feron gave a sad kind of laugh. "Besides, the Owahgena are only *sort of* my people. No one knows for sure." He thumbed toward the crowd. "I got to admit, they aren't happy about the whole thing. And like I say, I'm a little sad too that it went the way it did, but hey."

They went silent, listening to Balt shout over the PA system about how the project was going to turn a muddy old riverbank into a center of prosperity.

The crowd was eating it up.

Feron indicated toward the stage with a nod. "Yeah, they're assholes, all right."

That's when they heard Pegger steal the show. He stood and yelled loud enough that everyone could hear him. Surprised, Balt stopped speaking and scanned the crowd, until his eyes found Pegger.

"What you say is mostly bullshit," Pegger shouted. "And the rest is only half true."

Balt's face folded into a sympathetic look. He shook his head and then let his chin drop to his chest—the picture of condescension. "Mr. Cyr, we have been through this before, many times."

"Yes, we have. And nothing changes. You keep right on with your plan to desecrate the Chittenango River."

Balt spread his arms in a gesture of earnest explanation. "We are building a fishing community! Fishing does not desecrate a river."

"Overfishing does. So does catch-and-release fishing."

Balt's face morphed into a puzzled look. "Excuse me? How does catch-and-release fishing desecrate the river?"

Pegger was pumped now. "By terrifying, displacing, and humiliating the fish that live in it, just for entertainment, *that's* desecrating the river."

Balt smiled a broad, false smile, as if he could not believe his ears. He glanced at the crowd then back at Pegger. "I'm sorry, but I don't think fish *can* be humiliated." A wave of laughter went through the crowd. "We don't even keep them. We put them *back*. It's catch-and-*release*."

"That's the point!" Pegger roared. "Catch-and-release is not harmless. You try to convince everyone that you are just playing, that everybody is having fun. Not the fish, I can guarantee you that. You are torturing them."

"I think you are exaggerating."

The crowd turned to Pegger for a reply and he let the silence hang. Finally, in a calm, confident tone, he said, "Mr. Balt, how much fun would it be for you if one day you were walking along the river, minding your own business, when you saw a gold nugget in your path? You reach down to pick it up and, suddenly, a piece of steel comes up out of the water and hooks into your lip. It was a trap! The rope attached to the hook starts dragging you into the water. You struggle with all your might to free yourself, but the hook holds tight and the line keeps on pulling. When you are exhausted, you collapse, gasping for air. Helpless, and sure you are going to die, the rope drags you into the river and under the water."

"Mr. Cyr," Balt interrupted, leaning close to the mic for extra volume, "I am not a fish."

"Hold on Mr. Balt, I am not finished." Pegger turned to the audience as he continued. "Now, you *can't* breathe because you are underwater. As you are drowning, a monster grabs you around the chest and tears the hook out of your mouth, and in the process its barbs rip your lip, or tongue, or throat. He puts his thumb in your mouth and lifts you by your jaw for his fellow monsters to see. They laugh, measure your length, and take a picture or two of you. Then, after an infinitely long few minutes during which you can't breathe, the monster in his benevolence, he heaves you back up onto the riverbank. You lie there, disoriented, gasping for air, mouth bleeding, while he tells his friends what an exhilarating feeling it was pulling you in. Except, as you lie there paralyzed with fear, you realize it's not a part of the riverbank that you recognize. It's far from your home and, now on top of everything else, you are totally lost."

"That's not what it is like."

"How do you know? You just said you are not a fish."

Balt's voice was becoming shrill. "What you say is unrealistic."

"Is it? Scientists have shown time and time again that fish feel pain. And fear. And any school child will tell you fish cannot breathe out of water. Their life is no more a joke or less important than yours."

The crowd fell into a heavy silence. People treaded uncomfortably.

For a moment, Balt was at a loss for words. Then he turned back to his script. "Jobs!" he said, pounding the podium. "That's what Northern Lights is all about—jobs and prosperity."

The crowd came back to him with a round of applause.

"Mr. Cyr," Balt said, now that he was back on firm footing, "why don't you get back in that hot rod of yours and take your negativism someplace else?"

Pegger sank back into his chair, seething. "Goddamn Euros. Total bullshit." He sat clenching and unclenching his fists until he could no longer stand all the eyes on him. He stood and wheeled around, pushed through the crowd, and headed for his car.

Kent had heard enough. Feron and Lip-Lip had disappeared. He remembered that he'd left Barry back at the truck and he didn't want him there too long. He needed to get Lute, but when he looked over to where the Owahgena were sitting, Lute and Jodi were gone. Must be they left to keep an eye on Pegger. He started back toward the parking lot.

He was at the edge of it when he noticed that Pegger and Feron had crossed paths and were in a heated discussion. Pegger was seated in his Mustang, its top down. Feron was standing a few steps away restraining Lip-Lip. They were spitting angry words at each other.

Before Kent could get close enough to hear what they were saying, Pegger flipped off Feron and hit the gas. Tires spinning, gravel flying, the Mustang fishtailed out of the lot.

Feron spit tobacco juice, grumbled to his dog, and watched him go. Then he loaded Lip-Lip into a Silverado pickup. It was that year's model, 1999, all shiny and jacked-up, with oversize tires, and lots of chrome. On the back window were decals for Arctic Cat, Remington, John Deere, and a half-dozen other mainstays of country living. Through the window Kent could see a gun rack with a mean-looking rifle cradled in it. Two stack pipes rumbled when he started the engine. He roared out of the lot just as Pegger had done.

Kent heard rustling behind him, turned and saw Lute and Jodi.

"I was just looking for you," Kent said.

"Where's my dog?" Lute growled, but it was followed by a smile.

"Barry's watching him."

"How's he doing?"

"Like I've been telling you every two hours when you call for a progress report, he's doing just fine. Actually, he's doing superbly if I do say so myself."

"When can he come home?"

"Soon."

"That's what I want to hear."

Lute's mind went in a different direction. He pointed at Feron's truck getting smaller in the distance. "Where do you figure our ol' pal got the money for a truck like that?"

Kent followed the truck with his eyes. Sun glinted off the chrome like mirrors. He could still hear the big engine. He shrugged. "You don't need money to buy a truck, just credit."

"I know for a fact that The Ferret deals only in cash."

They digested that fact for a moment, then Lute said, "I saw him and Pegger going at it pretty good just now. What was that about?"

"I couldn't hear. Probably he was telling Pegger to butt out. Word is The Ferret is pretty tight with Mr. Balt these days."

"There's a rumor going around on the Rez that Feron is a partner or something."

"Partner?" Kent scoffed. "Feron's a high roller, all right. He just informed me that *he* sold Northern Lights the land. Did you know that?"

"Nope. I didn't know he owned it. Must be his smuggling business is down."

Kent laughed. "Yeah, that's probably it."

Any semblance of humor was blown away when Jodi spoke for the first time. "I'll kill that bastard if he touches my son."

Kent waited for the spiders to quit crawling up his spine. "Why would Feron come after Pegger? He's just full of hot air. His big talk, his big dog, his big truck—it's all for show."

Jodi pulled the earphones out of her ears. Her eyes went dark as she stared in the direction that Feron's truck had gone. "He's more than bluster, believe me. And he's not taking anything from me ever again."

Lute and Kent studied Jodi, then gave each other puzzled looks.

"What is that supposed to mean?" Lute asked.

She waved him off. "That's between me and Feron Munn." She jammed her earphones back in, cranked the music so loud Kent and Lute could hear it, and retreated back into herself.

The three of them stood there waving away blackflies. Jodi bent down and gave Lucinda a hug. Kent watched her—slender body, her smooth hair drifting down onto Lucinda. As cold as she was, there was warmth in there somewhere.

To keep his mind from going the direction it was starting to stray, he changed the subject. "Hey. I've got something for you two in my truck."

"What's that?" Lute asked.

"Follow me."

The three of them walked toward Kent's vet truck. Lucinda bolted ahead. They watched her rise up, paws on the door, and start barking into the open window. It was her happy, playful bark. They could see movement inside, but detail was obscured by shadows and glare.

When they got closer, Lute asked, "Is that Skippy in the truck? What's he up to?"

Kent didn't answer.

When they were a few steps away, Barry shifted his position and Otsi's head emerged out the window. He stretched toward Lute and let out the loudest, most joyful, coonhound bay Kent had ever heard.

Kent was reminded just how fast Lute could move. He and Jodi stood back as Lute raced the last few steps and leaned in the window. Otsi licked his face between howls and whines. Lute said something in Owahgena, then buried his face in the fur of his dog's neck.

When it seemed to Barry that the reunion had gone on long enough, he said, "He's doing great."

Lute opened the truck door and slid in next to his dog.

"He's going to be carrying that leg for a while," Kent said. "He may have a permanent limp. I hope not, but time will tell."

"We'll have him hunting again," Lute said, confidently. "You watch."

"He's come along faster than I expected. As far as I'm concerned, he can go home with you now."

Jodi pulled one earphone. She kept her eyes grounded, only giving Kent a quick glance. "Thank you, Doc. You saved Otsi for us. We owe you." She seemed conflicted, as if it hurt to say kind words to a Euro.

"You're welcome," he said, wishing he could extend the moment.

Jodi lit a cigarette and they watched Lute and Otsi reunite while she smoked it. She reached in and gave Otsi a pat. "Max really missed you. He wouldn't admit it, but I could tell. Every time I went to look for him, he was in your bed."

Kent chuckled, then cleared his throat loudly. "There is one thing." In a somber tone, and loud enough that he was sure Lute could hear, he said, "Otsi needs to be on antibiotics. For several weeks." He braced for a backlash from Lute.

Lute opened his mouth to provide one but closed it when Jodi gave him a threatening look and waved her hand. "Don't worry, Doc. You give *me* the medicine. I'll see that Otsi gets every pill."

Lute was wise enough not to argue.

"Good. I am going to hold you to that."

Barry helped Lute get Otsi to his truck and got him situated.

"How about I stop by tomorrow and take a look at him?" Kent suggested.

Jodi blew smoke skyward. "That works."

Kent and Barry climbed into the mobile unit. They were about to leave when Jodi stepped to the window. Her expression was cautious. She still avoided eye contact. "Are you going to the funeral this afternoon?"

"I'll be there," Kent said. "I owe Jimmy that much."

Jodi gave him a furtive glance then looked away again. "I think Pegger has them worried." She stepped back and slipped her earphones in before he could further the discussion.

CHAPTER 15

THE NEXT MORNING KENT WAS AT THE CEMETERY
as usual watching the sunrise and carrying on a lonely conversation
with Aubrey.

"The Northern Lights groundbreaking was a fiasco, as I warned
you it would be. Pegger Cyr got all fired up and tried to shame their
head guy, Benjamin Balt. He didn't have much luck. Then Feron Munn
showed up with that damn dog of his. You can imagine how that went."

Blackflies were annoying Lucinda. She snapped at the air and
shook her head. Kent waved away a swarm that was hovering over her.

"Yeah, Lip-Lip is the dog's name. He got all up in Lucinda's face.
Wolf hybrid? Whatever. He's a nasty thing. Did I ever tell you this? One
time I asked Feron how he settled on the name *Lip-Lip* because I had a
hard time imagining Feron read *anything*, let alone a classic novel. He
said, as far as he knew, it was just a name. It came with the dog when he
got him up in Canada. So I told him, Lip-Lip was the name of a mean-
ass dog in Jack London's novel *White Fang*. You should have seen The
Ferret's face light up. He thought it was awesome that his dog was named
after a famous bully."

Kent slapped his neck then rolled the dead blackfly between his
fingers. "He used to be a good guy, basically I mean, given his tough
upbringing. I used to enjoy having him around, but somewhere along
the line he got knocked off the track." He flipped the fly off into the

grass. "Anyway, Feron has Jodi worried that he might do something to Pegger because he's sided with Northern Lights and Pegger wants to shut them down."

A long silence ensued.

"I went to Jimmy Silverheel's funeral in the afternoon. Barry came with me. He liked Jimmy a lot, too. It was awful. There was as much anger at the funeral as at the groundbreaking. Lute was a mess." Kent exhaled a sad laugh. "Who wouldn't be? He actually saw Jimmy's head get blown off."

Kent tried to think of more to tell Aubrey, he didn't want to leave on such a bad note.

"Barry is doing well. He misses you, for sure, but he's got it under control." Another weak laugh. "He's turning into a great kid. He's doing better than I am, really. He keeps himself busy at the CVC. You can be proud of him."

Another void.

"Sometime today I'm supposed to stop by Lute's place to recheck Otsi."

He stared absentmindedly around the cemetery.

"Emily called me. She thinks Sim's foot is worse. So I moved up the recheck. I'm going to head there right from here."

Kent listened to the first rustling of the squirrels overhead. The sun was fully up. He wasn't eager to start his day.

"That's about it. I can't think of anything else to report."

He waited, half expecting her to speak. When there was only silence, he rose and whistled Lucinda over. *Another day begins.*

***

Kent tried to let his mind drift as he guided his mobile unit along the bank of the Chittenango River toward Orchard Hill Farm, but it went straight to Jimmy. He wondered if Merrill had been able to get anything off Otsi's bullet. And he wanted to tell Merrill about his conversation with Feron. It didn't sit well. Feron sold the land to Northern Lights for the resort. That in itself was grounds for concern. And Jodi seemed so convinced that Feron was up to something. What was that all about?

He let it go for now. "Lucinda," he said, thinking out loud, "Barry has it in his head that you and Otsi ought to have a family."

Lucinda turned from the window to face him. Her expression was neutral.

He prodded her. "What do you think of that idea?"

Lucinda didn't care what Kent was saying. He was paying attention to her and that was all she cared about. She smiled at him with her eyes.

"He's a blue tick hound, you know. Are you okay with that? I mean, there's all that interracial stuff, you being a redbone."

Her heavy brow rolled forward into a you-are-such-an-idiot look.

He chuckled. "It's a moot point if you don't come into heat, right?"

She turned back to the window.

Orchard Hill Farm was bustling when they arrived. The parking lot was full. Classes were in progress in both the indoor and outdoor rings.

Kent ducked under several sets of crossties and exchanged pleasantries with equestrians and stable hands as he made his way to Sim's stall.

When Emily saw him, she stopped stroking Sim's back and dropped the brush she was using into a pail of grooming supplies. Sim was standing at rest, head down, quietly munching some hay.

"Right on time."

"So you don't think your boy is improving," Kent said after a quick greeting.

"His upper leg looks swollen to me, and his lameness is worse."

Kent could see some puffiness above Sim's bandage. He placed the palm of his hand on it, like a mother feeling her child's forehead. "It feels a little warm."

He lifted Sim's tail and inserted a thermometer. While he waited for it to register, he asked, "Is he still eating?"

"Yep. No problem there."

He withdrew the thermometer. "One hundred and one."

"That's normal. Right?"

"Yes."

Kent unwound the bandage and noticed a patch of dried blood the size of a silver dollar on the gauze. He brought it close to his nose and detected a foul odor. When he inspected the wound, his level of concern rose. The sutures he had applied were under tension from pressure beneath. The skin edges that he had aligned were now spread slightly. When he touched the wound, Sim pulled his foot away.

"Sorry, buddy." He stood up and stared at Sim's leg in silence for a few seconds. "You are right. It's more painful than it was before. I think there is a little infection getting started. It looks mild and superficial, but we need to ratchet up our treatment. When I saw the wound the other day, I thought a topical antibiotic would be enough. I didn't think we needed to risk side effects from a systemic antibiotic for a minor ding like that. Now I'm thinking it would be smart to start him on one, just to be on the safe side. I want to knock out any infection before it can really get going."

Emily searched her father's face. "He's going to be okay, right?"

"Yes. He'll be fine. I'll give him an injection of Tribrissen now to get him started and leave you enough tubes that you can give him an oral dose every day for a week. I want you to soak his foot in a warm iodine solution, too. And keep up the Banamine." He saw a dark look cross Emily's face.

"There's no need to panic. You've ridden with me enough to know this sort of thing happens all the time."

"Yes, but this is Simpatico's Gift, *my* horse. It's not the same." Her mouth curled into a smile, but he knew she wasn't kidding.

He was silently thinking the same thing.

She talked quietly to Sim as her father used an alcohol pad to clean a small area on his neck and then injected a milky fluid into his jugular vein.

"His temp is normal and he's still eating well. You follow my instructions and I'll stop by day after tomorrow to see how he's doing. He should be coming around by then."

"Sounds good." As Kent climbed back into the vet truck, she asked, "By the way, is there anything new about what happened to Jimmy?"

"Not really. The Chief is waiting for a report on the bullet we got out of Otsi. And they are canvasing all around trying to see if anyone saw or knows anything. Have you heard anything?"

"Just a few rumors. Are they still thinking it was random gunfire from some idiot?"

"The Chief says they are not jumping to conclusions, but I think that's their working theory."

"It makes the most sense, really. Didn't he live by himself?"

"Yep. He never even married. He wasn't a gambler and always paid his bills. He drank some, but nothing out of line."

"Wasn't he a welder?"

"Self-taught. He had a small shop on his farm. Mostly did repairs on machinery for other farmers. They said he was pretty good at it. I don't think he made much money at it."

"I can't imagine why anyone would kill him. I'll keep my ears open. A lot of the help here at Orchard Hill lives out in the country. Somebody may say something."

"Lute has hinted that he thinks it's tied to all that's going on with the Northern Lights project. The police haven't found anything to support that." He gave a dismal laugh. "Lately it seems that Lute blames Northern Lights for anything at all that goes wrong anywhere in the county."

"He's got a grudge."

"In spades. But I have to say, Jimmy's death aside, I agree with him. You can say what you want about jobs and money flowing into Jefferson, but I don't buy it. Northern Lights is just as bad for our community as it is for the Owahgena."

He promised her again that he would stop by to recheck Sim in a couple of days and left.

CHAPTER 16

AFTER ORCHARD HILL FARM, KENT CROSSED THE bridge to the reservation side of the river then drove upstream for a mile or so to Lute's log cabin. Lute built it himself years ago and Kent both admired and envied his friend's construction skills. It was a beauty—tidy and in tune with nature, tucked in the woods, and hidden from the main road. The open space around it was minimal, as if the cabin had grown in the forest. There was a small barn, a large vegetable garden, and a half-dozen fruit trees of different varieties. The only oddity was the long, narrow pasture running from the barn out into the woods like a landing strip. Its odd shape was because not only was it a pasture for their cow and a few goats, it was also a rifle range—when the livestock were safely secured in the barn, of course.

He parked next to Lute's truck and eyed the range. Under a lean-to next to the barn was a heavy table anchored in the ground, where the shooter could steady a rifle. He squinted at a collage of targets tacked on a wood wall at the other end. His eyebrows lifted. It had to be three hundred yards away.

He heard a dog yapping inside the cabin and chuckled. *No need for a doorbell out in the country.*

He climbed a set of solid log steps to the door. Inside, he could hear Jodi scolding the dog to be quiet. The barking stopped and the door opened just enough for Jodi to squeeze out onto the porch. She teased the earphone out of one ear. It was a good thing she had a loud dog or she never would have heard him pull up. Her expression was distant.

"Yesterday we agreed that I would stop by and check Otsi today, right?" he reminded her.

"I remember."

She was wearing a flannel shirt, clean and crisp, top few buttons open. It fit close enough to show her contour. Her braid rode over her shoulders and down to her jeans. Sun rays reflected off the red cedar logs highlighting her skin. Kent tried not to stare. *She could be an L.L. Bean model if it wasn't for the earphones.* She lifted a half-smoked cigarette to her lips. *No, maybe not.*

"This is Max," she said, pointing at the feisty black and tan Chihuahua that was looking out through the screen and growling at Kent.

"Merrill warned me about that little guy. I'll put Lucinda back in the truck before there's a fight."

"No need for that. Max is like me; he gets along with animals better than people. They'll be fine together. Just don't *you* reach down and try to pet him. He'll take your finger off."

"Noted." Kent didn't doubt her for a minute. He guessed Max to be ten to twelve pounds and bet the little guy would not back down from a bear.

To be on the safe side, they watched as Lucinda and Max got acquainted. At first, the two dogs stood on the porch posturing, hackles up, circling stiff-legged, gathering each other's scent. Then, simultaneously, they relaxed, tails dropped to a normal carry, and they trotted off. Lucinda followed Max as he hopped down the steps and pranced around his yard stopping to let her smell bushes, tires, and clothesline pole, like a kid showing off his playground.

"Looks like they'll be fine. You were right."

"Otsi is in the back bedroom." She mashed her cigarette into an ashtray on the porch railing and led him into the cabin.

They crossed through an inviting country kitchen. Dried herbs hung in neat bunches along the ceiling. A heavy kettle, too big for the cupboard, sat on the stove. One corner was floor-to-ceiling shelves of mason jars filled with corn, squash, pickles, and other staples.

Jodi set her Walkman on the counter. She noticed Kent studying the larder. "We have a big garden."

"It smells great in here."

She pointed at the pot on the stove. "It's the herbs we've been brewing for Otsi. I like the smell, too."

"But he's getting his antibiotic, right?"

"Oh, yeah. But Lute insists on the tea. He figures it doesn't hurt."

Kent gave a quick shrug. "That's okay with me. If he wants to."

He followed Jodi into a large living room and was immediately hit with three images—a primitive Indian village, a man, and a small child.

The Indian village was a mural the size of a department store window. It was hand-painted in a rustic Native American style and depicted an idyllic pre-European Indian village on the shore of a river—no doubt the Chittenango. There were longhouses, canoes, and men fishing with nets or carrying game. Women with toddlers were drying fish on racks and tending vegetable gardens. A group of boys were playing the original version of lacrosse. It was easy to see that the artist had deep feelings for the culture and lamented the loss of it.

"That should be in a museum," he said.

"Pegger did it when he was in high school."

"It's fantastic!" Kent was speaking softly because of the other two things in the room, Lute on the couch, and a toddler sleeping next to him.

Lute seemed oblivious to their presence. He sat cross-legged, back ridged, eyes closed, chanting softly. His hands were working a string of tiny shells just as he had done in the CVC emergency room.

"What's he doing?" Kent whispered.

"Praying."

"For Otsi?"

"Yes…and for Jimmy…and the rest of us, too," she said, as casually as if she was discussing dinner.

Kent gestured toward the little girl. His eyebrows rose in a questioning look.

Jodi ignored him. "Otsi is this way."

As Kent followed her down the hall, he noticed the gracefulness in her stride. She moved like a deer, but it was offset by an uncomfortable tightness, something pent-up in her.

She opened another door and, as Kent entered, he smiled. Lute's man-cave. On the walls were guns of all types—long, short, new, old, with scopes and without—all polished to a parade shine and emitting the pleasant smell of gun oil. There were very old-looking longbows and hi-tech compound bows. There was a table in the center with a reloading press, several small pails of spent brass of assorted calibers, and all the tools for reloading ammo. Kent didn't see any gun powder but was sure there was a keg of it nearby. Lute would have it safely stored somewhere other than in the cabin—for obvious reasons.

Otsi was on the floor next to the table lying on a mattress of three stacked throw rugs. He was lapping from a bowl when they entered and immediately looked up. His eyes brightened and he started to rise to greet them.

They knelt quickly so that he wouldn't try to stand.

One glance told Kent that Otsi's pain level was near zero, his hydration was normal, and he may even have put on a little of the weight he'd lost.

"He looks great."

"He's feeling so much better that it's hard to keep him down," Jodi said proudly.

"I'm amazed. It looks like we got the bullet out and the antibiotics in just in time."

"It's all Lute."

"I doubt that." He reached over and picked up a well-chewed knucklebone and gave Jodi a questioning look.

"Don't blame me for that. That is all Lute, too."

Kent waggled the bone at Jodi. "I don't mind the herbs and stuff but this is how Lute is going to kill Otsi with kindness."

"I know." She took the bone and set it out of reach on the bench. "Sorry. Lute insists on the bones, too."

Kent rolled his eyes. "No big. We'll get his leg fixed first, then worry about pancreatitis."

"I know you and Lute have different ideas on whether they are good for dogs."

He exhaled a short laugh. "It's one of our many differences of opinion regarding medicine. Just remind him for me, 'All things in moderation.'"

Her dimples flickered into view then vanished as a wisp of a smile blew across her face. "Yeah. I think that's the best we can hope for."

Kent stroked Otsi's head. To Jodi he said, "How is the wound?"

"Better. At least I think so."

"Can I see it?"

"Sure. It's time to change the bandage anyway."

Kent was amazed at how strong the dog was. Jodi struggled to keep him still while he unwound the bandage.

She whispered in Otsi's ear—part in English and part in Owahgena—until he finally relaxed.

"You're good with animals," he said.

"I help them, they help me."

Kent thought about how much he relied on Lucinda. "I get that."

The wound was clean and odorless. It had closed to half of its original size. He flexed and extended the leg—full range of motion and very little pain.

"The wound looks great, too."

The corners of Jodi's mouth rose in a smile. This time, her dimples stayed.

"What was it exactly that you and Lute were doing for him?"

She sat back on her heels. "I fed him the teas that Lute made up. I don't know the recipes. He's got all kinds of herbs growing in our garden. And he collects stuff in the woods, too. I spoon-fed him until he could drink on his own. We coat the wound with raw honey twice a day."

Kent looked at Otsi's leg then back at Jodi. "I wouldn't be surprised if that helped a little. All the sugar in honey makes it hypertonic. That environment inhibits bacterial growth."

He missed it when Jodi rolled her eyes. "I'll let Lute know that."

As they worked together rebandaging Otsi's leg, Kent's elbow brushed Jodi's breast. It was his first touch of a woman in—forever. Even that slight contact felt good, but at the same time still forbidden. His eyes met hers for a split second. Hers were unreadable.

He searched for something to say to conceal his angst. "Cool gun room."

She rolled her eyes. He wasn't sure if it was because of his school-boy shyness or her family's unconventional hobby, but she went along. "We like to shoot."

"I knew Lute had a few guns, but nothing like this."

"Some are Pegger's and mine, too."

"I remember you used to hunt with Lute."

"I still get a deer every year, but mostly I hunt by myself now. We target shoot a lot." She indicated to the room with a nod. "That's the reason for all this stuff."

Kent put the last tape on the bandage and Jodi let Otsi up.

"I noticed your range out back."

"Yeah, I enjoy getting out there." She went dark for a second. "It's a great stress reliever."

Kent wondered what stress she was thinking about.

She bounced back. "Nothing like cranking Guns N' Roses in your headphones and blowing up pumpkins at three hundred yards to clear your mind."

"I bet."

She kissed Otsi on his forehead then stood up. "Plus, it empowers me."

Kent was considering her words as they tucked Otsi in, gave him a final pat on the head, and left the gun room. "It's still too soon to stop the antibiotics. Make sure he gets them all."

CHAPTER 17

IN THE LIVING ROOM, LUTE WAS STILL ON THE couch meditating. The little girl was still sleeping next to him.

Kent gestured toward Lute. He kept his voice at a whisper. "No wonder Otsi is getting better with all the prayers he gets."

"He's actually praying for me now."

"Really? How can you tell?"

"By the condolence beads."

To this point, Kent hadn't paid much attention to the string Lute was holding. Now he saw it was a fine leather thong about a foot long strung with tiny snail-like shells. Some were blue and some were white.

"Why condolence beads for you?" The second he said it, he wished he could pull the words back.

For several beats Jodi did not speak. Her face flushed. She took a step into the kitchen and picked up her Walkman. Kent thought, for sure, he was about to be shut out, and he kicked himself. As she lifted the earbuds, their eyes met, and she stopped. He could tell she was deciding whether or not to let him in. After a few more beats, she set them back on the counter.

"The Owahgena believe that when you lose a loved one, the spirits allow you to mourn for a brief period, then they expect you to overcome your grief and resume the life they gave you. To grieve too long is an insult to them. When someone can't recover and mourns too long, the shaman uses condolence beads to communicate between the spirit of the one who died and the mourner. He makes things right so that the mourner can refocus on living."

Kent was trying to get his head around that when Jodi spoke again, "I had a daughter."

"I didn't know that."

"Yeah. She was a few years younger than Pegger." Her tone told Kent that she was drifting back. "Our house burned and she died in the fire."

"I'm sorry to hear that."

"We were living in Canada then." Tears filled her eyes. "I was her mother and I didn't keep her safe."

She yanked a tissue from a box on a side table and wiped her eyes. Angrily, she held it toward Kent. "See, this is what I mean about needing the condolence beads. It's been so long and I can't stop crying. I can't let it go!"

In the silence that followed, Kent tried to think of something to say. Jodi found a pack of cigarettes on a side table and shook one out. She had her lighter poised at the tip of the cigarette when her eyes landed on the sleeping child. She cursed under her breath, then tossed the cigarette and the lighter onto the table.

"Do you think Lute's prayers help?"

Jodi pulled the flask from her pocket and waved it at Kent like it were a handgun. "How does one know? You want a drink?"

"Right. No, none for me."

Jodi leaned her head back and took a swallow just as Lute stirred on the couch. When she brought it down, she pointed at him with it. "He doesn't like that I drink so much." Then, frustrated, she said, "It's been years. I just can't get past it."

Kent's mind drifted to Aubrey. "I know what you mean." Then, as a half-joking afterthought, he said, "Maybe Lute should do his bead thing for me, too."

Jodi gave him a solemn look. "Oh, he does. Often."

That surprised Kent and, in a way, irked him that his private mourning seemed to be common knowledge to everyone else.

Lute emerged from his trance. He leaned over to an end table and carefully placed his beads in a small wooden box. He uncurled his legs onto the floor and stretched his shoulders. He gave no sign that he had heard their conversation.

"Did Jodi take you back to see Otsi?"

"Yes. He's doing great. I wouldn't change a thing. Like I told Jodi, keep him on the antibiotics until they're gone."

Lute smiled. "Will do. It wouldn't have worked unless you had gotten the bullet out."

Kent looked at Jodi then Lute. "And it looks like we pulled one over on the spirits."

Lute was confused for a second but recovered quickly. "You mean the bullet switch?"

"Yeah. The spirits must have been okay with the one from Jimmy."

"They let it slide this time but reserved the right to punish me in the future." There was no hint that he was kidding.

"They're tough."

"They're fair." He hesitated, then added, "Anyway, I'm sorry about the fuss I made."

"No problem."

The little girl on the couch rustled and sat up.

Lute glanced up at Jodi and his eyes narrowed. She gave him an almost imperceptible shake of her head. He held eye contact with her for a flash, then his face returned to an impassive expression.

"So, who is this little lady?" Kent asked.

Lute's eyes met Jodi's for a second time then broke away. "She is our niece."

With her straight black hair, skin, and high cheek bones like Jodi's, Kent had to admit that she was a cutie, and he said so.

Jodi and Lute were both like stone.

"She's staying with us while her mother is in rehab." Jodi said it as if it were easy for someone to understand that an Indian would be in rehab.

Kent knelt down to the girl's level. "Hi, there. What's your name?" No response.

"Her name is Wren. She doesn't talk much to strangers."

Kent stood back up and gave her a reassuring smile. "That's okay."

He let his eyes drift across the mural and saw Lucinda and Max through the window next to it. "Look at those two. They're best buddies already."

Lucinda and Max were in a tug-o-war over a bone that was half as big as Max. Lucinda was easily holding her end, while the feisty Chihuahua shook his head, braced his feet, and pulled with all his might.

"What he lacks in size, he makes up in determination," Jodi said, admiration in her voice.

Lute stood up from the couch. "Won't be long before Otsi's out there, too."

"I don't doubt that for a minute." Kent pointed a finger at his friend. "Just be sure he gets his meds."

"Don't worry. He'll get every dose," Jodi said.

"And his tea," Lute added, his tone defensive.

Kent gave him a thumbs-up. "I'm good with that. Whatever works."

Lute took that as a signal to test the waters. "I'm thinking of letting him have a knucklebone, too. I can tell he misses them."

"Oh, you're *thinking* of it."

"There was one in Otsi's bed," Jodi deadpanned.

Lute looked sheepish. "But he loves to chew on them."

Kent let him off the hook. "Will you at least boil them first to get the fat out? And not too many. The last thing we need at this point is to throw him into a bout of pancreatitis."

Lute scowled and said nothing. Jodi nodded affirmatively.

Wren held up her arms toward the window and began to whimper.

"She sees Max. The two of them are inseparable." Jodi stepped to the door and called the dogs in.

They bolted past her legs. Lucinda went straight to Kent. Max rolled on his back at Wren's feet. She immediately flopped on him. Her crying turned to laughter. Max's eyes bulged under her weight, but even so, he was smiling.

"Connected at the hip," Lute said.

As Kent watched Max lick her face, Feron Munn's comment about a missing toddler drifted back into his head.

They escorted Kent back to his truck and chatted for a minute more.

"Pegger in Albany today?" Kent asked.

"He is," Jodi said, and concern moved onto her face.

He caught it. "I know it worries you, but we need him, and we are all glad he's doing what he's doing. He's our best hope to stop Northern Lights. I know what Lute says, but they aren't stupid enough to resort to violence. Big corporations like those guys, their MO is to crush their enemy under an army of lawyers."

"That's easy for you to say. It's not your son we are talking about."

"I get that, I do. I have a daughter. I'd be worried sick if she were doing what Pegger's doing, but I'd be proud of her, too. You should be proud of Pegger."

"I am."

They mulled that over for a moment, then Kent redirected the conversation. To Lute he said, "Jodi said you were really praying for me in there."

Lute smiled a smile that revealed nothing. "I was praying that the Jets beat New England this year."

"Good. They need all the help they can get."

Kent's eyes drifted to the shooting range, then down its length. He could just make out tattered paper targets and the remains of bottles and pumpkins. He turned to Jodi and thumbed toward the range. "You can hit those?" His voice held disbelief.

Lute's chuckle was barely audible. "Now you've done it."

Jodi's lips curved into a thin smile. "Lute, hold onto Wren," she said and headed toward the range.

Lute dropped the tailgate of his pickup. He lifted Wren and they sat on it, legs dangling. He signaled for Kent to join them. "This will take her a minute or two."

It took two. Through the fence, they watched as Jodi came out of the barn carrying a rifle almost as long as she was tall. She eased into position at the shooting rest, drew in a deep breath and released it, then brushed a few stray hairs off her forehead. She raised the rifle and squinted into the scope. A breath or two later, Jodi's shoulder jumped back as a single round exploded from the muzzle.

Kent and Lute listened as the sound reverberated off the hills. Kent strained to see down the range, but at that distance with his naked eyes he had no idea if she'd hit her target. Wren clapped. Lute casually stared at his feet.

Jodi lowered the rifle and pointed at a three-foot long telescope mounted on a tripod standing a few feet away. She yelled to them, total confidence in her voice, "We've got a spotting scope. Come see for yourself."

Kent raised his hand in defeat. "No thanks, I don't doubt you."

Lute nodded. "Good decision."

CHAPTER 18

KENT ROLLED INTO THE JEFFERSON DINER AT JUST past six a.m. The parking lot was already more than half full and he recognized every vehicle. He'd gotten a mediocre night's sleep. He'd tossed and turned thinking about his trip out to Lute's cabin. Otsi's near-miraculous improvement was a good thing, of course, but something about Wren, their niece, didn't sit right. Lute had seemed uncomfortable when Jodi talked about her. On top of that, Kent hated that Jodi had to endure a mother's fear for her son, but what Pegger was doing was so critical. That part made his sleep restless. He'd bounced it all off Aubrey at the cemetery. She told him in her wordless way that she was happy for Otsi and that he was making too much out of the Wren thing. He needed some coffee.

He pulled open the door to the diner and a warm wave of breakfast smells rolled over him. The cashier looked up from the slips she was punching in. "Morning, Doc."

"Morning, Sonia. The Chief here?"

"Not yet. But he will be. Wouldn't be a day without him."

He grabbed a newspaper from a pile next to the register and returned friendly greetings as he worked his way to a booth. He sat so he could see the door. Coffee appeared in ten seconds.

He made it to the sports page and was stressing about why Bill Parcells, even with Vinny Testaverde quarterbacking, couldn't get the

Jets to the Superbowl when Merrill's silhouette darkened the door. Tall, wide, and in police uniform, he really did darken it, too.

The Chief glad-handed his way through the crowd as Kent had done, but with a lot more gusto, and slid into the seat across from him. "I saw your truck at the cemetery this morning."

"I stopped by."

"Jesus, Kent. Every day? It's morbid."

"Mind your own business."

"It's been, I don't know, how many months now? You've got to move on. Maybe on Sundays, but not *every day.*"

"I don't need a lecture."

The Chief eased up. "I know. It was bad. Really bad. Cancer is the worst."

Kent leaned across the table toward his brother and fired back. "I watched her starve to death and couldn't do a goddamn thing about it. I'd like to see how quick you'd forget."

Merrill raised his hands. "I'm sorry. I didn't mean it that way. I get it. I just hate seeing you down in the dumps all the time. I'd like…"—he waved his arms at the other patrons—"…we'd all like the old Kent back."

"Tough luck for you."

They drank coffee and scanned the specials in a brooding silence.

Merrill slapped his hand on the table. "Forget about me. I've got a big mouth."

"I'm glad you finally realized that." Kent tapped the newspaper. "So anyway, what's going on? Nothing about Jimmy in here."

Merrill shrugged, "That doesn't mean nothing has happened on the case."

"So you *do* have something?"

Sonia reappeared, topped off their coffee, and took their orders. Merrill ordered bacon and eggs. Kent ordered pancakes with strawberries.

"Whipped cream?"

"Of course."

"Attaboy," she said. "And anything to go for our girl outside?"

"Two scrambled."

She smiled. "Tell her I said hi." Merrill rolled his eyes.

"Coming up," she chirped, and strutted off.

"So, who shot Jimmy Silverheel?" Kent asked the second she was out of earshot.

"We don't know yet." Merrill's eyebrows rose. "But we did get a lead from the ballistics guys."

"On the bullet from Otsi?"

"Yep. It was pretty well beaten up, and they're not sure if they can match it to a specific rifle, if we ever find one, but they were able to determine that it is a .264 caliber."

Kent waited for more. "So?'

"That's an odd size, especially for sporting rifles."

"*You* know this?"

"I didn't then, but I do now. I had to do some research after they told me. It turns out Winchester developed the .264 back in the fifties. It's a relatively small bullet and they load it with a whole lot of powder behind it. It packs a lot of wallop even at long range, and yet has a surprisingly mild kick. You can shoot it all day without destroying your shoulder. For a few years, it was a real popular round for long range shooting like out west or for varmints around here. Then 7mm came along and changed everything. The .264 got left in the dust, but that's another story. Nowadays, there aren't many rifles around that shoot it, and most of them belong to gun enthusiasts. I guess they are considered sort of a cool novelty."

Kent sipped his coffee and rolled that around. "Are the Staties helping you?"

A wave of indignation crossed Merrill's face. "Yes, the State Police will be at every photo op until we solve this. But I have to give them credit, they're helping to check gun sales and transfer records to try to track down .264 caliber rifles, and they're helping with the canvasing. They've got a hell of a lot more manpower than we do."

Sonia arrived with their food and conversation waned for a moment.

When she was gone, Kent said, "So we still don't know whether it was a stray bullet or a full-on murder."

While he salted his eggs, Merrill said, "Think about this. There were three shots. The first one hit Jimmy in the head. The second one missed, and the third one hit Otsi in the leg. Granted, we don't know for sure that they were from the same gun, but if they were, and it was fired by a gun enthusiast, that means he or she knows what they were doing when it came to shooting. Would you expect they'd send off three strays?"

Merrill chewed a mouthful of egg and gave his brother time to think.

"No. Gun guys are safety nuts. They'd never fire a shot that they didn't know where the bullet would land, let alone three."

"Now, how about this? If it *was* intentional, and they got Jimmy with the first shot and kept on firing, they must have been trying to get Lute, too. Right?"

"Ugh!" Kent choked on his coffee. Through a napkin, he said, "I guess."

"So . . . who would want to kill Jimmy *and* Lute?"

"If it wasn't an accident, we're back to the question of whether all three shots came from the same gun. There could have been multiple shooters. Holy shit!"

"Don't get ahead of yourself. We still need a motive."

Kent was on a roll now. "What if someone wanted to create public unrest against Northern Lights?"

Nothing from Merrill.

Kent continued puzzling through it. "Do you think it's possible that someone would try to kill two guys on the river just to stir things up?"

"Who? Who would benefit from that? Shoot a couple guys on the river. Would the Indians do that? Send a message to Northern Lights that it's their sacred place and don't mess with it?"

"No. They wouldn't shoot *other Indians*. And besides, Pegger has made that message perfectly clear to them many times. I'm thinking the reverse," Kent said, waving his fork in the air. "What if some crackpot at Northern Lights decided to take out a couple of Indians to let *them* know they better back off?"

"Now you are sounding like Lute."

"And seriously, Merrill, do you think any of the Owahgena over there on the Rez would shoot *anybody*?"

"You never know."

"Come on. You know every one of them. It would be a stretch. To me, it's way more likely Northern Lights would do it."

Merrill thought a minute. "Pegger has been pissing them off lately, I'll admit."

"You should have seen him at the groundbreaking."

"Yeah. I heard."

Kent gave a little laugh. "He had a weird analogy of a person getting caught and released like a fish. It really made the crowd squirm."

"He's a smart guy and Balt knows it."

They swilled the last of their coffee and argued over the bill and the tip. They socialized their way out and, eventually, made it to the parking lot.

"Pegger the Potamologist," Kent said, opening his truck door. He let Lucinda run over to the grass. When she returned, he opened the takeout tray Sonia had prepared for her and set the eggs down. "There you go, girl. Pegger has taken the battle to Albany. He understands how the game is played and he has been lobbying—politicians and environmental groups—hard."

"He's been putting a lot of miles on that Mustang of his." Merrill laughed. "And getting a lot of tickets."

They watched Lucinda gobble her eggs.

Then Merrill said, "I don't know. I can't make myself believe that a big operation like Northern Lights, with so much to lose, would take a risk like that."

"I just reassured Jodi that nothing bad would happen to her son."

Both men mulled the horrible implications of that. Neither could come up with a comment, so they let it drop. Lucinda ambled back over, and Kent loaded her in. They agreed to keep each other posted as they headed off to start their day.

CHAPTER 19

BY THE TIME KENT GOT BACK TO THE CVC, THINGS were in full swing. Right off the bat, Beverly caught him in the hall. She was carrying a bundle of papers and envelopes and, as usual, was bouncing with energy. She walked with him stride for stride. Lucinda dodged her feet as Beverly updated Kent as to what fires needed to be put out, where he needed to be and when, what he needed to sign, and whom he needed to call. Merrill was number one on the "to-call" list. "The Chief wants to talk to you ASAP."

"That didn't take long, I just had breakfast with him at the diner."

"I don't know, I'm just the messenger. Here's a bunch of stuff I was about to add to the pile on your desk." She pushed her load toward him. "That box on top is the peanut brittle you like. Mrs. Bynacker and her daughter, Mavis, made it for you as a thank-you for fixing their gerbil."

He stared at the brightly colored box for a second. "It had a bad eye, as I remember. Really swollen. They don't have the money to do any kind of a work-up on a gerbil, so what was I going to do? I went with a tube of eye ointment and a Hail Mary." He wedged the lid off, folded back the wax paper, and took a piece. "It must have worked." He offered some to Beverly and savored the sweetness. "I love this stuff."

He held a piece of the candy down to Lucinda. She sniffed it politely then declined. He smiled. Lucinda didn't have much of a sweet tooth.

"Good work, Boss," Beverly said.

Kent took another piece of peanut brittle, then handed the box back to her. "Put this in the breakroom."

"You know it will disappear in ten minutes," she warned him.

"Better there than on my desk. It wouldn't last any longer there."

Beverly gave Lucinda a quick pat on the head and continued down the hall. Over her shoulder she said, "Don't forget to call your brother. He was insistent."

"What? Merrill? Insistent? No."

In his office, Kent fixed himself a cup of coffee, put his feet up on the desk, and dialed his brother. "Hey, Chief, Beverly tells me you want to talk."

"I no sooner walked into the station after I left you this morning and I got a call from the Staties in Atlanta."

"Georgia?"

"Yep."

He waited for more. Nothing. The usual Merrill tease. "What did they want?"

"Our help."

Again silence. Kent twisted the phone cord in his fingers imagining it was his brother's neck. "Doing what?"

Merrill went on at a frustratingly slow pace. "Well, it seems they have discovered a smuggling ring bringing in cigarettes and pot from Canada. They think it may be based in Jefferson."

"Of course it's based in Jefferson. We've known about it for years. It's Feron Munn and his Canadian Express."

Merrill's tone was even. "I agree."

"So that's not news, at least not to us."

"True. But it becomes a little more newsworthy when I tell you one more thing."

When the Chief didn't continue, Kent said, "Merrill, quit with the suspense bullshit and just tell me what they said. The whole thing."

"They had an informant."

"Okay."

"They've been watching these guys for quite a while."

"Up here or down there?"

"From what I could gather, they had been focused on both ends, the Canadian border and Atlanta, but not so much Jefferson."

"Isn't there some law enforcement courtesy thing where they are supposed to tell you when they come onto your turf?"

"Sometimes there's a breakdown in interagency cooperation," Merrill said, dripping sarcasm, "to say the least. Besides, like I said, they haven't been too concerned about Jefferson till now."

"So really there's nothing new."

"Well, there is one important fact."

Kent shook his head. "I'm going to kill you, Merrill. What's that?"

"Their informant is . . . was Jimmy Silverheel."

Kent pulled his feet off the desk and sat upright. "No."

"I couldn't frickin' believe it when the guy told me."

"That opens up some new possibilities."

"Most of the rest of his story was old news. They've determined that the smugglers are using a houseboat to pick up contraband up on the St. Lawrence."

"On the Mohawk Rez up in St. Regis. Because it straddles the St. Lawrence River which is the U.S.-Canada border."

"Right. It's perfect. It connects the U.S. and Canada *and* it's a sovereign nation. What could be better for smuggling?"

"A quick boat ride up the St. Lawrence to Lake Ontario, up the Chittenango River and, bingo, they are in *another* sovereign nation, the Owahgena Rez here in Jefferson."

Merrill summed it up. "The Canadian Express. Feron Munn has been doing it forever."

Kent thought for a moment. "There was a break in there. He disappeared a few years. Remember?"

"Yep. He hid out up in Canada for a while."

"And he did a stretch in prison one time."

"Sentenced to five. I think he did two. I'm pretty sure."

There was pause as their memories rolled over the hardscrabble road that was Feron Munn's life.

Kent asked, "Do they know anything about *who* shot Jimmy?"

"No. Actually, they got concerned because Jimmy hadn't reported in to whoever he was supposed to. So they started checking around. It took them a while to figure out he'd been shot."

"Jesus!"

"Anyway," Merrill went on, "I wasted my precious breath chewing the guy out for not looping us in. Then I told him that we know about Feron 'The Ferret' Munn and his Canadian Express. I told him what we know so far about Jimmy's death, too. Actually, I hedged a little more than I should have and told him we're starting to think he was murdered."

"It's not so big a leap now that we find out he was their informant."

"True. The guy seemed appreciative, surprised that we were on it, I'm sure, but he wouldn't admit it. Said he'd work with us going forward. We'll see how that goes."

There was a long, uncomfortable silence over the phone. Finally, Kent said, "Jimmy Silverheel was a snitch. Go figure."

CHAPTER 20

IT WASN'T FIVE MINUTES AFTER KENT HUNG UP with Merrill when his phone rattled again. He was still processing the news that Jimmy Silverheel was a police informant when he answered it. It was Emily and there was concern in her voice. She called him *Dad* instead of *Doc*. That was never good.

"Dad, I know you're busy, and I don't want to bug you, but you said to let you know if Sim wasn't getting better, and he's not. He's actually worse! He didn't eat this morning and his whole leg is swollen. I took his temperature and it's a hundred and three."

The call was short. He had the information he needed, and he knew what he had to do. The feeling that Aubrey was somewhere in the great ether urging him to hurry was so real it was eerie. He told Beverly where he was going and headed out the door. He pushed the mobile unit to its limit, and twenty minutes later he and Lucinda were turning into Orchard Hill Farm.

Lucinda heeled beside him as they approached Sim's stall. Emily was standing at its open door, staring in. She turned when she heard his footsteps and came toward him wiping her eyes. He gave her a one-armed hug, his heavy black medical bag dangling from his other arm.

"Any change?" he asked before he looked in.

She bit her lip, fighting back the tears, and shook her head.

When Kent looked into the stall, he saw why she had no words. Sim was standing braced along the back wall, head dangling to the straw, unresponsive. His injured leg was swollen like a stovepipe from his elbow down to the bandage that covered the wound. It was bad.

He throttled back his panic and reminded himself, *Never-let-them-see-you-sweat.* He withdrew a thermometer, a penlight, and a stethoscope from his bag and stepped to the horse. Emily stayed by Sim's head as Kent checked his vitals and examined him. It took five minutes and Sim did not move the whole time.

He removed the bandage and a fetid smell wafted up into the stall. The wound was gaping, pus draining, and a tendon exposed—Otsi all over again. He hoped Emily did not see his hands shaking as he returned his instruments to his case, then leaned against the stall wall.

Working to keep his tone calm, he directed his words to Emily but spoke loud enough that the half-dozen onlookers who were peering between the stall bars could hear.

He stated the obvious. "He's really bad."

There was a terrible silence.

"His temp is a hundred and four."

Emily made a choking sound. "That's up a degree from when I took it just before I called you."

"His pulse is up, he's dehydrated, and the lymph nodes in his left axilla are huge."

Emily slid her hand back and felt up into Sim's armpit. "I didn't notice those. It feels like he has lemons up under there."

"And then there is the wound itself. The infection is much worse. Whatever bug is in there is not susceptible to the antibiotics we have been giving him, that's for sure."

Kent was quiet long enough that the onlookers began to squirm. Emily couldn't contain herself. "So now what?"

"We transport him to the CVC for one thing."

"Good. That's where I want him, too."

"I'll bring a trailer around," someone said, and Emily thanked them.

While Kent rebandaged the wound he explained, "The first order of business is to correct his dehydration. At the same time we'll get a culture going to see what bacteria is in his leg, and more importantly, what antibiotic best kills it."

Emily put transport wraps on Sim's other three legs, switched his halter to one with a leather and fleece pad to protect his poll, and buckled on his blanket. "I wish we had done this in the beginning."

"Me too, Em," he said sadly.

She let her forehead fall against Sim's neck. "Hindsight is twenty-twenty."

Kent cursed himself. For his whole career he prided himself on making decisions that, in hindsight, proved to be correct for his patients. This time he blew it, pure and simple, for Emily and for the horse she loved. He'd give anything to have a redo.

Within an hour Simpatico's Gift had been admitted to the CVC Equine Intensive Care Unit and ensconced in a stall. Immediately, a team of veterinarians and technicians swooped down on him. They started an IV, collected blood samples, and took swabs from the wound for culture and sensitivity. Kent had them radiograph the leg, "just to be sure." He didn't want any horrible surprises like what happened with Otsi. There were no fractures or foreign material.

Barry and Emily stood side by side chewing their nails and watched it all.

"Doc, when will we know the culture results?" Barry asked.

"Depends on how fast the bacteria grows. Usually twenty-four to seventy-two hours."

Emily jumped in. "But you'll put him on antibiotics in the meantime, right?"

"Oh, yeah. We'll throw the pharmacy at him."

"Has he got blood poisoning?" Barry asked.

"That's the old term. Nowadays it's called septicemia. The infection has moved out of the wound and is attacking his whole body."

Tears rose in Emily's eyes again. "He could die."

Her words struck Kent like a mule kick in the chest. "We'll make sure that doesn't happen."

When he hugged her, and she could not see his face, he closed his eyes and sent up a prayer to the veterinary gods.

They all turned when they heard Lucinda let out a soft, sad howl. She was standing in the stall staring at Sim.

CHAPTER 21

KENT HAD BEEN SITTING ON THE BENCH BESIDE Aubrey's headstone for over an hour. As the sun came up, out came the blackflies. One got him on the ear and he scratched at it. Lucinda sneezed one out of her nose.

"So that's about all I've got, Hon. But I guess that's enough. Feron and his smuggling isn't big news. But Jimmy as a snitch? Now there's a surprise. I still can't believe it. All of a sudden there may be a reason mild-mannered old Jimmy got shot."

He waved his hand over Lucinda's head, shooing the blackflies, and tried to come up with more to tell Aubrey about. He didn't want to leave.

"And Sim. That situation has me scared to death." He watched a leaf drift down and settle on his knee, picked it up, and twirled it between two fingers. "That little nothing of a scratch on his foot has turned into a raging infection. He's really sick." He studied the pattern of the leaf's veins against the sunrise. "I know Em is tough. She's already been through more than any kid should have to—parents divorced, a deformed back, and getting shot. Then losing you—that's been a crusher. She could use you now. She's always held up so well, but if Sim gets a permanent lameness out of this and can't be ridden anymore, I'm not sure she will be able to handle that. I don't know if *I* can handle that." He crumpled the leaf in his fist and tossed away the shreds. "I dropped the ball, Hon. I should have treated him more aggressively from the start. Goddamnit, I wish you were here."

● ● ●

Kent headed his truck along the river toward the CVC. He was crawling so slowly that cars backed up behind him. He ignored them and listened to the radio as Jessi Colter sang about not being Lisa. He couldn't get Sim out of his head. After the cemetery, he'd called in for a progress report on the horse and the night crew said there hadn't been much change. He didn't want to think how he had blown it with Sim. He pounded the steering wheel. Why hadn't he taken the wound more seriously from the beginning? It was on the most important creature in his daughter's life, for Chrisake! "Don't worry, Em. It's just a little ding," he snarled mocking himself, then he pounded the wheel again. "Yeah, right." He cranked the radio.

It wasn't until a frustrated driver wheeled out to pass him on a dangerous turn and nearly caused a head-on collision that he pulled over on a wide spot in the shoulder and let a line of cars pass. In the distance he saw the bridge, peaceful water drifting under it. He thought about how it protected the Owahgena, kept them separate.

He wished he could draw the same strength from the river that the Owahgena did. For them it was easy and obvious; they had heard the legends of the river from their elders their whole lives. Envy rose in him. It must be nice.

He was rousted from his thoughts by the sound of a horn behind him. In the mirror he saw a police cruiser had pulled up close. Merrill leaned his head out the window. "You all right?"

"I'm fine," Kent yelled back.

Doubt shone on Merrill's face, but he let it go. "Okay, good. Listen, I've got some more news. Head to the diner and I'll buy you a cup of coffee."

When they slid into a booth at the diner, Merrill said, "I already ate. You want anything?"

"Coffee's good."

Sonia hustled up, coffee pot in hand. "You back again already, Chief?"

"Did you miss me?"

Sonia just smiled and poured. "What can I get you fellas?"

"Just coffee."

"Anything for my girl, Lucinda?"

Kent watched her pour, then took a sip. "No, I think she's good."

"Aww!" Sonia groaned. "I always feel sorry for her getting left out there in your truck."

"Health department regs. You know."

"Yeah, I get it." She spun toward the next booth, coffee pot extended.

"So, what's the news?" Kent asked, then waited while Merrill added cream and sugar.

"Remember, this is brother to brother. Don't go telling anybody. Not a soul. I just want to bounce this off you, to help me think it through. You okay with that?"

"I understand."

Merrill took a deep breath. "I got another call from our friends in Atlanta. Turns out we may have been underestimating the Canadian Express."

"Really?" Kent said, and he sounded disappointed. "What's The Ferret up to now? Trying his hand at coke or heroin? Those cartel animals will eat him alive."

"People," Merrill said, and let it hang.

"What people?"

"The Atlanta police and the customs guys think Feron is dabbling in human trafficking."

Kent leaned back, his face pinched. "No way! That's more out of his league than coke or heroin."

"They found twenty-six."

"Twenty-six what?"

"People."

"You have got to be kidding me. Where?"

"At a rest stop in Georgia, north of Atlanta. In the back of a semi that they believe originated in little ol' Jefferson, New York. The guy said they were all Koreans. He pointed out that we are all concerned about the Mexican border and it gets all the press, but it turns out there's a big Korean population in Canada, and a lot of them want to sneak into the States."

Kent picked up his coffee but then set it down hard without taking a sip. "I don't believe it."

"It gets worse."

"Tell me."

"Two were dead."

"Huh." Kent took a sip of coffee and considered what Merrill had just said. "Shit. Now it's a homicide investigation."

"It already was, with Jimmy and all. But now it's bigger. As if the Staties aren't enough, now we've got the FBI poking its nose in."

"Jesus! Because it's international?"

"Right. As usual, they aren't saying much. To Atlanta or us. The FBI does things its own way, plus they always claim to be overextended. This case may be a huge thing for us, but for them it's just another day."

"So how do they know the truck was from Jefferson?"

Merrill shrugged. "Like I told you before, they figured out what we've known forever. Feron takes his beat-up houseboat up to the Mohawk reservation on the St. Lawrence and loads up with *whatever* from Canada. We thought cigarettes and pot, maybe illegal furs and taxidermied animals that you aren't allowed to have in the States, that sort of thing. Then he brings it by boat to the Owahgena Rez here in Jefferson and somehow gets it loaded on trucks. Then off it goes."

"I have to give Feron credit," Kent said shaking his head. "Indian reservation to Indian reservation. Perfect."

"Makes a nice pipeline. It always has. But now they say he's transporting illegal immigrants."

"On that rickety old houseboat of his? Do you think it could hold twenty-six people?"

Merrill considered that. "Probably. The water would be up to the gunnels. You wouldn't want to be out in rough water with that big a load. I guess The Ferret's crazy enough to risk it for enough money. I'm sure the stowaways have no idea what they are getting into."

"He docks at the Rez, then what? He off-loads his cargo, and what happens to them?"

"At least some of them went to Georgia."

"I get that. But how?"

"They were in a tractor-trailer."

"Yes, but how does Feron connect with it? Who's truck? Feron doesn't have one. This is a small town. Somebody would notice a semi lurking around. Maybe even you guys."

"Very funny."

Kent started to say something but was interrupted as Sonia appeared next to them. She placed the check and a take-out box on the table.

Both men gave her a questioning look.

"That's for Lucinda. Tell her I said *hi.*"

Kent gave her a comical scowl. "You're going to make her fat."

"I should be treated as well," Merrill grumbled.

She shrugged. "Hey, that's why Doc tips me well. Unlike certain other people."

When she turned away, Kent dove back into their conversation. "So how does Feron get the people on a truck without drawing attention?"

They gave that some serious thought.

Gradually Kent's face morphed from frustration to enlightenment. "What about the construction site?"

"Northern Lights?"

"It would work. Big trucks in and out all the time. Lots of opportunity with the chaos of construction."

Merrill blew out a long sigh that ended with a nod. "Yeah, it would be a good cover."

Kent had it in his mind's eye now. "If I know The Ferret, and I do, it would happen at night."

"I agree."

There was another long silence. Finally, Merrill said, "There's something else. Feron stopped in at the station yesterday."

Kent feigned disbelief. "Feron set foot in the police station of his own accord?"

"Yep. He asked if we had a report of a missing girl. He was really cagey about it, like he is about everything. He wouldn't say why or give any details about the girl. When the desk officer told him no, he left. It didn't feel right."

"Sorry, I can't help you with that one."

Merrill relaxed back into his seat. "I guess we'll have to keep our eyes open and wait until I hear from Atlanta or whoever is in charge."

Kent stared at the dregs in the bottom of his coffee cup and said nothing. After a moment, he rocked back his eyes opening wide as if something had occurred to him.

"The look on your face bothers me," Merrill said. "What?"

Kent grabbed the box Sonia left for Lucinda and slid out of the booth without answering.

Outside, he and Merrill watched Lucinda gobble a large helping of scrambled eggs.

When Kent didn't continue the conversation, Merrill did. "What was that back in there? You had a strange look. What are you thinking?"

Kent kept his eyes on Lucinda. "I'm thinking we should do some bullhead fishing. Maybe a lot of bullhead fishing."

"What the heck are you talking about?"

CHAPTER 22

KENT, MERRILL, AND LUTE FLOATED IN KENT'S canoe under the bridge. The road deck overhead blocked the moonlight making the darkness and the wet smell of moss on concrete pylons even more dank. The canoe was tied to the lowest rung of a rusty service ladder attached to a pylon that ascended into the darkness above. It wasn't one of their favorite spots for night fishing, they knew it was only so-so for bullheads, but that wasn't the point. The point was, it was a good place to hide while they watched the Northern Lights construction site.

"I'm getting sick of this," Merrill said as he dug a mosquito out of his ear. "I think we need a new plan. Besides, my freezer is about full of bullhead."

"Don't bait your hook. Then you won't catch any more," Lute said, as if he were talking to a five-year-old.

Merrill replied in a sing-song voice. "How about I just catch and release them?"

"When you release the first one, be ready for a canoe paddle upside your head."

Kent smothered a laugh and reminded them to keep it down; sound carried over water.

Lute went back into his silence, but Merrill didn't. "Bait or no bait, that doesn't help my lack of sleep. What is this, the fifth night in a row, right? And I'm about bled out. Jesus, if Mother Nature doesn't get you with the blackflies during the day, she'll get you with mosquitos at night."

They let Merrill's complaints hang as the canoe rocked in a hypnotic to and fro, the water lapping against the hull.

Kent glanced at his watch as it glowed in the dark. "It's only eleven." He handed his brother a thermos of coffee. "Here, have some more of this. It will help keep you awake."

Merrill reluctantly took it and poured himself some. "I need sleep, not coffee.

Kent shifted from one butt cheek to the other and arched a kink out of his back. For the hundredth time, he lifted the binoculars that hung around his neck. He scanned the construction site on the far bank. Same old nothingness—darkness striped by shadows from a few dim security lights.

On the first night they'd fished, Merrill had told Lute about the bullet being a .264. Lute took the information in without showing much response. That bothered Merrill because, not only was he fishing for bullhead but he was also fishing to try and find out if Lute owned a .264. Lute hadn't taken the bait. Merrill brought it up the next morning at the diner with Kent.

"I know he's got a lot of guns. I need to know if he owns a .264 caliber rifle."

"Why?" Kent asked. "He didn't shoot at himself."

"It's important to the investigation that we find the gun. Maybe Lute had one and it was stolen."

"He'll question our friendship the second you ask him. He knows I saw his gun room when I was there to treat Otsi. He'll think I put you on to him."

"He'll be touchy."

"To put it mildly."

"You could let the state cops do it, as part of their canvassing."

"The problem with that is Lute's cabin is on the Rez. The Rez cops are handling the investigation there. They don't like other cops sniffing around."

"The sovereign nation thing again."

"Right. Unfortunately, they are really slow."

So, Kent and Merrill had agreed that they would double-team Lute to see if they could get an answer out of him, but only if they found a good opening.

Sitting there in the boredom of the night, Kent decided it was as good an opportunity as they were going to get. Trying to sound casual, he said, "So Lute, when I was at your place to see Otsi, I saw your gun room. I was really impressed. Lots of cool guns."

Lute's voice came back out of the dark, unusually sharp. "Yes, we have a .264 caliber rifle."

Kent cringed, Merrill got interested in baiting his hook, and an awkward silence ensued.

Finally, Lute said, "You could have just asked."

Merrill didn't respond. Kent signaled him with jerk of his head to say something. Nothing. He saw what was happening, it was just like his brother to let Kent take the heat.

"Sorry. We thought you might take it the wrong way," Kent apologized.

Lute shot back, "You're both assholes." He was quiet for a long moment then let out a loud sigh of resignation. "It belongs to Pegger."

"Are you sure it's there?" Kent asked. "I mean, it's not missing? Nobody stole it?"

"It's there. I checked the day after Merrill told me the caliber of the bullet."

"That's good to know," Kent said. "Thanks."

He glared at Merrill with a "there, are you satisfied?" look.

Lute spoke again. He drew out his words, as if he were thinking out loud. "Actually, it's the rifle you watched Jodi shoot on our range the day you were there. She shoots it the most. She likes it because it doesn't have much of a kick." He chuckled. "And as you saw, she's damn good with it."

Kent was about to say that he remembered when the sound of an engine carried across the water.

All three men froze, watching, listening, the way they reacted to the rustling sounds of an approaching deer when they were hunting.

The drone waxed and waned, muffled by trees and turns in the road, but it continued to get louder.

Lute said, "It sounds like a truck. A big one."

They began reeling in their lines.

Headlights came into view and flickered between trees as a semi moved along the riverbank. In the darkness it was impossible to make out any colors or signage. It turned into Northern Lights, moved slowly to a dark spot beyond the security lights, and stopped. There was an explosive hiss as air brakes set, startling the night creatures into silence. The engine went dead.

Kent watched them through his binoculars. "That's got to be them."

"Hard to tell from here." Merrill whispered.

Kent untied the canoe. "We need to get closer." He took up his paddle, but before he could get it in the water he felt the canoe surge forward as Lute, in the stern, gave a hard stroke. Merrill shuffled their gear to keep it all quiet and they approached the construction site.

Lute guided the canoe to quiet water close to shore. They were behind some bushes shrouded in shadows. "Okay. Drop her."

Kent eased the anchor over the side and into the water, careful not to clank it against the metal gunnel. He played out rope until he felt it hit bottom. As he tied it off, the current brought the canoe around parallel to the shore. Less than fifty yards from the truck, now, they settled back into their wait-and-watch mode.

For close to half an hour nothing happened. Just a truck sitting in the dark. Then they heard another vehicle. It sounded odd. Kent tried to get a read on its location, but it seemed to come from several directions all at once.

The sound became a roaring whine—tires with heavy tread echoing off the bridge surface. The vehicle was crossing the bridge.

Kent ducked, praying that the headlights wouldn't sweep over them.

"Keep still!" came from Lute, and it was not a request.

Merrill stated the obvious. "It's coming from the Rez."

"Uh-uh," Lute said, his eyes following the vehicle as it reached the other side. "And it's The Ferret's truck."

They watched as Feron Munn's big pickup turned into Northern Lights and worked its way to the semi. Its lights went out. The cab light in the big truck flashed on, then off as the driver got out. Through the binoculars, Kent saw the guy move to Feron's truck and the two men confer. After a moment, the driver moved to the back of his rig and swung open two big doors while Feron began loosening a tarp that covered the bed of his truck.

That's when Kent noticed a third vehicle coming up the road. It was smaller, moving much faster, and emitting a mellow rumble through its tuned exhaust pipes. It turned into Northern Lights.

"Jesus, that's Pegger," Merrill said, confirming what the other two already knew.

"Quiet," Lute said.

"What's *he* doing here?"

"Shut up, Merrill," Lute ordered in a hard whisper. "Listen."

Pegger's Mustang slid to a stop next to the trucks.

Through the darkness and the distance they watched the driver back away as Pegger charged at Feron. He pushed him hard in the chest, causing Feron to stumble back against his truck. Feron righted himself and held his hands up, warding Pegger off. Pegger roared angry words that they could not make out. At first, it sounded like Feron was trying to make peace, but as Pegger raved, Feron's tone became more combative. The driver stepped farther away.

When Pegger got right up in Feron's face, Feron shoved him back hard. Like magic, a gun appeared in his hand. He pointed it at Pegger. Pegger put his hands up and backed off a few steps.

Kent glanced over and saw Lute fixed on the scene through his binoculars. He heard him start a soft chant. For a second he wished Merrill had let Lute bring his rifle.

Pegger and Feron's argument ripped through the night for a minute or two more. Then they heard Pegger shout, "Fuck you, Feron." He stomped to his car, fired it up, and spun the tires as he disappeared back into the night.

The shoulders of all three men in the canoe sagged with relief.

They watched as Feron and the driver went back to loosening the tarp on Feron's truck. When they rolled it back, a head rose up slowly, cautiously, like a chipmunk coming above ground, then more heads appeared.

"I'll be goddammed," Merrill whispered.

Feron gave muffled orders to his cargo to climb out. He herded them into the trailer. The hinges on the huge doors creaked loudly as the driver closed them.

Feron and the driver exchanged a few more words and each climbed into his vehicle. The big truck roared south. Feron crossed back to the reservation.

Silence came down like a wet blanket. Kent, Merrill, and Lute each waited for the other to speak. When the void was as long as Kent could stand, he asked, "What was that all about?"

"We just witnessed the transfer of smuggled humans," Merrill said. "How many did you count?"

"I think seven."

"I had six."

"Why the hell was Pegger there?" Kent asked.

"That's a good question. Obviously, he knows what's going on."

Kent was incredulous. "Pegger couldn't be part of that, could he?"

"No," Lute said and left no room for argument.

They went quiet for another few seconds, each mulling over what they had just seen.

Kent broke the silence. "Pegger and Feron were arguing. Right?"

"Hello?" Merrill said, his tone sarcastic. "Did you miss the gun Feron was sticking in Pegger's face?"

"Maybe Pegger was trying to talk some sense into him. Get him to stop this crazy smuggling thing before he ends up back in jail."

"Do you think Pegger even gives that much of a damn about Feron?"

"He cares about the image of the Owahgena. Maybe he's worried about that. Feron using the reservations to work his scheme and all."

"Possibly."

Lute said, "That's got to be it."

CHAPTER 23

PEGGER WAS STILL WOUND TIGHT FROM HIS run-in with Feron last night at the construction site, but he had made up his mind and he wanted to get this over with. He took a deep breath, let it out, reminded himself that Feron was an animal, then stepped onto the springy two-by-ten board that served as a gangplank onto Feron Munn's boat.

How could a person live full-time on this jerry-rigged old thing? It was more like a raft than a boat, really—three party barge pontoons with a flat deck across them. In the center of the deck was an ancient camping trailer that had been backed on board, its wheels removed, then secured in place with cables. There was a rickety shack made of peeling wood and glass at the bow that served as a wheelhouse, and a cluttered walkway maybe five feet wide around the perimeter. It was skirted with sheet metal and a threefoot rail that kept the ropes, buckets, fishing gear, ice chests, propane tanks, and sundry litter from falling into the water. Toward the bow was a partially rebuilt small engine, parts strewn around the deck. A monstrous black outboard motor hung off the stern. Beside it were two red barrels labeled GASOLINE. The boat was definitely set up for distance, not for speed.

Tiny vibrations when Pegger stepped aboard were like a doorbell for Feron's feral senses. Before Pegger could knock on the door, The Ferret called out an unwelcoming "Who's there?"

"It's me."

"Door's unlocked. Come on in."

"You have your gun?" Pegger asked, only half joking after last night.

"Am I going to need it?"

"No. Last night was enough."

"You're safe. Come on in."

As he touched the door handle, Pegger heard a growl that could have been a bear. "How about your dog? Where is he?"

"Lip-Lip's tied up. He won't bother you."

Pegger eased into the trailer. The air was hot and smelled of a sweaty woodsman, his dog, and a poorly kept kitchen. The space was claustrophobic and as disheveled as the deck. He swallowed hard in an attempt to clear the greasiness from his throat.

Lip-Lip was sitting bolt upright on a dirty dog bed. He was secured to the far wall by a short chain. His eyes were fixed on Pegger. Feron was sitting at a small table.

Pegger avoided eye contact with the dog. "How can you live on this shit hole?"

Feron was unfazed by the insult. He massaged the deer tattoo on his arm. "I like being able to move around."

"It's disgusting."

"There's only me and Lip-Lip. Plus, most of the winter I live in my trapping cabin. I got some of my stuff there, too."

Pegger had heard about Feron's cabin—its sloth was legendary. He had no problem imagining it to be worse than what he was standing in now. He pushed a pair of moldering hunting socks off a plastic chair and sat across from Feron. "I apologize for last night."

Feron suddenly seemed interested in a torn fingernail and said nothing.

Pegger continued. "Today we have cooler heads, right? So let's sort things out."

Feron remained fascinated with his fingernail.

Pegger went on, "We can't keep doing this."

Now Feron turned and looked directly at Pegger, his eyes narrowed. "Doing what?"

"You know what I'm talking about. Smuggling."

Feron went back to his fingernail.

Pegger ran his hand through his hair. Talking to Feron was like prodding a mountain lion. "Don't you get it? You jeopardized our whole operation. Smuggling people is way too dangerous. They escape. They talk. They die. And if they do, the cops come after you like hell won't have it. It's not the same as moving drugs and contraband. This thing has gotten way out of hand."

The glint in Feron's eyes sharpened as his temperature began to rise. "You know, you came to me when, a year ago? And pitched me this big plan you had. You were going to help me build my pissant—that's the word you used, *pissant*, I remember—little smuggling operation into a real money maker. Oh yeah, good luck was about to shine down on ol' Feron. We already had the reservations at each end, but now—now a distribution terminal was moving right into town. That's what you called Northern Lights, a smuggler's dream distribution terminal."

"That's right. And I believed it. Way out in the boondocks with nobody watching. Trucks in and out all the time. It would have been perfect. I said to you, 'Why do cigarettes and pot when you can do heroin and coke, right?'"

Feron spit a nail fragment toward the floor. "Yes, you did. And I agreed."

"Correct."

"And everything has been going smooth as silk."

"Yes, but back when I originally talked to you, I thought Northern Lights was going to be a small operation. I could live with that, and so could the Owahgena and the river. What I didn't realize was that the liars were really planning to make a giant resort."

"That is your problem, not mine. On one hand you're fighting to get rid of Northern Lights, and on the other you're planning to use it for your own smuggling business." Feron let out a little laugh. "That's messed up. You can't have it both ways."

Pegger spread his arms wide, palms up. "And that's why I'm here. We've got to stop."

Feron shook his head. His voice ratcheted up. "You know, you are just like your uncle and the rest of the Owahgena, and the Stephenson brothers, too, for that matter. You always try to keep everybody else down, keep everything for yourselves. I was raised Owahgena, I did my best to respect our traditions." He paused, confused, pondering his own words. "I still think of myself as Owahgena, but I was always second best, no matter how hard I tried. I finally just gave up and said to hell with it. I built my Canadian Express and now I have something good, something that makes me more money than anyone else on the Rez. And, once again, you want to take it away from me."

Pegger wasn't falling for Feron's self-pity. "That's bullshit. You never gave a damn about the Owahgena."

Feron shrugged hard. "I don't care if you believe me or not. We agreed to be partners, fifty-fifty."

"We did. Originally."

"Well then, I disagree. If we can do heroin and coke, we can do people! I don't give a damn if you're having a crisis over whose side you're on. My advice to you is to keep faking it like you want to block Northern Lights, same as you've been doing right along, and get rich with me by expanding our operation to include smuggling people. You said yourself you wanted to get rich."

Pegger made a frustrated noise. The way Feron put it, he really was a conflicted mess. "I wasn't faking it, and I'm not faking it going forward. What you are saying is crazy. Don't you get it? We need to stay under the radar. No matter how big Northern Lights gets, it can't hide us for long if we smuggle people. Customs and the border patrol don't want the hassle of dealing with the Indian reservation. Too much red tape and bad public relations. Besides, they've got bigger fish to fry than us. Unless—" Feron opened his mouth to reply, but Pegger stopped him with a raised hand. "Unless we give them so big a reason that they can't ignore us, and human trafficking is *way* too big. And already we have the problem of the missing girl. That's a perfect example."

Feron flashed an embarrassed look. "Yeah, I screwed up there."

"How the hell did you lose a kid?"

"I don't know. Me and the semi driver were so busy trying to get rid of her mother's body, I guess we just missed her when we loaded them on. But I'll fix it. I'm looking for her, and when I find her, I'll fix it."

"You sure as shit better."

Feron stood, leaned toward Pegger, hands on table. His sudden action caused Lip-Lip to raise his head. He spit his words. "Wait a minute. You—the guy that convinced me that we had to eliminate Jimmy—are accusing me of drawing too much attention to our smuggling operation?" He held his palms out and moved them up and down like a scale. "Murder versus helping people across the border? I don't think so."

Pegger balled his fists against the back of his head. "We had to eliminate Jimmy."

"No, we didn't! We could have worked it out with him. Jimmy was my friend."

"He was a snitch."

"I could have turned him back. Made him a double agent. He could have really helped us that way."

"Jimmy was weak. We should never have brought him into the operation in the first place."

The anger in Feron's eyes was rising by the second. "Bullshit. Jimmy was not weak. But he was just another little guy, like me, at least in your eyes. You figured it was nothing to eliminate him. I don't know what the cops had on him, but it must have been big to turn him, because Jimmy was loyal, and he was my friend. Hell, he was helping me get stuff across the border when you were still in diapers." Feron's thoughts shifted, "And then you wanted to make a show of it. We could have lured him off into the woods or something and killed him secret like, but no, downed him right next to your uncle?"

Pegger shot back. "Because I thought it would generate some anti-Northern Lights sentiment among the Owahgena and maybe even with the politicians in Albany."

Feron snorted a laugh. "How'd that work out?"

The words were like a gut punch to Pegger. "Not the way I'd hoped."

"I'd say so. See? It's *you* who's weak, not Jimmy, you hot-shot college know-it-all. You don't know shit! I'll tell you what came of it. I'm the number one suspect. Everybody in town knows that I'm Benjamin Balt's go-to guy when it comes to getting the locals on board with Northern Lights. If they think Balt wanted to shoot an Indian for some reason, the first person they're going to point a finger at is me."

"That's bullshit."

"It's not. I can see it every time I look at Lute, that's what he's thinking."

Pegger went quiet, letting Feron simmer down. When he thought it was safe, he said, "Okay. We are still good. You—we—did a few runs of people and we made it." He stood as if concluding the meeting. "But enough is enough. No more, we are done. Period. Do you understand?"

"Why you sonofabitch!" Feron roared. "You're not my boss. You can't fire me. I'll do as I goddamn well please."

Feron's right hand slid behind his back and came around holding his revolver. "I should have shot you last night. Hell, I'd shoot you right now if it wouldn't make such a mess. Maybe I will anyway."

Pegger stared down the barrel of Feron's gun for the second time in two days.

"You know," Feron said, his face breaking into a hard smile, "I should have done a better job years ago." He waggled the gun in Pegger's face. "Do you know what I'm talking about?"

"No," Pegger said, but it was mostly air.

"Well, let me tell you a little story. A lot of years ago up in Canada, I helped a guy collect a debt from that worthless father of yours, Dewey." Feron's eyebrows creased into a question. "You've got to agree, he was an asshole, right?"

"Uh-huh." Pegger's memories of his father were few and vague, but the ones he had were bad—terrible fights between Dewey and Jodi, moving from one dump of a house to the next, usually at night, and in a hurry.

"It didn't go well that night. We didn't get the money and we ended up torching your house."

"That was you?" Pegger shouted. He had made it out of the burning house, but his little sister had not. The sounds of her screams still haunted him.

"Yep. You were just a little shit. Too bad about your sister. I always felt bad about that." Feron shoved his gun to within inches of Pegger's nose and smiled. "Now I'm wishing it was you instead of her."

The veins in Pegger's forehead bulged like ropes. He was *partners* with the monster who killed his father and sister and had ruined his life and his mother's, too. The realization caused bile to push up into his mouth. "I should have remembered you!"

Feron's smile went bigger. He fueled Pegger's churning emotions like he was feeding a fire. "Nah, you kids were upstairs. Good thing, too, because you didn't have to see me shoot that sonofabitch father of yours for not having the money he owed."

Pegger's face turned purple. Gun or no gun, he didn't care. He swung his fist at Feron's head, but he was no match for the big woodsman. Feron easily dodged the blow then delivered one to Pegger's midsection, driving the air from his lungs. Pegger bent over and retched loudly. Feron stepped closer and stabbed his elbow down hard between Pegger's shoulder blades knocking him to the floor. Then he stepped to a chair and eased into it as if he didn't have a care in the world. He shook out a cigarette and took his time lighting it. With a satisfied look on his face, he watched Pegger slowly push himself off the floor and crawl to the door. He used the knob to pull himself to his feet then stumbled down the gangplank without another word.

Pegger let himself collapse into the Mustang and sat there in a daze. He wasn't sure he could drive until finally he turned the key and the familiar roar of the engine cleared his head. He gripped the wheel as if it were Feron's neck and slammed his foot on the accelerator. Gravel sprayed in all directions as he fishtailed to the road. All this time, he and Feron had been living in the same town. He cursed himself for not remembering him from that awful night in Canada.

Feron listened with satisfaction to the sound of Pegger's car heading away. He looked over at Lip-Lip and chuckled. "There, I guess we set him straight. Now all I have to do is find that damn kid."

CHAPTER 24

PEGGER ROARED WEST ALONG ROUTE 20 ON HIS way back to the reservation after a miserable day of lobbying in Albany. He rolled his head on his shoulders and massaged his neck. It had been three days since his beatdown by Feron and his neck still hurt. He had the Mustang's top down letting the cool evening air wash over him. It thundered in his ears, pushing out thoughts of the day and scrubbing away the grime of politics in the capital city.

He was exhausted. He'd left Jefferson at five to make an eight o'clock breakfast meeting with a Sierra Club lawyer. After that he dropped in and glad-handed, cajoled, and begged as many state senators and assemblymen as he could until his late-afternoon meeting with the DEC Commissioner. That was the big one, Department of Environmental Conservation—the important one. He knew that support from the DEC was essential to win the battle against Northern Lights. It was a platform from which they could really plead their case and mount public support. Plus, it had a slew of lawyers who knew how the natural resource encroachment game was played. The DEC had clout.

The meeting hadn't gone well. He gunned the Mustang as he thought back about the frustrating afternoon. In previous meetings the commissioner had been cordial and receptive when Pegger laid out the Owahgena's concerns. Pegger had tagged him as an ally. But today the commissioner made him wait forever. Then he had been short and argumentative. Pegger sensed that some person or group with deep pockets had swayed the commissioner to keep his distance.

It had been a long bad day in Albany, pure and simple. And to make it worse, he couldn't stop thinking about Feron. Their fight writhed in his mind like a viper, making it hard for him to focus during the day's meetings. What a shit show that had been.

But now he had made up his mind. He thumped the wheel with new-found conviction. It was over. No more smuggling—not drugs, not people, not anything. He hated himself for getting mixed up with Feron and betraying the river and his heritage. Now he would go back to the way it used to be, and he would redeem himself by winning the fight against Northern Lights. He had just gotten tired of being poor. He had let his desire for money take him down the Euros' slippery slope, the one Lute had warned him about, had preached to him about, time and time again; white men's money will smother your soul. His mother had warned him over and over about the Euros' false promises of happiness. She had guided him to beat the Euros at their own game. Get an education; learn to use their laws against them. He had done that, a PhD, for Chrisake. He really was proud to be Owahgena. He held the Chittenango River to be sacred, just like any of his ancestors would have. He knew his mother and Lute were proud of him. He knew the Owahgena counted on him. Winning against the Euros, that's where the happiness lay for him. That's how he would get his life back on track.

For a brief moment he felt better, cleansed by his promise to do better, but the darkness returned as he thought about Feron. The Ferret would never stop smuggling, he was sure of that. He was just as sure that if he got caught, he'd take Pegger down with him. Then there was the fact that Feron admitted killing his father and sister.

He squeezed his eyes shut so hard it hurt, but the horrible thought lingered in his mind. He would have killed Feron a long time ago if he had known. He let out a guttural curse in Owahgena that was lost into the wind.

He'd do it soon—he had no choice—*then* he'd have his life back. He grimaced. He was doing it again, plotting another murder. What had happened to him?

His stomach rumbled and he realized that he hadn't eaten all day. Suddenly he was hungry. He glanced at his watch—it was too late to fix any supper at home, besides, he was too tired. He was almost back to Jefferson. He'd grab something to eat at Kolbie's. God, he wanted this day to be over.

● ● ●

Kolbie's Tavern was only a couple miles off Route 20, just outside of Jefferson, but to get there you descended into the forest, making it seem more remote than it actually was.

Years ago, it had been a respectable little tavern situated nicely to do business with fishermen in summer, hunters in fall, snowmobilers in winter, and loggers year-round. But after several ownership changes, the building and its reputation had decayed. Nowadays it was a hangout for social misfits with big mouths and big trucks. Patrons were hardcore drinkers, both whites and Native American. The kitchen was in back, consistent with their mindset that food was pretty much an afterthought. Even so, it managed to push out nachos, pizzas, and a decent burger on paper plates.

Pegger glanced back over his shoulder as he entered the bar and approved of the way his Mustang glittered like a diamond on the beach, among the mix of jacked-up trucks and pitifully rusted-out cars. Jerry, the owner and bartender, looked up from his endless handmopping of the bar top and nodded hello. Pegger nodded back.

It was early by Kolbie standards and the crowd was light. Pegger slid onto a stool. When Jerry Kolbie worked his way to Pegger's end of the bar, he ordered two slices of pizza and a Genesee. While he waited, he tapped his fingers to the jukebox—Tanya Tucker.

Only one table was occupied. On it were enough empty longnecks to make it obvious that the three burly guys around it had been there all afternoon. One gave Pegger a blurry-eyed glance and nodded a silly smile. He didn't recognize the man. The serious, silent drinkers were along the back wall, holed-up in the shadows like rodents in burrows, where it was too dark to make out their identity.

He was turning back to the bar when his eye caught the flash of a match igniting. The flame from it beamed out of the darkest corner of the bar room like an acetylene torch. As a hand brought the match to the tip of a cigarette, it illuminated Feron Munn's face. He was smiling at Pegger with his mouth but not his eyes.

"Shit," Pegger said to nobody, mad at himself for deciding to stop at the bar. Madder yet that he had given Feron the pleasure of startling him. Why hadn't he noticed Feron's truck in the lot?

The Ferret raised his beer bottle slightly in the hint of a toast, then blew the match out and descended back into darkness.

Pegger said, "Shit," again and spun on his stool back to the bar. His pizza arrived and he ate fast, chewing hard, in uncomfortable silence, wallowing in thoughts of his disappointing day, his life, and the man in the corner.

He was just getting into his second slice when the Genny and the hours on the road maxed out his bladder.

"I'll be right back," he said to Jerry, signaling him to keep an eye on his food. He weaved his way back to the men's room, waited for one guy ahead of him, took his turn at the urinal, and returned to the bar.

The whole process couldn't have taken more than five minutes, but as he slid onto his stool, he noticed a matchbook at the edge of his plate. He examined it. On the cover was a promo for a motel in Cornwall, Canada. Half the matches were gone. On the inside flap there was a scrawled note: *You are not my boss and I'm not stopping my business.*

Angrily, Pegger turned to Feron, but the booth he had been in was empty. He held the matchbook up to Jerry. "Did you see where this came from?" He knew the answer before he asked.

"Munn put it there on his way out."

"Did he say anything?"

"He asked me if I'd heard anybody talking about finding a little girl, is all. Which I haven't. I've got to say that was weird even for Feron."

Pegger shook his head. "Jesus. Okay, thanks, Jerry."

Jerry set another bottle of Genny in front of him. "He also bought you a beer."

Pegger ignored the beer and fumed in silence for a few more bites. He threw some money on the bar, picked up the rest of his pizza, wrapped it in a napkin, and headed to his car.

Feron was long gone, which was fine as far as Pegger was concerned. He would deal with him later. He climbed into his Mustang and fired it up. For a moment, he sat there listening to the rumble of the tuned exhaust, trying to relax. He untangled the pizza from the napkin, took a couple of angry mouthfuls, then tossed the rest onto the seat beside him.

Today had been one allaround crappy day. He was dog tired and he wanted to get home. Fifteen minutes to go and he'd be crawling into his bed. He spun out of the lot without looking for traffic.

He hadn't gone a mile when his hands began to feel numb, his vision blurred. *I'm more tired than I thought.* He slapped his cheeks, took a couple of deep of breaths, and focused on the road. He swerved right and his wheels caught the shoulder. Gravel sprayed against the under carriage. He horsed the Mustang back onto the road. *Jesus, that beer really hit me.*

Usually, when he was behind the wheel, he and his muscle car were as one, but now it was like the car was revolting against him, refusing to be controlled.

His eyelids grew heavier and the headlight beam closed into a tiny tunnel. His head sloshed like a halffilled water jug. He thought about pulling over, sleeping it off, but he wanted to get home. *Dammit!* He slapped his face again, hard this time, and sucked in more of the night air.

The Mustang bucked, almost throwing him out. Then it was bouncing and scraping down an embankment toward the woods. The sound of wrenching metal and shattering glass filled his spinning head.

His vision was almost gone. He couldn't tell how to correct the car's path. Through the tunnel of lights in front of him, he saw a huge maple tree. It was old and gnarled, probably a hundred and fifty years old. In its life it had stood up to storms and disease, pesticides, and men—the little Mustang would be nothing. It was the last thing Pegger saw.

CHAPTER 25

"I LOVE NIGHT DUTY," BARRY SAID. "IT'S WHEN ALL the cool cases come in."

Kent still hadn't fully caught up on his sleep since their bullhead fishing adventure. The investigation—searching for the .264 rifle, Jimmy being a snitch, Merrill's next move, all of it—scraped around in his mind like sandpaper. And then to top it off, there was Sim's tenuous condition. Emily's horse had not improved since transporting him to the intensive care unit, and that was scaring the hell out of Kent. Barry's enthusiasm was a welcome distraction.

A tech rolled Cocoa, a four-year-old chocolate Lab out of the operating room. This was her second pregnancy. The first one had gone like clockwork. She had started into labor in the family room at eleven and the owners watched her push out four beautiful pups by morning. No problem. So this time, when Cocoa went into labor in the afternoon, they thought, *Oh, good, here we go again.* The first pup came uneventfully, but then nothing. They watched and waited. And waited. And waited. Nothing—no more labor, no more pups. Mom's abdomen was still huge so they were sure there were more pups in there. By supper time, they were concerned. By midnight, they were flipping out—and called the CVC.

A cesarean section, twelve pups, and two hours later, that's where they were.

"How's she doing?" Barry asked.

The tech pushing the gurney stroked Cocoa's ear gently. "She's fine. Stable. She's starting to wake up."

Barry was kneeling next to an incubator box. The soft mewing of newborn pups came up into the room like a lullaby. "Nice. All the pups look like they're going to make it."

Kent snapped off his surgical gloves and followed Cocoa out. "Let me check your work."

Exaggerated indignation rolled onto Barry's face. "My work is beyond reproach."

"Uh-huh. Trust, but verify, my good man. That's what the president would say." Kent admired the pups. "I love that sound."

Barry held up a fat pup that wiggled and cried. "Looks more like a bulldog at this point." He set it back in the box.

"I lost track. What's the tally?"

"Five boys and eight girls total, counting the one born at home. Nine black and four chocolates."

"That's a nice litter."

Barry watched Kent examine each pup. He could tell Kent was enjoying the moment. The timing was right, so he asked, "Doc, wouldn't it be cool for Lucinda to have a bunch like this?"

Kent rolled his eyes. "Don't start that again. As much as you'd like her to, it ain't happenin'."

They went quiet, pondering the new lives that squirmed before them. Kent was the first to break the silence. "It would be nice, though."

He watched the pups and let his mind drift. After a long moment he asked, "I'm going over to the Equine Unit to check on Emily. Did you get over to see Sim this evening? I haven't heard anything since I left the office at six."

Thoughts of Sim's struggle to live deflated the moment.

"On my dinner break I went over and sat with Emily. She hasn't been eating enough to keep a bird alive, just stuff from the cafeteria.

I took her some spaghetti and meatballs, her favorite. I thought that might pick her up a little, but she didn't eat enough to say so. She's so tired—and scared."

"Thanks for doing that."

"No problem. As far as Sim's condition, no change. He just stands in the corner of his stall, head down, drooling. He's totally out of it. And the swelling in his leg hasn't come down at all." He stroked one of the pups with his fingertips. "I feel like we should do more."

Kent reminded Barry, "The cultures showed *Pseudomonas*. That is one of the toughest bacteria to kill. We've got him on massive doses of the combination of antibiotics that should work best to knock it out. And as you know, we've got him on fluids and other medicines to keep up his strength while the antibiotics do their job. We are all doing everything we can."

"I know that, but"—Barry gave Kent a pleading look—"but it's not working. You don't have to be a veterinarian to see that he's slipping away. I feel like we are just sitting around watching him die."

Kent gave him a pat on the shoulder. "Hang in there. I'll go over and check on Em and see if there is anything else we can do."

As he left the OR, Lucinda gave him her I-need-a-potty-break whine. He opened the door for her and she dashed to a patch of grass. In the dim glow of a parking lot security light, he watched her and wrestled with Barry's words. The kid was right. At this point they were just waiting and watching, giving the medicines time to do their job. It was always such a frustrating, frightening time, the wait. He'd already used every weapon in his arsenal. There was nothing else he could do but wait.

Out of the corner of his eye, he saw a set of headlights turn into the lot and recognized Merrill's cruiser. It came to a stop three feet away and the window rolled down.

Kent spoke first. "Mighty late to be making your rounds."

Merrill didn't smile. "I called and they said you were finishing up some surgery in there. So, I figured it could save some time if I just came on over and picked you up. Get in."

"What's the big hurry?"

"Pegger crashed that damn Mustang of his."

When Kent didn't move, Merrill repeated, "Get in," more forcefully. "We're going over there."

Kent helped Lucinda into the back seat and climbed in. "Jesus. Is he all right?"

"He's dead."

"Ugh! What happened?"

"I don't know the details yet. My patrol guys just called me at home. Somebody driving by noticed his car over the bank and reported it. I guess it's bad."

The crash scene was surreal, like the movie set of an alien landing. The darkness of the country road was shattered by the whirling, flashing lights of police cars and first responders. Men in reflective gear waved flashlights to guide traffic. Police cars, an ambulance, firetrucks, and a tow truck were parked at all angles, the lights from each strobing the next, their radios barking tidbits of conversation from far-off dispatchers.

Merrill wove the cruiser through it all until he nosed up to a yellow crime scene tape. He and Kent were out of the car before it stopped rocking.

Merrill greeted the officer in charge who, in low tones and gestures, gave him the lay of the land.

Even in the distorted light, Kent could make out a set of tire tracks that veered off the highway and coursed through deep grass down into a gully. It was littered with shreds of chrome trim and diamonds of window glass. At the far end of it, taillights of Pegger's Mustang reflected back at him like wolves' eyes. Kent squinted at the car for an instant, then moaned softly when he realized that it was wrapped around a massive maple tree.

Merrill stepped back over to Kent, raised the yellow tape, and said, "We're waiting for the medical examiner, but we can go down. Don't touch anything."

Kent swallowed hard and ducked under.

One glance told him the car was totaled. There wasn't a piece on the front half of it that wasn't broken, bent, or missing. The trunk of the tree, its bark ripped through to glistening white wood, was lodged two feet into the engine compartment. Pegger had flown through the windshield and now lay on the hood. First responders had covered his body with a blanket, but his left arm dangled in sight.

Merrill took a corner of the blanket then raised his eyebrows to Kent. Kent braced himself and nodded. Merrill lifted the blanket.

Pegger's eyes were still wide open. There was a deep gash across his forehead that never had a chance to bleed.

"He didn't suffer. That's for sure," Merrill said, lowering the blanket. "We're lucky the whole thing didn't explode. The way he drove? It was bound to happen sooner or later."

Kent studied the wreck for a long time without replying. Then he turned, took a few quick steps into the darkness, and with his hands on his knees, he retched hard. He stood, wiped his mouth with his sleeve, and stared up at the stars.

He was drawn back by the sound of voices up on the highway, loud and argumentative. He could make out terse commands from the policemen and angry replies from a voice he instantly recognized. He reached the Mustang in time to see Merrill already scrambling up the path.

"Shit," Merrill said, over his shoulder. "Lute's here."

"I know. This is going to kill him."

At the top, two officers had Lute face-down on the ground. A third one was snapping cuffs on his wrists. Lute was struggling and spitting vicious demands for them to let him see his nephew.

Merrill put a hand on the cop's shoulder and waved him off Lute's back. The officer shifted just enough to give Merrill room. Merrill squatted close to his friend's face, "Lute, it's me, Merrill. You gotta stop."

"I gotta see Pegger," Lute shouted, still struggling.

"You settle down and I will make that happen. But not until you do."

Lute let out a roar like a trapped bear, then went quiet, considering his options. Just as Merrill was thinking that he might have to let Lute cool off in the back of his cruiser, Lute sighed, almost a whine, and forced himself into a calmer tone. "Okay. Get these bastards off me."

On Merrill's signal, the cops lifted Lute to his feet. He glared at them and they glared back.

Merrill kept a firm grasp on Lute's arm. "You okay?" he asked, testing the waters.

"Yes, goddamnit, I'm okay," Lute snarled.

"You going to cooperate if I take the cuffs off?"

The policeman holding Lute's other arm gave Merrill a wary look.

"Yes," Lute said, still working hard to control his anger.

Merrill held for a moment, studying Lute's face. Then to one of his guys, he said, "Take off the cuffs. I got him."

As Lute rubbed his wrists, Merrill moved square in front of him. "You can go down there with Kent and me. You can look—if you want—but you can't touch anything. Understand?"

Lute nodded.

Merrill raised the tape for a second time and the three of them descended toward the wreck.

Lute began an Owahgena chant, barely above a murmur, as he approached the Mustang. It rose louder as he circled it. He gestured for Merrill to lift the blanket.

"You sure?" Merrill asked him.

Lute was shaking like a sapling in a windstorm. "Yes."

Merrill lifted the blanket and Lute's chant turned into a hideous gurgle as an invisible hand clutched his throat. Then it stopped, leaving an eerie silence.

Lute studied Pegger's face long enough for Merrill's arm to get tired. Before their eyes, Lute's shivering stopped. His demeanor morphed from flailing anguish to cold, terrifying self-control. He leaned in close and, like a forest creature, sniffed the air near Pegger's face. Ignoring Merrill's instructions from before, he lightly stroked Pegger's lips with his finger then brought it to his own mouth.

He signaled Merrill to replace the blanket, then stepped back around the Mustang and peered over what was left of the passenger-side door. Kent and Merrill watched in silence. They hadn't paid much attention to the interior before and now they looked over his shoulder. It was strewn with papers and notebooks. Pegger's suit jacket was half on the seat and half on the floor. Lute reached in and lifted it.

"Don't touch anything," Merrill reminded him.

Lute didn't seem to hear him. He lifted the jacket higher and stared at the half-eaten slice of pizza that was hidden under it. He touched his finger to the pizza, then put his finger to the tip of his tongue. His expression was inscrutable.

Merrill sighed in frustration. Trying to be as sensitive to his friend's agony, he said, "Lute, remember, you agreed not to touch anything."

Still, Lute didn't respond.

Merrill held, hoping his message got through.

In a tone that chilled Kent like sitting through six hours of wind and sleet in a duck blind, Lute asked, "When can I have his body?"

CHAPTER 26

KENT DROVE PAST TIRED TRAILERS AND PREFAB homes on his way through the Owahgena reservation and thought about how what he was seeing contrasted so severely with Pegger's sylvan Iroquois village mural. He imagined how it must have been in that era long ago when the Indians lived in harmony with nature, before Europeans' greed, whiskey, and smallpox decimated the tribes.

It had been four days since the crash. The police had ruled the cause to be unsafe speed. Merrill went along with it, officially, but unofficially, he and Kent weren't buying it. And they knew Lute wasn't either. Kent was worried more than ever about his friend. Lute had pulled back, told them he wanted to be alone. Kent had reached out to him and gotten a huffy response to mind his own business and was more than a little surprised when Lute invited him to the longhouse ceremony. He hoped it was a peace offering.

He found one of the last places in a crowded parking area next to a grassy patch that was the reservation's version of a village green. The longhouse sat in the middle of it, and it struck him that he'd never been inside it. He had been friends with Owahgena his whole life. He'd grown up hunting and fishing on their reservation and, at times, even though it stuck in Lute's craw, he had made veterinary calls there. Heck, he'd played lacrosse on the field right behind that building. The Owahgena had always welcomed him, and he had always enjoyed their company.

They had invited him into their homes many times, but never into their longhouse. He joined the solemn line of mourners approaching it and noticed no other whites.

It was relatively new, built with modern materials, but designed in the style of a traditional longhouse—long, narrow, and low. The exterior walls were vertical logs with a natural stain and there were only a few small windows. The roof was arched and layered with broad, irregularly shaped shingles that imitated the elm bark ones that would have been used in the old days. There were five large holes evenly spaced along the ridge line, and each one had blue smoke curling up out of it. There was a small windowless wood door at one end, and it was easy to imagine it replaced by a blanket or hide back in the day. An American flag hung out front on a pole with blistered white paint. It seemed out of place and embarrassed to be there.

The longhouse was big enough to hold the whole tribe and was the meeting place for most major events, including council meetings and spiritual ceremonies. Iroquois ceremonies were awash in secrecy and mystery, and those of the Owahgena were the most secretive of them all. The longhouse was the heart of their culture, and it was rare for whites to be allowed inside.

Not surprisingly, everyone on the reservation had turned out for Pegger Cyr's funeral. Many were wearing traditional Iroquois clothing. Others had pulled worn suits and dresses from the back of the closet.

Kent felt a soft tap on his arm. He turned and there stood a high school age girl. She was wearing a dark gray shift and matching low pumps. Her features were Owahgena but otherwise she looked like any other teenager dressed for church.

She held out her hand. "My name is Jenny. Luther and Jodi asked me to escort you."

Kent smiled. He hadn't heard Lute called Luther since their school days. "Where are they?" he asked and immediately realized it was a dumb question.

"Luther is inside." She pointed toward the longhouse. "He is part of the ceremony. Jodi should be arriving any minute."

"And you are my escort?"

"Yes," Jenny said politely. "You can't go inside alone."

"I was by myself at Jimmy Silverheels funeral."

Jenny nodded understanding. "I saw you there. It was an honor for Jimmy that you came, but you were at the cemetery, not in the longhouse."

"True."

There was a sudden rise of chatter from a group behind them and they turned to see what had their attention. Jodi was approaching on foot, and alone.

She was wearing a dress of soft leather with beadwork designs that were foreign to Kent. It looked very old but cared for like a family treasure. Her hair was in a braid down her back. Once again, he was struck by her beauty and wondered how he overlooked it in the past.

"She walked?" Kent asked, surprised. "Alone?"

Jenny nodded, and in a tone beyond her years, she said, "The mother of the deceased can do as she chooses."

Members of the group went to her and greeted her with sad eyes but did not speak. Jodi continued toward the longhouse.

When she saw Kent, she stepped toward him. Her face held a smile that told him her mind was in another place. "Thank you for coming. Pegger thought the world of you," she said. It sounded mechanical.

She offered her hand, he took it, and a cold wave of memories, as cold as her skin, flowed over him. All the sad smiles, soft murmurs of sympathy, and limp handshakes of well-wishers, the emotions that were churning in Jodi now came rolling back over him like a tidal wave. He understood why she had shut down. He had done the same thing on the day of Aubrey's funeral. It was the only way to survive the ordeal.

"I'm sorry, Jodi," he said, and it sounded so pointless he wished he had said nothing at all.

She squeezed his hand then turned and, surrounded by the women of her tribe, she entered the longhouse.

Jenny gestured toward the door and reminded him to duck his head as she held it open for him. Kent noticed as they passed through it that men went to the left and women to the right.

He raised his eyebrows to Jenny.

"Custom," she whispered.

She steered him to a small section off to one side and settled onto a bench. She patted the seat next to her. "Guests are here."

Kent sat and was immediately taken by the eeriness.

On both sides, running the full length of the room were several rows of low, backless wooden, benches. They rose only a few inches off the floor. Each was filled with attendees sitting cross-legged on earth tone-colored cushions—men to the left, women to the right.

The walls were paneled in cedar and decorated with rattles and drums made of turtle shells and deer hooves. There were knots of dried corn, tobacco, and sage hanging at intervals. Down the center of the room was a slate floor with five fires in rings of field stone. Smoke from them rose up through the holes in the roof. The center fire was larger than the others and had benches around it. The air was thick with the smells of herbs, tobacco, wood smoke, and people.

Jodi and a couple of women that Kent did not recognize were seated at the central fire. She reminded Kent of the tiny songbirds so often brought to his office, stuporous because they were in shock. Lute sat on the other side of the fire. Like Jodi, he was dressed in leather and beads that looked old and regal. On his head was a skullcap with a set of deer antlers and two eagle feathers, one standing up, the other dangling. His face was painted black with splashes of white. He was chanting softly and shaking a turtle shell rattle. Other men to his side accompanied him on small drums. Between him and the fire was a plain wooden casket. It was closed.

Lute received an invisible signal when everyone was seated, and his chanting stopped. The room descended into a heavy silence. He let it linger just long enough then exploded into a loud, wailing song that jolted the crowd. The ceremony started in earnest—drums thumped, rattles shook, and masked dancers invoked the spirits by placing sage, cedar, and tobacco on the casket.

Lute was standing in the circle holding a lance that was decorated with carvings and feathers. It looked old and strangely vicious in a way that made Kent suspect it had killed many an enemy of the Owahgena, both beast and man. Lute was thrusting its point skyward, stabbing at the spirits, and shouting loudly in Owahgena.

The five fires threw heat and smoke into the crowded space. The air became stifling. Kent's eyes burned. Just when he thought he may have to leave, he felt a rush of cool fresh air come from behind him as someone opened the longhouse door to enter. It felt wonderful.

At the same moment, Lute's gaze caught the new arrival. It took him just a heartbeat to focus through the smokeveiled air. When he did, he froze, his singing stopped, and the spear dropped to his waist.

Kent watched Lute's face shift from recognition, to disbelief, to anger, and then he saw Jodi's do the same thing. He glanced back, craning his neck to see who or what had shocked them. It was Feron Munn.

Jodi jumped to her feet, screaming. "Get out of here!"

The heads of the shocked faithful spun from Lute, to Jodi, to Feron, and around again. The quiet screamed, then rose into murmurs as outrage boiled through the crowd and the entire tribe turned on Feron. Kent stared at his old friend and felt an unexpected pang of sadness for him. The rough old woodsman had made an attempt to dress for the occasion with a tattered charcoal sport coat, over an equally worn collared shirt, and khaki pants. His boots were properly tied. He literally had his hat in hand.

Jodi shouted again for Feron to get out.

Feron stood there, the picture of humility, absorbing the brutal judgment of his people. His eyes reached out to Lute.

Lute stepped to Jodi. He bent so that their foreheads touched. With his thumb, he wiped away tears of anger and whispered to her. She listened to what he said, then shook her head violently and struggled to get away. But Lute held her shoulder firmly. There were more whispers, more crying, more struggling, until Jodi dropped her head to Lute's chest. He signaled the tribal women to assist, and they guided Jodi back to her seat. She fixed her eyes on the casket and seemed to move to some distant place. Her hands went for her ears and Kent's heart sank when he realized that she was groping for her earphones that were not there.

Lute recovered his lance and turned to Feron. He drew it back, aiming at him, and the clan gasped. The two men held, eye to eye. Feron never moved, for all the world looking as though he would welcome it piercing his chest. Finally, Lute brought the spear down to his side. Several elders approached him. They whispered among themselves then nodded and dispersed.

One signaled the crowd to sit and be silent. One escorted Feron to a bench and gestured for members to make room. Feron sat, staring at his knees, until finally he raised his head. With eyes red and full of tears, he frowned around the room, asking the clan the questions that had determined his life's path. *Why am I never accepted? Why can't I ever get it right?*

The people sent furtive glances in any direction except toward Feron's and were relieved when Lute resumed Pegger's death ceremony.

CHAPTER 27

PEGGER'S ACTUAL BURIAL FOLLOWED RIGHT
after the longhouse ceremony in a small cemetery on the reservation.
It was outside in the fresh air—Euros were welcome, and Feron was
gone. Heads were cooler.

The ceremony was like a Christian burial except Lute, in native
garb, presided instead of a preacher. The family was seated next to the
grave in folding chairs. Jodi was still in her traditional dress of leather
with beads, still beautiful, and still in a daze. She had Wren with her
now and was rocking the child on her lap in a somniferous rhythm and
staring blankly at the ground in front of the casket. Most of Lute's words
were spoken in Owahgena and even though he couldn't understand
them, Kent judged from Lute's tone that he was simmering in anger
more than in grief. Mercifully, Lute being Lute, he was brief.

Kent was standing off to the edge of the small crowd waving his
hat to ward off blackflies when Merrill came up behind him.

"I was wondering if you were going to make it," Kent whispered.

"Me too, for a while. How'd it go at the longhouse?"

"To say it got rowdy would be an understatement."

Merrill flipped his hand at a fly on his face. "What happened?"

"Feron showed up."

"What, the dumbass was going to pay his respects?"

"Jodi went nuts."

"Oh, man."

"She was yelling at him to leave."

"She sure has it in for Feron."

"Lute wasn't happy either."

They both swiveled their gaze toward Lute. The ceremony was winding down and he was surrounded by fellow mourners.

Merrill said, "He still doesn't look happy."

"No he's not. I gotta tell you, Lute is one scary guy when he gets mad. I thought he was going to throw a spear at Feron."

Merrill considered that until he remembered something. "The guys from Atlanta called again this morning. It turns out the Korean illegals they have in custody are finally feeling safe enough to open up. When they started talking, it came out that on one of the trips a woman died. And, to make it worse, she had a kid with her. A little girl, just a few years old. They are both missing. The cops figure the mother's body will turn up sooner or later, but the last anyone remembers, the girl was still alive and hanging with the rest of the group. No one knows what happened to her. Of course, Atlanta wants us to keep an eye open for her."

Kent's glance shifted to Jodi and Wren, then away before Merrill noticed. "We can do that."

The crowd was starting to disperse. Kent gestured toward the grave. "I'll catch you later. I'm going to give them my condolences."

Jodi was receiving words of sympathy from a few stragglers and he waited for them to leave before he approached. The light rose in her eyes when she saw him. She shifted Wren to her other arm and extended her hand. "Thank you for coming, Doc."

He wanted to tell her that he knew how she felt, that he felt the same emptiness in his chest every moment of every day. He wanted to tell her that what they say about it getting better with time is a lie. But, instead of making the moment about himself, he said, "Pegger is— was—half my age, but he was a good friend. I'll miss him."

He was surprised when she said, "I am going to need your help."

"Of course, anything. How?"

Surprise became confusion when she said, "To grieve."

"Me?"

"You deal with the loss of Aubrey every day."

"Not very well, believe me. I certainly haven't got it figured out."

"I know you visit her grave all the time."

"Who told you that?"

"Lute." She set Wren on the ground but kept hold of her hand. "Will you help me?"

"I'll do what I can, if you think it will help, but don't get your hopes up."

With her free arm, she hugged him. When their cheeks pressed together, a wonderful heat surged through him.

When they released, Kent asked, "How's your niece doing with all this?" He studied her reaction.

"She's fine," Jodi answered a beat too fast. "She doesn't understand all that's going on."

They stared at the casket in silence for a moment, then Jodi said, "I apologize for what happened in the longhouse."

"Forget it. A lot of people don't like Feron, for a lot of reasons."

Her face hardened. "You have no idea."

He was searching for something to say when the pager on his belt chirped. The message read: *Urgent, call the office.* With a half laugh he read it aloud to Jodi. "Never a dull moment. I can call the CVC from my truck."

"We'll walk with you."

Jodi and Wren stood by as Kent leaned across the driver's seat, legs out the door, and made the call. It was short. Sim's condition had deteriorated. They needed him there ASAP.

Kent apologized even as Jodi reassured him that she understood and encouraged him to get going.

He was steering his truck back up onto the main road when a glint of sunlight off chrome caught his eye. It came from Feron Munn's jacked-up pickup parked along the back side of the cemetery in a poor attempt to hide behind grave markers and trees. Feron was scanning the crowd. Kent's first thought was *Good, at least he's got enough sense not to join the group again.* He followed Feron's line of sight. It settled on Jodi, and Jodi was staring knives back at Feron. She snatched up Wren, wrapped her in her arms, and turned back to Pegger's grave.

CHAPTER 28

KENT SLID HIS MOBILE UNIT TO A STOP AT THE equine entrance of the CVC.

Emily was waiting. She stepped to him, crying like he'd never seen her cry before. He hugged her as she said between sobs, "He just went down. He's dying."

He held his daughter for a moment, silently praying that she was wrong. "Let's take a look."

When he entered the stall, Sim was every bit as bad as Emily had described. The once magnificent stallion now looked pitiful lying on the floor of the stall. The only sign of life was the heaving of his chest. An oxygen mask had been thrown over his muzzle and it fogged with each gasping, grunting breath.

Veterinarians and technicians were swarming over him like ants. One team was at his head, attempting to switch out the mask for a breathing tube. Barry was with another team collecting vital signs and shouting them out. Someone yelled for a water blanket. "We need to warm him up." They unrolled a plastic blanket over him that looked like a child's swimming pool. The stall became more and more congested as techs wheeled in monitors and other equipment.

Kent bent down by Sim's head. He felt his ear—it was deathly cold. He lifted Sim's eyelid—the scleral blood vessels were barely visible. He glimpsed at the membranes in his mouth—they were the color of clouds before a thunderstorm.

"He's dying, isn't he?" Emily said, over his shoulder.

Kent raised his eyebrows to the veterinarian in charge, knowing that he'd overheard the question.

"He is in deep shock," the young doctor said. "And getting worse by the minute. His body functions are shutting down. The infection has overwhelmed his whole body." He turned back to one of the other doctors and said, "Push the fluids."

"We've got two lines going in full bore," the second doctor replied. She pointed at a tube snaking out from under the water blanket near Sim's hind legs. The first drops of golden liquid were just starting to drip into the clear plastic bag connected to it. "We got a urinary catheter in to keep track of his output, too." Then she recited the mantra of the ICU—*It's all about saving the kidneys.*

Emily had heard her father say it a hundred times. "It's the job of the kidneys to remove toxins from the body. If they shut down, the battle is lost."

Barry touched Emily's arm. In the most reassuring tone he could muster, he said, "We aren't giving up, Em."

She wanted to beg her father to do all that he could, but she knew he already was. Why hadn't anything he had done from day one worked? For all of the CVC's expert staff, laboratories, and critical care equipment, she was about to lose Sim, her horse that was so much more to her than a horse.

The stall filled with a putrid smell that caused several of the hardened team members to gag. Emily couldn't make herself look as a crew removed the bandage from Sim's leg. She already knew what they were seeing—massive swelling from shoulder to hoof, skin pulpy and mottled black, and ulcers the size of a man's hand that were oozing green pus. She'd seen it get worse day by day.

In frustration, she asked, "Doc, what's *doing* this to Sim?" Even though he'd explained it to her many times over the last few days.

"*Pseudomonas aeruginosa* is the name of the bacteria," he reminded her.

"I know that's what the cultures showed, but we've had him on a half dozen different antibiotics. Why haven't they killed it?"

"*Pseudomonas* is the worst of the worst. It's resistant to most antibiotics. And there's a lot of different strains of *Pseudomonas*—all bad."

Emily dropped to her knees and touched her forehead to Sim's neck.

Kent stood watching her. His heart ached for his daughter. He knew she was terrified. Her lifelong dream, all that she had worked for—the Olympics on Simpatico's Gift—was slipping away. He hated himself for not treating Sim more aggressively from the start. Hindsight was cruel.

When she finally lifted her head, Barry extended a hand and helped her to her feet. Her eyes glistening with tears, she said with cold resignation, "Sim is going to die, isn't he?"

Kent said softly, "We don't know."

"No!" came out of Barry so forcefully it jolted the others.

CHAPTER 29

THE CLOCK ON THE SIGN IN FRONT OF THE BANK
read 6:15 as Kent drove through Jefferson. It had been two days since
Sim crashed. The stallion was still alive but hanging on only by the most
tenuous of threads. Kent was in constant terror for Sim and for Emily.
Both of them had been living at Sim's side. He hadn't slept enough to
say so. He was exhausted.

The CVC dispatcher was amazed when she told Kent about an
early-morning call for a calving and he agreed to take it. He was actually thankful for the diversion. He was on his way back from it now. It
turned out to be just a front leg back causing the elbow to lock in the
birth canal. It was an easy fix—happy cow, happy calf, happy farmer.
He needed happy. It was a tiny moment of brightness in an otherwise
dark two days.

He still had time to swing by the cemetery to talk to Aubrey before
he checked in on Sim again, but strangely, this morning he didn't feel
its usual draw.

He was waiting at one of the few traffic lights in town, listening
to George Jones sing a sad country song, when without really knowing
why, he hit his turn signal and, when the light changed, directed his
truck toward the reservation.

A few minutes later, he pulled up in front of Lute's cabin. Lute was rocking on the porch, already soaking up the morning sun. Otsi was stretched out at Lute's feet doing the same thing.

Max came charging off the porch all bad and bristled, barking like he was rabid. When Lucinda leaped from the truck, his barking stopped, and his tail began to wag.

In response to Max's ruckus, Otsi raised his head and glanced their way. He sniffed the breeze, identified Kent and Lucinda, determined they were not a threat, and dropped his head back down—all in the lazy motion hound dogs made famous.

As Kent stepped onto the porch, Lute coiled his string of beads and slipped it into the breast pocket of his flannel shirt. "What brings you out to the boonies this early in the morning?"

Kent motioned toward Otsi. "That guy. I thought I'd see how he's doing."

Lute patted his knee and Otsi pushed himself up and licked his hand. Lute stood and took a few steps. "Otsi, come," he said. "Show Doc how your leg is doing."

Otsi rose on his three good legs and walked to Lute, bearing just the slightest amount of weight on his injured one.

Kent raised his eyebrows, impressed. "Not bad."

"He's going to have to take it easy for a while, that's for sure, but I think he's coming along pretty well." There was pride tempered with modesty in Lute's voice.

"I'd say so. I have to admit, I'm amazed with his progress. You've gotta love those antibiotics."

"I'm hoping he'll be ready to go coon hunting with us this fall."

Kent raised his eyebrows. "We'll have to see about that."

Lute's voice went serious. "I heard Em's horse isn't doing well."

The words sucked away Kent's self-satisfaction at Otsi's remarkable recovery. "That's an understatement."

Lute didn't mince words. "Is he going to make it?"

Kent was slow to answer. When he did, it was just a shrug.

Lute stroked Otsi's head. "I know you and I don't agree on what's the best type of medicine. Never have. We are what we are. But the only reason this guy is with us today is because when I was losing the battle, I swallowed my pride and let you take a try. That day when I brought Otsi into your office and I didn't want to leave him, you said to me, 'No treatment works all the time. If the one you are using isn't working, you have to try a different one.'" He let his words settle a moment. "I'm willing to do that for you, try my medicine on the horse, that is."

Kent couldn't imagine anyone making medical decisions for Em's horse other than himself. Sim was *his* patient and his alone. The horse was too important, he meant too much to Emily. She would be crushed if he bailed out on her now. No way was he going to suggest to her that they treat Sim with potions made of herbs and roots. He put the idea out of his head. His reply was quick and sharp. "I know what I said. Thanks, but no thanks. I've got it covered."

A lesser friend might have been insulted. Lute just shrugged.

The screen door creaked, and Jodi stepped out drying her hands with a dish towel. She looked as tired as he felt. Why wouldn't she be? Two days ago she buried her son. She pulled her earphones out. "Morning, Doc."

"I came to check on Otsi."

"He's doing pretty well, wouldn't you say?"

"Lute and I were just saying that."

Wren squeezed past Jodi's legs and out onto the porch. In a flash, Max was at her side.

"Good morning, young lady," Kent said, bending as close to her as he dared with the little guard dog eyeing him.

Wren smiled up as she petted Max's head.

"Does your dog have a name?" Kent prodded.

Wren's eyes twinkled at the attention, but she didn't speak.

"Are you staying with your aunt and uncle?" he asked in baby talk.

Jodi pulled her back to her side.

Kent straightened. "She's quiet. How much longer is she going to be with you?"

Jodi veered the subject, "Can you stay for breakfast? I was just about to call Lute in. French toast."

"Sounds great."

Lute held the door for them and as Kent slid by him, he said under his breath, "I didn't know Indians ate French toast."

Lute shoved him into the cabin, "You are *such* an ass."

A half-hour later, Kent stepped back out onto the porch, rubbed his belly, and stared out at the rifle range that now had a cow and a few goats grazing on it. Man, it was a long way to the targets. Jodi, Wren, and Lute were watching the dogs eat their serving of French toast. His pager sounded. The message on it read simply: *Call the office.*

"It never fails," he said with a smile, but his chest tightened as his fear for Sim skyrocketed.

He made the call from his truck. The emergency was for a down horse. That was the bad news. The good news was that it was not Sim.

Kent allowed himself to breathe again. "I've got to go."

Lute nodded. Jodi indicated *okay* with a wave of her hand.

"One of the Syracuse Police horses is down in the street right in the center of town. It's trapped."

"What, one of the mounted patrol horses? Wow!" Jodi said.

"Something about getting its leg caught."

"Sounds exciting. The poor thing needs your help. You better get moving."

Kent called Lucinda to load up, closed the door, and was about to pull away when a thought struck him. He lowered the window. He glanced at Lute hoping he'd be okay with the idea, then turned to Jodi. "Do you want to ride along?"

"I'd love to, but no." She rubbed the top of Wren's head. "I've got to keep my eye on this one." It was obvious she was disappointed.

Lute cleared his throat. "I haven't got anything going this morning. You go ahead. I'll watch her."

Jodi shook her head. "No."

"Go ahead, Jodi. Wren and I will be fine. You know you want to."

"It is a pretty unique call," Kent coaxed.

Jodi scanned the perimeter as if reassuring herself that no danger lurked nearby. Finally, in a pleading voice she said, "Lute, you promise me you won't let her out of your sight, even for one second."

"I promise."

She turned to Kent, still hesitant. "Okay, I guess I'm in." She gave Lute a threatening you-better-do-as-I-say look, then kissed Wren on the top of the head.

CHAPTER 30

JODI BIT HER THUMBNAIL AND TWISTED TO watch through the rear window of the vet truck as Lute and Wren got smaller in the distance. To Kent, her angst seemed excessive, but he chalked it up to her having just lost Pegger. When she could no longer see them, she sighed, resigned herself that Wren would be safe with Lute, then turned to the excitement at hand. "It's going to take us forty-five minutes to get into downtown Syracuse. Is the horse going to be okay for that long?"

"The mounted patrol officers know first aid and how to handle emergencies. We should be all right." He sounded more confident than he was. "Plus, we'll get there faster than usual."

"How? We need a helicopter."

A moment later, as they were going through Jefferson, Merrill's cruiser pulled away from the curb in front of them and accelerated hard, siren wailing. Kent sat up straight and gripped the wheel with both hands. He coaxed his truck to within a couple of car lengths of Merrill. "We don't have a helicopter, but we've got the next best thing."

"Wow! A police escort!"

With Merrill leading, they flew through the village, blowing past traffic lights and stop signs. Jodi went wide-eyed and white-knuckled. She clenched the console with one hand and the door handle with the other. Lucinda whined in the back seat.

"Mounted patrol horses get the royal treatment," Kent told her. He pressed the gas pedal harder. The truck grunted indignantly then lunged ahead doing its best to keep up.

When they reached the village line, Merrill cut his siren and peeled off as a county sheriff's cruiser took the lead.

Jodi gave Kent a questioning look.

The brothers exchanged a quick salute. "Change of jurisdiction," Kent explained.

The same maneuver occurred in DeWitt and again as they entered the City of Syracuse.

"They've really got this relay thing down," Jodi said.

Cars pulled to the shoulder to let them through and pedestrians jumped back to the curb. Kent leaned toward the wheel.

Jodi could see he was on a power trip. "You must have wanted to be a fireman when you were a kid."

Eyes still fixed on the road, he smiled. "No, I always wanted to be a vet, but I've said right along that vets should be allowed to have sirens."

Jodi smiled. "Yeah, that's true, they should. I never thought about that."

They slowed as they approached a crowd—firefighters, police officers, and onlookers. Two men swung aside a sawhorse construction barrier and waved them through the opening.

Jodi saw the horse first. "Awww."

It was on its side, wild-eyed and covered in sweat from struggling. A woman police officer wearing a mounted patrol uniform was on his neck, trying to calm him. The horse's hind leg was caught in a narrow cut in the pavement and contorted in a twist that made Kent cringe. A vision of Sim's grotesque leg flared in his mind, paralyzing him until he could force it away. He jumped to the back of his truck, pulled out his medical bag, and handed it to Jodi. "Carry this," he said. "They'll know you're with me."

Within seconds, Kent had a dose of sedative in the horse. While they waited for it to have its effect, he asked the officer, "This your mount?"

She nodded. "Yes. His name is Azucar and I'm Officer Johnson."

"You are doing the right thing, Officer. Hold his head down, it makes him less likely to struggle." She nodded again.

He patted the horse gently. "Don't worry, Azucar, we'll have you on your feet in no time. What happened?"

Officer Johnson pointed at a 6inch-wide, 18inch-deep channel in the macadam. Kent could see cables running in it. "They are laying new conduit. No big deal, Azucar is as steady as they come. He doesn't mind bucket loaders, jackhammers, or anything else. It was my fault. I asked him to back up to let a car pass and his foot slipped into the cut. It happened so fast. He tried to pull it out, but when he couldn't, he panicked. He slipped and fell, then his leg was twisted so that he *couldn't* get back up." She brushed away tears, trying to maintain a command appearance.

"Are you hurt?"

"No. I'm fine."

"Lucky for you. You could be in an ambulance right now."

She sniffed back more tears. "I'd trade places with him in a heartbeat."

Azucar relaxed and Kent moved back to the leg. It was wedged sideways in the narrow groove. The heel of the steel horseshoe was caught under the blacktop. His pastern was bent in a way a pastern was not intended to bend. There was no way to get a splint on it.

"This may not have a happy ending," Kent whispered to Jodi.

He scanned the crowd and saw a heavy-set man wearing an orange vest and hard hat. "Al, we're going to have to knock out some of the blacktop—carefully."

Al gave Kent a quizzical look. Then he remembered his name was on his hard hat. "Oh, yeah, Doc. I got you. No jackhammer. We've got chisels."

Al vanished into the crowd and returned faster than Kent could have hoped. He was lugging a maul that would have made John Henry proud and had a couple of his coworkers in tow. They were carrying an assortment of cold steel chisels.

Kent inspected the chisels and picked one that was the diameter of a broom handle and half as long. He ran his thumb along its blade and a chill crept up his back at the thought of it being pounded inches from Azucar's foot. He handed the chisel back to Al.

Loud enough for them all to hear, he said, "Here's what we are going to do—or at least try to do. Al, this is the piece of road that's got to go." With his finger, Kent traced a semi-circle around a section of blacktop next to Azucar's hoof.

Al nodded and clenched the maul. One of his helpers positioned the chisel.

"Officer Johnson, you stay on his head. Our guy here is sedated, but even so, he might be startled by the hammer and start struggling again."

Johnson tightened her grip on Azucar's bridle, "Got it."

He looked at Jodi. "Put your weight on his shoulder. Be ready to hold him down."

Jodi took a position with both forearms supporting her weight on Azucar's shoulder.

"I'll try to steady his leg." He gripped the horse's fetlock with both hands. He scanned his crew to see that everyone was in position, took a deep breath, and nodded to Al. "Gently."

Al lifted the huge maul and tapped the chisel lightly, if such a thing is possible. It made a loud clank. Nothing happened—Azucar was not disturbed, but neither was the blacktop.

"Again," Kent said. "A little harder."

Al did his thing with a little more gusto. The sound of steel on steel made Kent wince. He felt the ground vibrate and Azucar shudder.

The blacktop did not give.

"Jesus," Kent said, and took a breath. "Okay, everybody, be ready. Al, put some stank on it."

Al raised the maul above his head and brought it down as if he were driving a railroad spike.

Chips of blacktop flew, stinging Kent's face. Azucar snorted like a bull and raised his head, sending Officer Johnson flying. He yanked his leg violently trying to free it. Kent held on and tried not to think about how if his fingers were crushed between the hoof and the road, he would be out of work for weeks—or worse.

Jodi dove forward, dropping all of her weight on the thinnest part of Azucar's neck just behind his head. She put her mouth so close to his ear that Kent thought she was biting it. But no, she was whispering. Fast words. He could not make them out, but he could tell she was pleading with the horse and consoling him at the same time.

Azucar's head sank back down. His leg relaxed. Officer Johnson grabbed his bridle and climbed back into position, shoulder to shoulder with Jodi.

Jodi kept whispering into Azucar's ear.

Kent examined the trench. "We made some headway that time, but not enough to get his foot out."

"Can you give him more tranquilizer?" Officer Johnson asked.

"Not safely. The next step would be to anesthetize him. That would be more dangerous, even if we had the equipment." Kent held the leg and considered his options. "Let's try it one more time."

A buzz went through the crowd. The chisel guys got back into position. Johnson held Azucar's head, and Jodi whispered furiously into his ear.

On Kent's signal, Al drove the hammer down hard and it rang the chisel with the same deafening toll. More of the roadway sprayed away. Azucar's eyes widened, but he did not move.

When Kent opened *his* eyes, the ditch was wide enough for him to lift Azucar's foot free.

There was a communal sigh of relief as those in front sent the good news back into the crowd.

Kent felt the leg. No fractures, at least none that he could feel. There was a cut where the sharp edge of the trench had torn the skin, but the deeper structures seemed okay.

He yelled for someone to bring a trailer around. "This guy needs to go to our hospital for Xrays."

Within minutes Kent had the wound cleaned, sutured, and bandaged. "Okay, guys," he said, "we're going to try to get him up on his feet. *Slowly*! He'll be wobbly and confused from the sedation, he's only working with three legs, and his steel shoes are slippery on the blacktop."

On Kent's signal Jodi and Johnson slid off Azucar's head. As the thousand-pound creature rose to his feet, Al, his helpers, and a half-dozen cops all joined in to support him. The crowd clapped and cheered. Kent noticed a crew from the Syracuse newspaper snapping photos.

A few minutes later, Officer Johnson approached Kent as they closed the tailgate of the horse trailer. She extended her hand. "I just wanted to thank you personally. You are the best."

"You're welcome. It's what we do."

"By the way, Doc." Johnson gestured toward Jodi, who was loading gear back into the vet unit. "I can see why you have that girl for an assistant. She has an incredible way with horses."

Kent thought back to how Jodi had talked Azucar down from near panic. She hadn't been just babbling the mindless chatter that most horsemen use to settle a nervous animal. She was *talking* to him, actually telling the horse something, he was sure of it. He could tell by the way Azucar responded. "She's good with animals, that's for sure."

"It's more than that, Doc. She has a gift."

Kent and Jodi headed back to the CVC at a much more relaxed pace. Jodi bounced in her seat like a kid at the circus. "That was amazing! Flying into the city with a police escort. Then helping the horse. You have an awesome job."

Kent was just as high on the moment and laughed out loud at her enthusiasm. Her energy buoyed him, and he was struck by how badly he had let his love of veterinary medicine slip.

For a few miles they drove in silence, reliving the rescue. When Kent spoke again, his voice was sober. "You should know that it's not all fun and games. We don't always have happy endings. It can be tough."

Jodi's mood deflated. "I know that. Death is part of life. The hard part. I've seen plenty of it."

He wished he hadn't shifted the mood. A long minute passed. Then he breathed out the words, "Tomorrow morning, then."

"What about it?"

"Do you want to see the not-so-much-fun side of the job?"

"Yes, I do."

"I'll pick you up just before sunrise."

Jodi studied her hands in her lap, debating. "Maybe. I need to check on Wren, see how Lute did with her today. Then I'll have to get up the nerve to let him do it again tomorrow."

CHAPTER 31

THE DAY WAS A SAD ONE BECAUSE IT WAS
Virginia Wolfe's last. Kent had agreed to abide by the owner's tradition,
so they were euthanizing the wonderful old mare at sunrise.

Putting a horse to sleep was always a depressing event, but now,
as Kent thought about Sim and how Emily's poor horse was suffering,
the reality of the procedure as the one that might turn out to be the
most humane treatment for Sim really struck home. Kent had already
discussed that terrible possibility with Aubrey at his last few cemetery
visits—no one else—and she had refused to consider it.

Jodi was sitting in the passenger seat.

All had gone well yesterday while Lute watched Wren, so Jodi was
less apprehensive about letting him do it again this morning. Lute, for
his part, had stated that Wren had proven to be an excellent vegetable
garden weeder, and that he was happy to take her.

Jodi had been ready and waiting when Kent picked her up, and
much to his delight, her Walkman was nowhere to be seen. Lucinda
was hanging her head over the seat, enjoying the attention that Jodi
was lavishing on her. She was rubbing Lucinda's jowls and chattering a
stream of silliness. Kent smiled in the dark.

He turned his mobile unit through the majestic gate of VinChaRo
Farm just as first light was appearing on the eastern horizon.

Jodi recognized where they were. "This is the St. Pierre's estate," she said, obviously awed.

"Correct. Elizabeth has been my client for years, and she's also a very good friend of mine."

The long driveway coursed between white board fences separating pastures. They passed the mansion house and pulled to a stop in front of the main barn. Before he could get out, Elizabeth appeared at the door. She was the matriarch of VinChaRo Farm and looked the part—mid-seventies, ramrod posture, keen blue eyes, and attired in pressed jeans and a leather jacket.

"Good morning, Doc," she said. Kent picked up a sadness in her voice. That was unusual. "Don't get out. Osvaldo is already up on the hill with Wolfie. We can drive up. I'll just hop in with you...oh, you have a rider with you this morning." Elizabeth hadn't seen Jodi in the dim light. "Never mind. I'll grab my Jeep and meet you up there."

Kent looked back and forth between the two women, but before he could speak, Jodi was over the seat into the back with Lucinda. Kent wasn't sure if he or Lucinda were more amazed at her agility.

He nodded a silent thanks to her. "We have room, Elizabeth. Hop in."

Elizabeth pulled herself up into the truck. "Good morning, Lucy." She let Lucinda lick her ear a time or two then pushed her to the back.

Kent introduced the two women.

"I'm sure you're learning a lot from Doctor Stephenson, but I hope you don't have to experience too many calls like this one."

"He warned me," Jodi said softly.

Elizabeth drew a deep breath then sighed heavily. "You won't have to drive me back, Kent. I'll walk. I know I'll need the time to myself."

Kent was familiar with the lane that snaked its way up the hill to the final resting place for all VinChaRo horses. Over the years, he'd made the trip more times than he cared to remember.

"Osvaldo started up with Virginia Wolfe a while ago. She has to go slow these days. She's so old and lame now. She's just a rack of bones. It breaks my heart. She's been a wonderful broodmare." In the half light, Kent saw Elizabeth tease a tissue from her pocket and touch her eyes. "But it's time. I hate seeing her like she is. She's not happy anymore."

They rode in silence as the truck rocked and swayed its way up the farm lane.

After a long minute, Elizabeth said, "Emily told me about Simpatico's Gift. Is he as sick as she says?"

"He's pretty bad."

"If something happens to that horse it will break my heart."

The anvil on Kent's shoulders took on more weight. Elizabeth had a special relationship with Emily and Sim. She had given the horse to her as a special birthday gift after Kent had thwarted an attempt by an egotistical horseman to destroy VinChaRo Farm."

He wondered how much detail Em had given her. "Yeah, we are all thinking the same way. But he's getting the best care possible."

"I'm sure of that," Elizabeth said, and there was not the slightest hint of doubt in her tone. "Horses, they give you the best moments of your life, and the worst, right?"

"That's for sure."

Elizabeth drifted for a moment. She broke the silence with "This is the right thing to do, isn't it, Doc, what we are doing for Wolfie?"

Kent spoke slowly, "Yes, it is. She's led a long and happy life, thanks to you. Now she's old and dying. Like you said, she's not happy anymore. To keep her going when we can't help her is unnatural and selfish. Still, knowing that it's right doesn't make it easy." It was so much easier for him to talk in the abstract about the death of *someone else's* horse than to even consider it for Sim.

They drove a little farther and stopped at the end of the lane, a few steps from where Osvaldo was standing with Virginia Wolfe. He was holding a lead rope that dangled loosely to her halter. She was nibbling at a clump of grass. Osvaldo had been VinChaRo's stableman forever. He looked like he would cry at any moment. He gave them a sad wave.

Jodi followed a step behind Kent and Elizabeth, sensing that this was a one-on-one moment for doctor and client. She realized that she was privileged to be there, and out of respect, remained silent.

A few feet beyond Osvaldo and Wolfie was a freshly dug crater with a pile of dirt next to it. A hundred feet beyond that, partly hidden by trees, was a yellow backhoe, its driver observing from the cab.

A breath-taking sunrise sent streaks of pink and magenta into the morning sky, and Kent stopped for a moment admiring it. Then he stepped to his truck and retrieved a small syringe. Virginia Wolfe hardly noticed the tiny needle prick when he gave her the sedative in her hip muscle.

He recapped the needle. "Elizabeth, I've told you this before, but I'm going to say it again. I think it's a wonderful tradition that you put the horses down at sunrise."

"Thanks. They deserve the honor."

They watched Virginia Wolf in silence for a few more minutes. As she got sleepy, her knees began to quiver and her head dropped. On Kent's instruction, Osvaldo led her to within a few feet of the grave.

Kent filled a large syringe with the deadly blue euthanasia solution, and a picture of Sim flashed in his mind for a second time. He stared into the blackness of the hole for a long second, then shook it away.

Osvaldo noticed. "Are you all right?"

"Yes, I'm okay."

On cue, Elizabeth stepped to the old brood mare and patted her neck. She whispered something like "Bye, Wolfie. I love you. You have been a good friend." Then she nodded to Kent and started down the hill on foot.

When Elizabeth was out of sight, Kent administered the blue liquid into Virginia Wolfe's jugular vein. She hardly reacted until the solution swept through her nervous system a few seconds later. She sighed deeply, went down on her knees in front, then her back legs, and rolled onto her side.

Jodi gasped and covered her mouth with her hand. Kent had almost forgotten she was there.

He listened to Virginia Wolfe's chest with his stethoscope then nodded to Osvaldo, who had tears flowing down his cheeks. Osvaldo waved to the backhoe operator, and Kent heard the engine fire up.

It was full daylight by the time they finished rolling Virginia Wolfe into the grave and covering it.

"Need a ride down, Osvaldo?" Kent asked.

"No, thanks." The man nodded toward the grave. "I'm going to do some raking and finish work."

Kent and Jodi reloaded their gear and started down the hill without a word.

Elizabeth was almost to the barn by the time they caught up to her. She waved without looking up as they passed.

He glanced over at Jodi. Lucinda's chin was resting on her shoulder so that their heads were leaning together. Her eyes were distant and impossible to read. "Are you okay?"

"Yes," she said but didn't look at him.

He wondered what she was thinking about. Had it been a mistake to bring her along to witness more death? Were the wounds from Pegger's death still too raw? The next time he looked over, she had pulled her Walkman out of some pocket and plugged in her earphones, closing out the world.

CHAPTER 32

ABOUT THE TIME KENT AND JODI WERE GOING through Jefferson on their way back to the cabin to drop her off, she pulled out one earphone and turned to Kent. "Thank you." She paused, then she added, "I'm glad you took me with you. Also, I'm glad I saw what the hard part is like—I think."

"My pleasure, if you can call it that."

"The owners feel so awful even though you are doing the right thing for their animals."

"Yep. They are upset, of course, because they are losing a friend and they are going to miss them, but most understand why and appreciate our help."

"I don't know if I could do it. That was a really dark moment."

"Did you see that sunrise? It was amazing. Elizabeth St. Pierre does that for every horse. The respect that she shows her animals is inspirational as far as I'm concerned. That's the kind of thing I try to focus on in those moments."

They went quiet for a while, until Jodi turned to Kent. "You might not believe it, but I wanted to be a veterinarian." Her face reddened as she spoke, and he realized that it was hard for her to open up about herself.

"You would make a good one."

She leaned her head against the window. After a few minutes, she asked, "Did Lute ever tell you why I came back to Jefferson?"

"In case you never noticed, your brother does not freely offer information."

She chirped a laugh. "So that's a *no*?"

"A *definite* no."

"You guys are good friends."

"We are."

"I hardly remember you guys as kids. You were older than me."

"And we never really paid much attention to you back then." He gave her a smile. "You were mostly a nuisance, you know, in the way. Although I do remember Feron sniffing your way some as you got older. The rest of us thought that was a little weird. I remember once he said something about you having a nice set of…well let's just say… you were developing well. Lute got pissed and threatened to beat the shit out of him."

"Feron Munn." The name floated out under her breath. "Yeah, he was a jerk to me back then. It got worse. He mostly waited until you guys weren't around."

"Last I knew you were a teenage bride. Right?"

"Yes. And off to conquer the world with my new husband."

"To tell the truth, Lute and I didn't much care for the guy."

"Dumont Cyr. *Good ol' Dewey*." She gave a sad little laugh. "Another bad life choice. He was going to get me out of the crazy pagan Indian world. Teach me the white man's ways. Yeah, right."

"How did that go?"

Jodi gave Kent the side-eye. "The way living with a lazy, drunken gambler always goes."

"Uh-huh."

"Took me a few busted lips and black eyes to figure it out."

"Not good."

"Yeah, I was gone a long time," she said, remembering. "The only reason I stayed with Dewey was because of my kids."

Kent was confused. "Kids? Plural?"

Her shoulders sagged. "You only know about Pegger. I had a daughter, too."

"I didn't know that."

"She died in the fire."

"What fire?"

She didn't respond. She was already reliving the experience in her mind. "One night these guys came barging into our house. Really it was more of a shack back in the woods up in Canada near the St. Regis Reservation. Dewey preferred Canada back in those days because he was in so much trouble in the States. Anyway, they came to collect some money Dewey owed them. A gambling debt. It was a lot and, of course, he didn't have it." Tears welled in her eyes. "Thank the spirits that the kids were upstairs in bed. There was a lot of shouting and fighting. He told them he didn't have the money. They thought he was lying and threatened to kill me and the kids. They beat the shit out of him."

She hugged herself and her voice dropped to a whisper. "When they finally realized he wasn't going to be able to come up with the money, they decided to take it in trade." She stroked her arms, wiping away the filth of that moment. "They did me right there on the kitchen table. They made Dewey watch. The whole time, I remember being so scared that the kids would come downstairs and see. Thankfully, they didn't."

She pulled out a cigarette, lit it, and let the smoke drift up as a frightening calm passed over her. Kent thought that was the end of the horrible tale.

She spit the next words. "Then they torched our house."

"Oh my God. With all of you in it?"

"Dewey was already dead. They shot him right after they were done with me. Pegger made it out, but my daughter didn't."

Kent could barely keep his truck on the road. "Did they catch the guys?"

"No," she said with a strange resignation. "I never even reported it. I just left. Lute took us in. I don't know what I would have done if it weren't for him."

"Does he know all this?"

"Parts of it. As much as I think he can stand."

"He's tough."

"I know, but that's not where it ends. If he knew the whole story, he would kill someone and ruin his own life in the process."

Kent gave her a curious look.

"I never thought I'd ever see any of those bastards again." She took a long pull on her cigarette, deciding whether to go on. "But I have. Many times."

Kent wheeled the truck onto the shoulder and brought it to a jarring stop. He turned to face her. "You *know* where they are?"

"Take it easy. See. This is why I can't tell you guys. You get crazy." She rolled the cigarette in her fingers and watched the smoke rise. Then she nodded, "Yeah, I know where *one* of them is, anyway."

"Why haven't you told someone?"

"I just explained that to you. Because it would destroy Lute. He would kill the guy."

"That sounds like a great idea to me, too."

"The bastard has ruined *my* life, and I'm not about to let him destroy Lute's life, too."

"Who is this guy?" Kent asked between clenched teeth.

Jodi turned back to the window. Her whole body quaked but she didn't make a sound. Kent waited. Finally, she turned back and looked into his eyes. "I will tell you because I want…I need to be sure someone else knows. Just in case something happens to me."

"Nothing is going to happen to you."

A sad smile waved across her face at Kent's naivety. "You don't know that."

"I will protect you."

"I want you to promise me that you will never tell Lute. Not ever."

Their eyes held.

"Jodi, I'd never do anything to hurt you or Lute."

"That's not a promise."

"It's as much as I can give you."

She took one last pull off her cigarette, crushed it into the dashboard ashtray, and blew a long, thin plume of smoke toward the ceiling, deciding.

Finally, she said, "Feron Munn."

Kent growled like a cornered bear and dropped his forehead to the steering wheel.

CHAPTER 33

THE REST OF THE TRIP BACK TO THE CABIN WAS quiet except for the sound of the mobile unit's engine and Lucinda panting in the back seat. Jodi's revelation that Feron had raped her and killed her daughter had been like a pipe bomb exploding in Kent's head. Several times his face contorted as particularly foul thoughts of how he'd punish Feron raged in his head. Jodi succumbed to her earphones and flask, between cigarettes. In a moment of gallows humor, she offered her flask to him. He declined.

Lute's truck was gone when they reached the cabin, and Kent saw tension rise in Jodi's face. He read her mind.

"I'll wait here while you go inside to make sure Lute and Wren are okay."

"Thanks," she said and darted into the cabin.

A moment later she returned on happier legs. Her face was red, embarrassed to be such a worrier, but lit up with a smile. She waved a note, then handed it to Kent. It was a scrap of a brown paper bag and he recognized Lute's heavy-handed penmanship scrawled on it. *Wren wanted to go berry picking. Upper meadow. Back by noon. Cobbler tonight?*

"They don't seem too distressed."

"That's pretty obvious. Sorry, I guess I'm the only one with all the stress."

"Not the only one."

She glanced up at the sun, checking the time. "They won't be back for a couple of hours. Do you want to come in?"

"I could use a cup of coffee," Kent admitted. "I need a lift."

In the kitchen, Jodi quieted Max. He expected her to start making coffee, but instead, she took his hand and pulled him farther into the cabin.

He balked, confused.

She tugged a little harder, with her eyes as much her hand. "Who said anything about coffee?"

She led him down the hall past the gun room that Otsi had been in and into a bedroom. It was neat, slightly stark, but warmed by the burnished gold of log walls and the sunlight that filtered through lacy curtains. There was a huge bed. Its frame was of hewn logs, its coverlet was a blanket with Native American patterns in rich colors. On the bureau was a picture of a young boy and a chubby little girl sitting at a picnic table with their parents, all smiling—a happier time in Jodi's life. The air held the scent of a woman who was attuned to herbs and nature. The sole incongruity was a monstrous Kiss poster on one wall—Gene Simmons in full garb with his shocking makeup, demonic eyes, and tongue protruding as if it would drizzle spit on the bed.

Kent's eyes were drawn away from the poster as Jodi sat on the bed and tapped next to her, asking him to join her.

The room was suddenly like an oven. He felt his blood pulsing through his jugulars like a horse at the Kentucky Derby. Aubrey's face appeared in his mind, but only to look lovingly at him, then receded back into the ether. Her image was so vivid he gasped, then froze.

In a voice that was soft and sympathetic, as if she were soothing an injured animal, Jodi said, "Are you okay with this?"

He sat. "I'm not sure."

She leaned over and kissed him, and any apprehension he'd had was washed away by a tidal wave of wanting her. He wrapped her in his arms and eased her back onto the bed.

First, they made love the way it's done to cleanse the soul—hard, fast, noisily—thrashing away the demons. They lay there a while and did it again, this time slowly, each striving to satisfy the other, and submerging themselves in the pleasure. When they were finished, they lay tangled in each other until their breathing settled.

Jodi picked up on Kent's smile. In an airy voice, she said, "Sex, the best remedy for those hopelessly mourning the loss of a loved one."

He rolled onto his back and she rested her head on his chest.

"Beats the hell out of Lute's string of beads."

She gave him a playful swat. "Don't mock my heritage."

They both laughed then went quiet for a while. Eventually, Kent's expression returned to its pre-sex seriousness. "There is a problem with this, you know."

Jodi's heart sank. "What's that?" she said, gritting her teeth for an answer she didn't want to hear.

Kent held the moment just long enough, then pointed up at the poster. "Gene Simmons has *got* to go!"

CHAPTER 34

LUTE AND WREN RETURNED ON SCHEDULE WITH a basket full of berries. Wren smiled through blue lips and, after Lute demonstrated, she stuck out her tongue for Jodi to inspect. Lute told Jodi about their adventure while Wren bobbed her head in agreement. It had been fun—lots of berries, wading in the creek, seeing a deer—but now, Wren was hungry for something other than berries and she needed a nap. Jodi was more than happy to handle that, so Lute excused himself with a vague comment about needing to run some errands.

Midafternoon was quiet time at Kolbie's Tavern. A few of the resident rodents shifted in the shadows when Lute entered. He eased himself onto a stool at the bar and waited for Kolbie to swirl his rag over to him.

"What will you have?"

"Just water."

In the nonjudgmental way of a good barkeep, Kolbie set a glass of water in front of Lute. "Anything to eat?"

"No, I'm good."

Kolbie resumed his perpetual mopping of the bar top, down its whole patronless length and back. When he reached Lute again, he leaned on the damp surface with one elbow. "I was sorry to hear about Pegger."

Lute shrugged and nodded. "Thanks."

"He tipped better than most."

"He was generous."

"I liked him." Kolbie made another excursion down the bar top. When he was back in front of Lute, he paused, struck by a thought. "He was in here the night of the accident. Had a couple of slices of pizza and a beer or two. I wouldn't even remember except the cops came in the next morning asking questions."

"Was he drunk?"

"Nah," Kolbie drawled, shaking his head.

Lute was pretty sure Kolbie's definition of drunk was different than the cops'. "He was just drinking beer, no hard stuff?"

"No hard stuff. Like I said, just beer. Only a couple, or maybe three, while he ate. He wasn't in here long. Feron Munn bought him one. I remember that."

Lute stiffened. "Did they talk?"

"Nope. I remember because it was kind of strange. Like they were mad at each other. Or, on purpose avoiding each other. Ya' know what I mean?"

"Uh-huh."

"You get a sort of feeling about that stuff when you tend bar as long as I have. They were eyeing each other. Pegger was there and Feron was over in that corner." Kolbie pointed first at a stool then at a dark corner of the room. "Not friendly like." He made a few slow swirls on the bar. "The strange thing was that when Pegger went back to take a leak, Feron comes up to me and buys him a beer." Kolbie raised both hands, palms up. "Then he leaves. Never said a word to him."

"When did Pegger leave?"

"A few minutes after that."

"Would you know if they talked out in the parking lot?"

Kolbie shook his head slowly. "Probably not if it was normal talk. If they got into a pissing match, I'd probably have heard about that."

They went quiet until Lute asked, "Feron come in here much these days?"

Kolbie huffed a short laugh. "It's an odd day he doesn't make it. You never know when, though."

Lute stood slowly. Pulled a money clip from his pocket and started peeling off a bill.

Kolbie waved him off. "Put that away. It's just water."

Lute gave him a tight-lipped smile and slipped his money back into his pocket. "Thanks for talking to me."

"No problem," Kolbie said and resumed swirling his rag on the bar.

● ● ●

After Kolbie's Tavern, Lute loaded back into his pickup and spent a good part of the afternoon driving around and petting Otsi, who lay on the seat beside him chewing a knucklebone. He was thinking about the two recently dead people in his life, Jimmy and Pegger. The cops were getting nowhere on Jimmy's case. He almost felt sorry for Merrill because he knew Merrill really was trying, but he was so dependent on the State Police, and they didn't give a damn. All they were doing was chasing down owners of .264s. Then what? Merrill had even said that they weren't sure if the markings on the bullet were in good enough shape to tie it to a specific rifle even if they did find one. He let out growl of frustration.

When he passed the site where Pegger crashed, he slowed. He studied the tire tracks that were still visible through the tall grass leading to the maple. In the daylight he could see a huge gouge in the tree's bark. Reflexively, he clenched his fists. Otsi yelped as Lute's grip tightened on a fold of his skin.

"Sorry, buddy," Lute said, startled.

Yeah, it was the car crash that killed Pegger all right, but what caused the car crash? Or who? He was pretty sure he knew the answer, and this time he wasn't going to wait for the cops. But, pretty sure wasn't good enough. He needed proof. How could he get it? That was the problem.

They drove for a few more miles on Jefferson's back roads until Lute said, "We need to go back."

Otsi cocked his head, a quizzical look.

"To Kolbie's," Lute answered.

• • •

Kolbie's lot was empty—except for a few tired pickups that were there more often than they were not. Lute could have parked right in front but, instead, he eased his truck around to a secluded corner angled off to one side.

He backed in behind a rickety storage shed. It, along with the kegs and barrels and discarded bar items around it, plus a massively overgrown lilac bush, hid him well but still allowed him a view of the front lot.

He shut off the engine and waited. And waited. An occasional vehicle crept in, an occasional vehicle weaved out—Kolbie's usual dejected tedium.

He was about fed up with the blackflies endlessly bumping their heads into the window glass and the sound of Otsi's teeth grating on the bone when The Ferret's big pickup crunched the gravel into the lot.

Feron slid out, lit a cigarette, and headed into the bar.

Lute checked his watch. It was six-thirty. He figured Feron would have a few beers, something to eat, and a few more beers. That would take a couple of hours, at least.

He cranked his truck and rattled off to his next stop.

CHAPTER 35

THE LANE THAT LED TO FERON'S HOUSEBOAT wasn't much more than a couple of tire ruts. Lute eased his truck along it like a cat stealing up on its prey. When he was close enough to make out the boat, he stopped and surveyed the area. There were a few others moored along the shore, mostly sad little fishing boats that looked like they hadn't been used in months. A few more were turned upside down in the weeds. Otherwise, all quiet, no one in sight. Feron's houseboat, like a derelict, rocked slowly in the current.

Lute opened the door to his truck gently using both hands, trying to preserve the silence, but the old door creaked loudly. He waited and watched—nothing changed. He told Otsi to sit tight and headed toward the boat.

The gangplank, two weathered boards that bridged from the dock to the deck, sagged under his weight causing the houseboat to shudder just enough to send tiny ripples from the pontoons. He held again, watching and listening. When he was convinced that there was no one on board, he continued up onto the boat. The heel of his boot made a dull thud that he hardly noticed as he stepped on board, but the roar that followed, he would hear in his sleep for years to come.

Lip-Lip slammed against the flimsy screen door and tore through it like it were paper, coming at Lute with bared teeth and fury in his eyes.

Lute screamed like a girl. "Sonofabitch!"

In the split second that it took him to recover and spin, Lip-Lip was on him. Red-hot wires of pain shot up Lute's leg as the big dog clamped onto his calf, driving teeth through skin and muscle.

Lip-Lip yanked hard and Lute went down on the deck. With his free leg, he kicked LipLip in the face, but the dog held tight, shaking his head to maximize the damage inflicted by his teeth.

In the distance, Lute heard Otsi barking furiously and knew he was going ballistic. He cursed himself for not leaving a window down. Maybe the two of them could have fended off the brown monster.

He felt himself being dragged farther onto the boat. He held onto the planks and kicked again. His eyes met LipLip's and he knew there would be no mercy.

In desperation, he pulled himself to the gangplank and rolled hard to the side. His body dropped off and he dangled above the water as the big dog strained to hold Lute's weight, cheating gravity. Lute's leg paid the price, and another scream exploded from his throat. Lip-Lip braced his front legs, his jaw muscles bulged like a fists as he sank his teeth into Lute's shinbone. He strained, trying to haul Lute back up on board. For an infinite second Lute dangled above the water, prey in the mouth of a predator, until finally Lip-Lip's jaws fatigued and released. Lute tumbled into the water.

The *river*, The Creator's wonderful river. It felt cool, soothing. He let himself sink into it and the current carry him downstream. When he figured he was far enough away from the boat, he force himself to the surface, and looked back. LipLip was standing on the deck eyes fixed on him.

He drifted a little more then swam to shallow water and crawled up onto the shore. He rested there and, in Owahgena, thanked The Creator for rescuing him. He was pretty sure LipLip would not pursue him. Lip-Lip was a watchdog, his only concern was *his* turf, Feron's boat.

He lay there letting his head clear. Then he tested his torn leg—he could support weight on it. It hurt like hell, but at least the bones weren't broken. He drew a deep breath and mustered the strength to hobble back to his truck in a large arc. He stayed along the tree line keeping the weedy meadow full of rusty boat trailers and discarded chunks of docks between him and the houseboat. He passed in front of a small barn that was mostly hidden by overgrown vines and approached his truck from behind, so that it was between him and LipLip. As he got closer, he could see Otsi's eyes fixed on him through the glass. Now he thanked the spirits that he had *not* left a window down. Otsi, still recovering from the gunshot, would have fought to his death.

He slid into the cab panting and let his head fall back. He grimaced as each beat of his heart sent a throb down his leg. When he caught his breath, he reached behind the seat and withdrew a small first aid kit he kept mostly for blisters, slivers, and fishhook punctures. He pulled up his pant cuff and covered the wound with what little salve there was. He used all of two small rolls of gauze to cover it. Blood seeped through even before he finished. He eased his pant cuff back down and leaned back again.

LipLip. He hadn't thought about LipLip.

In defeat, he reached for the key in the ignition and was about to crank the engine when he paused. *No!* He had to see for himself. He had come to confirm his suspicion. *Did Feron kill Pegger, or not?* He had to know. He released his hold on the key and turned to Otsi. "So now what?"

Otsi gave him a let's-get-the-hell-out-of-here look.

He rustled his dog's ears trying to think of a way to salvage their disastrous mission. He needed to search Feron's boat. That's when he noticed the knucklebone on the floor, the one he'd given Otsi earlier. He stared at it. *I wonder.*

He groped behind the seat again until his fingertips touched what he was after. *Yep. Still there.* He withdrew a length of braided wire secured in a coil by dried-out electrical tape. It worked for raccoons and coyotes, even an occasional bobcat. But this would be more of a test. He pulled it across his chest, stretching it as hard as he could. It held. The only way to know for sure was to try it.

He fashioned a loop in one end and checked to see that it slid smoothly. Then, he opened the truck door just enough to slip the wire out, shook it onto the ground forming a flat circle a foot and a half in diameter, and threaded the rest of the wire back into the cab.

LipLip, still on the deck, watched the whole process with a jaundiced eye. But, when Lute held the knucklebone out the window and whistled to him, his expression turned more inquisitive. His tongue dropped out of his mouth. Lute smiled and mumbled the Owahgena equivalent of *sucker*.

The bone was too much of an enticement for a dog that probably hadn't eaten in hours. Wary but no longer growling, LipLip crossed the gangplank, nose high, drawn to the scent of the bone. Lute waved it, teasing him.

Otsi whined—*that's my bone*. Lute shushed him.

When LipLip was too close for comfort, Lute dropped the bone. It landed into the center of the wire loop with a delicious thud. LipLip lunged for it, and Lute yanked his end of the wire. All hell broke loose.

LipLip felt the noose tighten around his neck and became a giant, snarling mass of angry canine. He reared back with all his strength. The wire slid through Lute's hands, cutting his palms. It made a hideous metal-on-metal scraping noise as it rubbed through the crack under the door. Lute struggled to keep the door from opening.

Otsi let out a bellow. Instinctively, LipLip lunged at him through the glass.

Lute hauled in the slack. He gained enough to throw a loop around the steering wheel. The wire pulled tight as a guitar string when LipLip fought to free himself. The big dog's claws made raking sounds on the outside of the truck. Lute held the door handle and beseeched the spirits to give the old wire strength. His whole truck shook.

Then, as the noose deprived LipLip of air, his roars became gurgles. Gradually, he sank out of sight. The wire slackened as he settled onto the ground.

Lute eased to the window and glanced down. LipLip was flat on his side, his neck lifted into a revolting curve by the wire. His eyes bulged like huge white marbles. His tongue was workshirt-blue.

Lute continued to hold the door closed, but slackened the noose hoping he had not killed the dog. He watched. Nothing for a long moment. He jiggled the wire and, finally, LipLip drew in a deep noisy breath.

Lute did the same and thanked the spirits.

LipLip, still dazed, rolled up onto his belly. Lute played out enough slack so that the dog could breathe, but no more, then secured the wire to the steering wheel. He removed his belt, looped it through the door handle and the steering wheel, then tested the door to be sure it would open no more than the crack needed to allow the wire to pass under it.

He checked LipLip again. He wasn't happy, but he was breathing and conscious—good enough for now.

For a second time, Lute told Otsi to sit tight then slid across the seat and out the passenger door: *Attempt number two to check out The Ferret's boat.*

CHAPTER 36

LUTE BALLED HIS FISTS TRYING TO FORCE OUT THE pain in his hands from the wire cuts. His clothes were still dripping river water and he was limping like a Civil War soldier as he crossed the gangplank onto The Ferret's houseboat for the second time.

He scanned the deck—a couple of overflowing garbage cans, some old tarps, a huge ice chest, and a beat-up gas grill. There was a greasy transmission pulled from something, a half-dozen frames for stretching animal pelts, several propane tanks, and gas cans. Toward the bow, there were some snowmobile parts. All of it in disarray.

Hanging off the stern was a tired-looking Evinrude that had to be at least a couple hundred horsepower. The paint on its cowling was blistered and smoke-stained from chronic overheating—the result of being pushed too hard on too many night runs up the St. Lawrence, no doubt. A couple of spare barrels of gasoline sat next to it. Risky, near a hot engine.

"Floating junkyard," Lute said under his breath.

He pushed his way inside the boat. The air was foul with the smells of bacon and beer, dog, and man sweat. The confined space inside was just as cluttered as the deck.

Along one wall there was a camp stove that had been jerry rigged to sit on a countertop. A cast iron skillet with congealed grease rested on it. Two rusty white propane tanks were below it. The wall behind it was charred from a long-ago grease fire.

Opposite the stove was a table with two cheap plastic chairs. On it was the stub of a candle, a tuna can brimming with cigarette butts, and a box of Diamond strike-anywhere wooden matches. His head bumped a gas lantern that hung from the ceiling.

"Pig sty," he whispered to nobody. The place was a fire waiting to happen. It was amazing that Feron hadn't blown himself up yet.

His toe caught on Lip-Lip's bed and he tripped, his shoulder striking a rack holding several rifles. They clattered noisily and started to fall until he steadied them. There were partial boxes of ammo for the weapons on a shelf below their stocks. He remembered what Merrill had said about the bullet that killed Jimmy being a .264 caliber. He sorted through the boxes. There were .30-30's, .30-06's, and .308's, but no .264's. Disappointing, but that didn't mean The Ferret didn't have a .264. Lute had seen a rifle on the rack in his truck. Maybe that was a .264. Or, maybe he got nervous and dumped it.

He pushed open a narrow door and stepped through into another room. On the wall was an ancient calendar with a picture of a redheaded, fair-skinned beauty whose massive breasts were barely concealed by corny Indian garb. She smiled seductively at Lute. He figured that the room had once been a bedroom, but now it was empty except for a wooden bench that ran along three of the four walls. *So this was where the human cargo spent the trip.*

Another door opened off of that room into a space so small Lute would have barely fit. He looked down. There was a toilet seat fixed over a hole in the floor. Through it, he could see directly to the surface of the Chittenango River. An angry sound rolled up his throat—another sign of Feron's lack of respect for the river.

He returned to the kitchen and stood there for a long second trying to think like Feron. Where would he hide poison? His eye caught a jelly cupboard hanging on one wall. In it were everyday staples—canned goods, a crumpled bag of pancake mix, cooking oil, and the like. On the top shelf, partially hidden by a molding, were several containers. He pulled one down, a pottery cookie jar—six hundred bucks in cash. *Classic Feron.* The next one was a dented Crisco can, most of its label missing—two nickel bags of weed, one half empty. He lifted down a wooden tray that held a dozen or so small glass bottles. He set it on the table and read some of the labels. A sly smile of recognition moved across his face.

Here was Feron's secret treasure, his pride and joy. Like Lute, and many other trappers, Feron formulated his own scents to lure game. They were closelyheld secrets—best one for fox, best one for mink, for muskrat, beaver, bobcat. The list was as long as there were furbearing species. Lute had grown up with these and knew them well. Begrudgingly he had to admit that Feron's were primo—pungent as hell, but like a fine wine to a trapper.

His smile was quickly replaced by a scowl as he opened and sniffed them one by one like a hound dog searching for a scent. With only a few left to go, he brought one to his nose, and there it was. This one was *not* a lure—it was poison. He drew back and stared at the bottle, startled to be holding the evidence that confirmed what he had suspected all along. He smelled it again, this time longer, more analytically. Yes, this was it, no doubt about it, the same smell he had detected on the pizza in the Mustang and on Pegger's lips. He read the label even though he didn't need to: COYOTE MIX #1. He slipped the bottle into his pocket, glanced around to see that he had left no clue that he had been there, and headed back across the gangplank.

When he got to the truck, Lip-Lip, still secured by the snare, was chewing on Otsi's bone. Otsi was staring down at him through the window, dejected. Carefully, keeping his distance, Lute wiggled the noose off the big dog and said in Owahgena, "No hard feelings. You were doing what you were taught to do. But next time, I will kill you."

He and Otsi drove away. It would have been convenient if he had found .264 ammo so he could tie Feron to Jimmy's murder, but it wasn't essential. He knew for sure that Feron poisoned Pegger. *Now, to find Feron—and kill him.*

CHAPTER 37

AS LUTE PULLED AWAY FROM FERON'S HOUSE-
boat, he glanced in the mirror and saw Lip-Lip on his feet and slowly
working his way up the gangplank. The big dog wasn't happy, but he
would be fine. Lute begrudgingly gave that one up to the spirits.

At his cabin, he tried to hide his injuries from Jodi. It was hopeless.

"Why are you limping?" she asked the second he crossed the
threshold. When she got a better look, she added, "Your pants are
all bloody."

Lute ignored her and headed straight to the bathroom. She
followed and, when he closed the door, she pushed it right back open.

"Something got you," Jodi said, her voice stern but motherly. "I
want to know what happened."

A wave of anger caused the veins on Lute's forehead to swell.
The siblings stared at each other. Lute blinked first. As his expression
relaxed, he said, "It was a fox." He turned to the sink and began washing
his hands. Instantly, the crusted blood turned the water red.

Jodi wasn't buying it. "A fox did that to your leg *and* your hands?"

Lute turned to her, paused a moment, then let out a sigh of defeat.
"Okay, here is what happened. I was up in the woods where the ginseng
grows. You know the place."

Jodi leaned against the door jamb. "I've got plenty here. You could
have asked."

"What you've got is dried. I need fresh."

She nodded, still dubious. "Okay."

"At the meadow, I stumbled on a fox den and momma fox wasn't happy that I showed up." He sat on the edge of the bathtub and pulled off his jeans.

Jodi gasped. "That was some fox! What about your hands?"

"I had to climb a tree to get the damn thing to let go of me, and the closest one was a thorn apple tree." He folded his leg into the tub and turned on the water. Again, red water. "Can you help me get a poultice on this?"

Jodi held, considering whether to ask more questions. Thinking better of it, she went to collect what she needed for a poultice. When she returned, Lute was daubing his leg with a towel and grimacing.

"I started a tea for you," she said. She knelt, applied a layer of white paste to the wound as thick as cake icing then wrapped it. "This is going to take days to heal." She wrapped his palms.

Lute stood, testing his leg. It hurt like hell. He opened and closed his fists. He could still use his hands, even with the bandages.

"Thanks," he said.

"Get into bed. I'll bring you the tea."

"No. I don't think so."

"What?" Jodi snapped, pointing at his leg. "You need to be off of that."

Lute limped out of the bathroom. Jodi followed. He stopped at his gun rack, pulled down his .30-06 deer rifle and took a box of shells from the drawer below it.

Jodi braced her arms on her hips. "What are you doing?"

"I'm going to kill that fox." He headed out of the cabin.

"Lute, you know that fox was just protecting her kits. If you kill her, they will die."

As he slammed the door of the truck, he said, "You're right. Don't worry."

● ● ●

Jodi sat on a porch rocker with Wren on one knee and Max on the other. The peepers were tuning up and night was settling in. She gently twirled a lock of Wren's hair in her fingers and watched the little girl's eyelids get heavy as she thought about Lute's fox fiasco. Somehow, it didn't add up. She was deciding how to follow up with him on that when a sedan with lots of miles on it wheeled in and braked hard in front of her. Instantly, the driver's door swung open. It was Barry. With one foot on the ground, the other still in the car, he blurted, "Is Lute around?"

Jodi held Max back with a firm grip on his collar. "Slow down. You're going to run over my chickens."

"Where's Lute? I need to speak to him right now."

"He just left."

"Where did he go?"

"He said he was going to kill a fox that bit him."

Barry thought about that for a second. "That's weird."

"I'm thinking the same thing."

Barry focused again. "Which way did he go? I need him. It's real important."

She described where the ginseng grew. "He should be over that way."

Barry was familiar with the area. He thanked her, ducked back into the car, and headed toward the ginseng patch.

When he got to the place Jodi had described, he called out and made a quick search of the area. Nothing, no Lute, no truck, no nothing. He headed back toward town at highway speed on the country roads, until he remembered Pegger's encounter with the maple tree and forced himself to slow down.

He needed Lute, and fast. Where was he? He was passing Kolbie's Tavern when he got his answer. He came up on Lute's truck from behind and it was chugging along so slowly that he almost rear-ended it. He could see Lute scanning Kolbie's parking lot as if checking to see who was inside the bar by the vehicles out front.

Without so much as a glance at his mirrors, Barry pulled left into the oncoming lane and hit the gas. He flew past Lute, moved right, and hit the brakes. Lute skidded to a stop within a hair's breadth of Barry's bumper.

Barry was out first and, as he ran toward Lute's truck, Lute shouted out of his window, "What the hell are you doing, Skippy? You could have killed us both."

"We need your help."

"Who's *we*?"

"Me…and…and Emily."

"For what?"

"To treat Sim."

"That's up to Doc. You know where he stands with my kind of medicine."

"Sim's really bad, Lute. Really bad." The words caught in Barry's throat. "Doc is talking about euthanizing him."

Lute clenched the wheel, his palms burned. Silently he cursed Doc for not letting him treat the horse back when he had asked.

Barry pleaded, "We can't let Sim die, Lute. It will kill Emily. You can do stuff Doc and the CVC can't. I've seen you do it. I saw what you did with Otsi's leg."

Lute stayed quiet. Barry implored him with his eyes.

Finally, Lute pounded the steering wheel and growled something in Owahgena. "I'll head to my place and get what I need."

Barry's knees went weak with relief. "Thanks, Lute. I'll follow you."

● ● ●

"Is Doc inside?" Lute asked when they were in the CVC parking lot.

"No. He's home."

Lute gave Barry a wary look.

"Sim has been here in the equine ICU for over a week, now. Doc has done all he can. So has the rest of the staff. Now they are all just waiting," Barry explained. "The crew told Doc to go home, get a shower and something to eat. Maybe some sleep. He is so beat, he didn't argue. They agreed that they'll make a final decision in the morning." Barry swallowed hard. "I'm not a doctor, but it looks really hopeless to me. I can't just sit there and watch Sim die!" He turned to Lute, hope shone in his eyes. "That's when I decided to find you. I told Emily and she was all for it."

Lute stared off into the darkness across the near-empty parking lot. "Doc saved Otsi's leg, not me. He took the bullet out." It sounded like a sad admission of failure.

"That's bullshit, Lute! I saw Otsi's leg. Even after the surgery, it was a mess. It was amazing what you did, how fast he recovered. Doc was amazed, too, but he couldn't admit it."

"I offered. Basically, he called my medicine a waste of time."

"I know. I heard. He's so dedicated to his type of medicine, he can't accept any alternatives."

"Where's Emily?"

"Inside. You couldn't pry her out of Sim's stall."

"So, Doc doesn't know I'm here?"

Barry pursed his lips. "Nope. I purposely waited until he went home to get you."

Lute's eyes burned into Barry's. "Jesus, Skippy! That's wrong and you know it."

"Doc would not have agreed to it," Barry snapped. "That's why I waited." He took a breath and his tone became respectful again. "Sim is suffering terribly in there. He's dying. I know it. So does Emily. One look at the faces of the crew and you can tell they all know it, too."

"You are asking me to go behind my friend's back. Deception is a precarious road."

"I am asking you to *help* your friend, even if your friend won't ask for it. Help him do what he wants more than anything, to save Sim's life. It's what Emily and all the rest of us want, too. We are out of options."

Barry waited as a series of expressions rolled like clouds across Lute's face—anger, confusion, guilt.

When he didn't speak, Barry started again. "Lute, remember Otsi's leg? Doc saw that what you were doing to fix it wasn't working. You couldn't see it yourself because you were too close to Otsi. Doc begged you to let him try, you did, and it worked. This is the same thing, only this time, Doc is the one who is too close. He can't help it; he knows how important that horse is to Emily. He won't let himself share his responsibility to his daughter with anyone else. Period."

Barry paused, hoping for a response from Lute. Still nothing came. He went on, "Emily and I came up with the idea of you treating Sim. You are our last hope, Lute. Please."

There was a long, uncomfortable silence as Lute stared out into the parking lot. Finally, he drew a deep breath and let it out. When he spoke, it sounded like it was against his better judgement. "I'll take a look."

Barry nodded, dizzy with gratitude. "This way," he said, and led Lute into the CVC.

CHAPTER 38

FOR ANYONE WHO HAD ONLY EXPERIENCED THE daytime chaos of patient care at the Equine Intensive Care Unit, the nighttime stillness was unnerving. It was dead quiet except for the sound of exhaust fans rolling softly like far-off thunder. The lights were low. The matted rubber floor was damp from recent hosing with a disinfectant that gave off a medicinal humidity. Thousand-pound creatures lurked in the darkness.

Barry led Lute down the main alleyway, both on their tiptoes.

"Where is everybody?" Lute whispered.

"Emily and I worked the schedule so that we'd be the only ones here on night watch," Barry said. Then, when he noticed Lute's stride, he asked, "Why are you limping?"

Lute waved his hand, dismissing the question. "It's a long story. I'll tell you about it some other time."

"It looks pretty bad."

Lute huffed a disgusted sound, stopped, and turned. He thrust out both of his palms so Barry could see the bandages. "Look, Skippy. See, my hands are sore, too. So you don't have to point that out, either. I don't want to get into it." He motioned for Barry to keep walking.

Barry got the message and did not pursue Lute's injuries.

They stopped at the door marked SIMPATICO'S GIFT.

Just then, the stall door opened as Emily rolled it from the inside. She pressed her head to Lute's chest and hugged him. "Thank you for coming."

He wrapped her in his arms. "Hmmm."

Sim was lying under a blanket on a thick foam pad. A huge mechanical bellows was pumping rhythmically, sending air through a tube into his lungs. An IV line trailed down to his neck from a large plastic bag of clear fluid hanging overhead. His injured leg was wrapped from elbow to foot in a thick tan bandage.

Lute shook his head slowly then said something in Owahgena. He squatted next to Sim, gently drew back the blanket, and put his ear to the horse's chest. After a few heartbeats, he replaced the blanket and turned to Barry and Emily. His eyes shifted between the two, then settled on Emily.

"If I do this, you need to know two things. First, there is a good chance it won't work, and second…" he hesitated… "it could cost me your father's friendship forever."

Emily's face collapsed into a soup of guilt and despair. Barry took her hand, but she pulled it back and covered her face. Her shoulders quaked.

"Forever," Lute said again, as much for himself as Emily.

Through her hands, she said, "I'm so sorry, Lute. I don't know what else to do."

Lute did not move. For a long moment, the only sound was the hissing of medical machines, until he sighed and said, "Then we'll do it." He mumbled something under his breath in Owahgena.

Barry and Emily brightened.

"I'm going to get some stuff out of my truck," Lute said, as he stood. He waved his hand around the stall. "Get rid of all this stuff."

The blood drained to Barry and Emily's feet.

"How much of it?"

"All of it."

"Even the respirator?" Barry croaked, his mouth so dry he could barely speak.

"*Especially* the respirator. Now."

Barry and Emily stared wide-eyed at each other as the gravity of what Lute was asking them to do struck home. Tampering with a patient's treatment plan without authorization was the mother of all breaches in hospital protocol. They would probably be banned from the CVC forever.

"Get going," Lute ordered and left.

When he was gone, Barry shot Emily a worried look. "Are you okay with this?"

Emily's brows V'd into a determined look. "We did what we had to do."

Barry nodded and, together, they crossed the point of no return.

By the time Lute got back, they had disconnected everything. The equipment sat outside Sim's stall like someone was planning a medical equipment garage sale. Emily and Barry were crouched against the stall wall, petrified. The only sound was Sim struggling to breathe.

"The blanket, too. *And* the bandage." Lute said.

Without a word, they followed his instructions.

Emily studied her horse lying there, his fetid leg exposed. He looked like he could die at any minute. Her heart ached.

Lute set down a crumpled cardboard box. The label on the side of it indicated that it had originally held a vacuum cleaner from Walmart.

"A *Walmart* box?" Barry said.

"Indians shop at Walmart, too," Lute said flatly.

"I get that. Sorry. Never mind."

"What's your point, Skippy?"

Barry kicked himself for mentioning the box. "I mean, a cardboard box for a medical bag? You know what I'm saying?"

Lute focused on the contents of the box. "It's not the box *or* bag . It's what's in it."

Emily rolled her eyes at Barry. She mouthed the words, *don't be such an idiot!*

He shrugged and took a place along the wall. The two of them went silent as they watched Lute work.

He took a beaded leather skull cap from the box and straightened its two eagle feathers, one up and one down. He tossed back his hair and set it on his head.

Almost as an afterthought, he turned to the pair. "You are sworn to secrecy. You are never to say one word about what you see here to anyone. Ever."

Both nodded.

Lute held them in his stare. "Ever!"

They both nodded more vigorously and agreed loudly.

As he began a low, rhythmic chant, he set a small clay dish near Sim's head, crushed something that looked like dried grass into it, then lit it with a match.

Emily recognized the smell of sage. She glanced up at the fire alarm above and prayed the exhaust fans would draw out the smoke from Lute's fire.

He placed dried corn and tobacco around the horse, then took ten precious minutes sitting cross-legged, chanting, shaking a turtle-shell rattle with one hand and stroking Sim with the other.

He rose, took a large tin from the Walmart box, and coated Sim's leg with a thick white paste. Instantly the stall smelled of menthol and herbs.

He filled another dish with red powder, lit it, and set it within inches of Sim's nose. As he chanted, he blew the smoke gently across the horse's nostrils. Sim's muzzle quivered, he snorted, then descended back into stillness. Lute left the smoking dish in place and pulled a plastic gallon jug from the box. Its worn label said *two percent milk*. He threw Barry a quick look, daring him to comment.

Barry felt Emily's nails sink into his hand and kept his mouth shut.

A thin smile appeared on Lute's face, then disappeared as he went back to work. Using a loofah that may have come from Walmart, he painted a brown liquid onto Sim's neck and body. The air in the stall changed once again, this time to a more acrid smell like turpentine or coal ash.

When he had Sim's coat wet, he set down the jug and loofah, turned to the two onlookers, and said, "Just so you know, I'm going to be at this for the next few hours."

"When will we see improvement?" Emily asked. Then her eyes dropped. "I mean, *if* we see improvement."

"I don't know," was all Lute replied. He turned back to Sim and became lost in his chanting.

The heavy air, monotonous chant, and late hour were too much for Emily and Barry. Before long they were both asleep.

Just before dawn, Lute loaded his Walmart box back into his truck. He nodded hello to a couple of sleepy-eyed employees reporting for the early shift, and they returned hellos and curious looks. He stared at their backs as they entered the building. *I've got to get the hell out of here. Doc will be pulling in soon and the shit's going to hit the fan.*

He pushed Otsi to his side of the seat and roughed up his ears. "Thank you for being patient," he told him. "Let's get out of here. Quick."

They headed away from the CVC.

CHAPTER 39

DUSK WAS A QUIET TIME FOR JODI. WREN WAS
fed, bathed, and tucked in for the night. Now, she had a few minutes
to herself. She meandered slowly back to the cabin from the chicken
coop carrying a basket of eggs. She didn't have her Walkman, instead
she hummed a Joni Mitchell song about clouds and seeing life from
both sides. She stopped and drew in a breath of the evening air as it
floated her way from the forest. She was happy for the first time in a
very long time. The feeling was strange—and wonderful.

She thought of Kent and how they'd made love after the sad
Virginia Wolfe call. He was the one that had finally lifted the weight
she'd carried for so long. Her unsettled youth, bad marriage, loss of a
child. Finally, all those bad memories were receding into the past. The
past, where they belonged. She wanted to move on. Even Pegger's death,
still fresh and painful as it was, was at least bearable with Kent in her life.
She felt strong again, in control of her life for the first time in a long time.

Their sex had been almost violent. That thought made her smile.
Violent men and violent sex were not all that strange in her life, but they
were in Kent's. He was genuinely concerned about her. He had asked
if he was being too rough— was she okay? —until she told him to stop
asking. They had squeezed and scratched, rolled, and sweated, oblivious to the animal sounds they made as they vented pent-up emotions.
They were two people struggling to finally free themselves from the

suffocating loss of loved ones. When they were finished, lying together in tangled sheets, they had laughed loud, satisfying, cleansing laughter.

As she approached the cabin, Max began to whine. She scanned the yard and house. All seemed to be as it should. "Patience, Max. I'll feed you in a few minutes."

She settled into a rocker on the porch and, out of habit, tapped out a cigarette. She stared at it for a moment, deciding whether to light it, then returned it to the pack. She leaned her head back and searched the sky for the night's first stars.

She thought about the thing with Lute and the fox. That was weird. Then there was Barry's visit a short while ago. What was that all about? Why was it so important that he find Lute? And then, from the garden where she was picking peas, she had seen Lute and Barry come roaring in just long enough for Lute to grab a box from the cabin and take off again without so much as a wave.

"I guess I'm not in the loop," she resigned to Max. He whined again and this time he followed it with a yelp. She reached down and brought him up into her lap. "What? You want some attention?" She schmoozed him.

Usually Max was quick to show his appreciation for Jodi's lap by curling into a cute little ball, perfect for petting. Not tonight. His tiny feet treaded on her thighs. Staring straight at her, he yelped in her face, even louder than before. She tousled his ears gently. "What is your problem?" He let out a full bark. "All right. You win," she told him, pushing herself up out of the rocker. "Between you and the mosquitos, it's not that much fun out here anyway." She set him back on the floor. "Your majesty," she said as she held the door for him, "I'll have your dinner ready momentarily."

Those words normally would have sent Max into a spinning frenzy in front of the cabinet where the dog food was stored. To Jodi's surprise, he headed down the hall toward the bedrooms.

She followed, curious now. When she saw him digging at the bottom of the door to the room where Wren was sleeping, curiosity changed to concern.

She eased the door open and let her eyes adjust to the dark. She clutched the knob for support as she realized that Wren was not in bed, where she had left her less than an hour ago. An invisible hand reached into her chest and clenched her heart. She glanced around the room— no Wren. This could not be happening. The spirits had gifted her with a second chance, beyond anything she could ever have hoped for or deserved. They had given her Wren. Now she had failed *again*. She was a terrible mother!

Panicked, she searched the rest of the cabin. No Wren, anywhere. The haunting wail of a doe that had lost its fawn rose from her throat. She moved back into Wren's room. This time searching more carefully, looking for clues.

That's when she noticed a long, clean slice in the window screen. She hugged her chest and bit her fist as a tidal wave of dread washed her knees from under her. She buckled to the floor. *Yes, she was a bad mother. She had not protected her gift from the spirits.*

For several minutes she stared up at the cut window screen, her pulse pounding in her ears. She tried to think of other explanations, but there were no others. She staggered to the kitchen, braced herself stiff-armed on the counter, then retched into the sink. It had to be Feron Munn. She spit his name like the vomit. She knew he had been search-ing for Wren, and he had found her at last. Wren was just lost cargo to Feron, a loose end to tie up to protect his smuggling operation. She had tried to keep her little girl safe like a good mother, but even so, The Ferret had managed to get to her. She was positive Feron had taken Wren. He'd crept back into her life and taken a child from her—again!

She needed to call the police. She picked up the phone and dialed in the number, but as it was ringing, she ended the call. What was she thinking! She couldn't call them. If the authorities found Wren, they'd sure as hell identify her as the missing Korean girl and take her away. Her chest filled with ice at the thought. She loved Wren, and she wasn't going to let that happen.

She let out an angry curse in Owahgena, then picked an egg from the basket she'd set on the counter and smashed it into the sink. For several minutes she stared at the mess of vomit and egg oozing into the drain, deciding what to do. Finally, she slammed the counter with her fist, grabbed a pad of paper, and scribbled a note to Lute. As she headed out the door, she thought, *Where was Lute, anyway?* She needed him.

CHAPTER 40

FERON MUNN'S BODY SHOOK WITH THE SAME MIX of exhilaration and fear that he felt when he was on a smuggling run. He had been half-running and half-walking for a good hour now. Down Jodi's trail from Lute's cabin to the river, then along the river toward his houseboat. He was tired but the rush gave him strength. He had carried the little Korean girl the whole way. He shifted her to his other shoulder. One thing he did find amazing, and lucky for him, was that she never made a peep. She'd even smiled at him a time or two, when she wasn't sleeping in his arms.

Wren, they called her. Feron smirked. He knew what Jodi was trying to do; make the kid into an Indian, her Indian, make this kid a replacement for her daughter. *Uh-huh. Like a kid would just drop out of the sky.*

No, she was *his* girl, and his problem. He cursed. How could it have happened? How had they managed to lose a kid? He cursed again. What if it had been an adult, someone who could tell the authorities what was going on? What then? Where would they be now? He shuddered at the thought. But it no longer mattered—he had her. He'd throw her in with the bunch going out tonight and that would be the end of it. She'd be gone. Good riddance.

He'd searched all over for days trying to find the damn kid, sweating bullets the whole time that the police would get her first. Then he had gotten the break he needed at Pegger's burial when he saw that Jodi had a little girl with her. It had taken a minute to click, then, *Wait a minute, Jodi's only kid is Pegger.*

Getting his hands on her was going to be the hard part, but good fortune had smiled down on him, and it turned out to be easier than he had imagined. He had worried about slipping past Lute and that hound dog of his. But as it turned out, Lute wasn't home, just Jodi and the kid. He'd snuck back to their cabin along the river trail, then found a spot in the woods that provided a good view and waited. For a couple of hours as afternoon became evening, he watched, and slapped bugs. Jodi tended her vegetable garden and mothered the girl. She talked baby-talk to her. She showed her tomatoes, bugs, beans, and what-not, teaching her, and encouraging her to talk. She laughed and played with Wren and that little dog of hers. No one had ever given him that kind of affection, and it made him uncomfortable and weirdly jealous watching it.

Thankfully, there had been no sign of Lute.

It was almost dark when Jodi called to the girl. Feron could hear her voice drifting in the evening air. She told her to finish what she was doing; it was time for a bath and to bed.

For a while Feron watched lights click on then off in various windows and was soon pretty sure he knew which room the girl was in.

He was deciding how he was going to deal with Jodi—he didn't want to create any more loose ends—when she reappeared on the porch. He heard her say to that little dog of hers, "Come on, Max. Let's go feed the chickens," and she started toward the coop, shooing a few stragglers along ahead of her.

Perfect.

He crept to the window of the room he was confident that Wren was in, drew his hunting knife, and sliced the screen. It hadn't taken him more than a couple of minutes to pull himself inside, wrap the sleeping girl in her blanket, and slip back out into the woods.

Now, he was almost to his boat and he still had enough time to meet the tractor-trailer that was due tonight at Northern Lights. He would toss the girl in with the others, end of story.

He pushed on harder. It was dark now, but when he broke out of the woods the moonlight shone on his boat and he could make out Lip-Lip's shadow on the deck. His spirit buoyed. He repositioned Wren to his other shoulder and trudged on. When he climbed the gangplank, Lip-Lip raised his head from the huge bone he was gnawing.

"Where did you find that bone, big guy?" He patted Lip-Lip's neck as usual and was surprised when the big dog yelped. "Sorry, boy. What's the matter?" He examined Lip-Lip's neck more closely and saw where hair was missing. "Ouch, that looks like it hurts," he said, but there wasn't much sympathy in his voice. He pondered the wound for a few seconds, then smiled. "Some dog didn't want to give up that bone, did he? You had to fight him for it. Good boy, it's yours now. Don't worry, your neck will heal."

Inside, with Wren still in his arms, he poured himself a shot of Jack Daniel's and threw it down his throat. No time to waste. He grabbed a flashlight, whistled for Lip-Lip to join him, and led the way back onto dry land and across the meadow to a small barn. It was old, crooked, paint long gone from its rough-cut wood siding. Mostly covered in vines and tucked into the edge of the woods, it was as inconspicuous as any building could be, perfect for hiding contraband.

He rattled through the key ring until he found the one he was looking for, twisted it into the lock, and threw back the hasp. He heaved open the door on its rusted hinges and shined his light into the blackness inside. It fell on the terrified faces of a truckload of Asians sitting cross-legged on the dirt floor. They squinted back at him.

He did a quick head count—he'd learned his lesson about that. They were all there, and all still alive. They looked too exhausted to put up a fight, but to be on the safe side, he slapped his thigh, drawing

Lip-Lip near him and into the beam. The illegals cringed back at the sight of the huge dog.

Feron drew a calming breath and tried to smile. To a young man who understood a little English and had become their de facto leader, he said, "Time to leave. Get ready. Be quiet."

He waved the flashlight beam over the group again and found a woman he guessed to be in her twenties. She was obviously weak, but she seemed to have more strength than the others.

"Here," he said to her and flopped Wren, blanket and all, into her lap. "You are in charge of this kid, now."

The woman looked from Feron to Wren, confused. As it registered in her fogged brain that she was being assigned extra responsibility, she protested, "No, no!" and pushed Wren back at Feron.

In an instant, Feron had his gun in the woman's face. There was a collective gasp from the others.

"Shut up!" he hissed at her in a loud whisper. "I told you no talking." In a calmer voice, but one that left no room for discussion, he added, "Now take the girl." He waggled his gun and the woman obeyed.

He turned to the rest of the group. "Follow me. And don't make a sound." He gestured to the young man to translate. When he did, the others began to stir, collecting their few possessions.

Feron led them out into the night. They had to hurry, the semi to Atlanta wouldn't wait forever. When he reached his truck, he dropped the tailgate and ordered them into the back. He kept them moving with shoves as they climbed. Even so, it took longer than he wanted to get them all wedged in.

"Don't make a sound," he said as he slammed the tailgate. They all nodded. They didn't need a translator.

With a downward wave of his hand, he signaled them to duck their heads, then he pulled a tarp over them. He was securing it when he heard a sound in the darkness. *A dog barking?* It was faint but too close for comfort.

CHAPTER 41

AFTER THE LONG NIGHT AT THE CVC TREATING
Sim, Lute was dog tired and drove back toward the reservation slowly.
The wire cuts still stung his palms like fire and his leg, last time he
looked at it, was dangerously swollen and turning purple. He could still
walk, but barely. As beat as he was, he still focused on his next move
to get Feron Munn.

As they crossed the bridge, he stroked Otsi and watched the first
streaks of orange light the sky.

"Home first," he said. "You must be starving. Sorry I had to give
your knucklebone to that beast of Feron's."

Otsi didn't know exactly what Lute was saying, but he did know
he was getting attention. Plus, he knew the word *bone*. So, he wagged
his tail.

"I could stand to eat something, myself. And I'm going to see if
I can do something more for all these little dings LipLip gave me." He
opened and closed his fists slowly. "Then I'm going to kill The Ferret. I
found the poison he used to kill Pegger. That's all the evidence I need."

When he pulled up to the cabin, he noticed Jodi's old Volkswagen
Beetle was gone.

He shook his head. His first thought was that his sister had
relapsed to her old behavior and spent the night with some worthless
guy she'd picked up at a bar. He hoped he was wrong. Since Wren had

arrived, Jodi had tempered her lifestyle. She'd stopped the bar-hopping and eased up on her flask. She had become quite the homebody and Lute was glad to see the change. But why else would she be gone at this hour? And who was watching Wren if she was carousing? Then it struck him, and he felt ashamed for accusing his sister. Maybe Wren was the *cause* of her absence.

He dragged himself from his truck up onto the porch. There was a note tacked to the screen door. He pulled it down and his question was answered. In Jodi's handwriting, scribbled in a rush, it read: *Wren is missing. I went to look for her.* He could hear the distress in Jodi's voice as he read the note and felt even more ashamed for thinking his sister had been tramping. What else could go wrong? It was as if the spirits were creating delays to protect Feron. First, a whole night treating Sim, and now he had to find Jodi and Wren. He huffed a guttural sound. Well, the spirits would not succeed. He was going to get Feron no matter how many obstacles they put up to block him.

He glanced back to where Jodi's car was usually parked. She must have already searched the property— the cabin, the outbuildings, the woods—if she's gone to search elsewhere. An image of The Ferret wedged back into his head.

Kent had just left Sim's stall at the CVC and his mind was a maelstrom of conflicting emotions as he raced toward his soon-to-be-ex-friend's cabin on the reservation.

On the one hand, he was furious. He jerked the wheel causing the mobile unit to pitch dangerously and muttered angry words under his breath about Lute. As if there wasn't enough hassle in his life, Lute had crossed the tenuous line they had held ever since the two of them had made life choices to follow different paths of medicine. A growl rolled up Kent's throat. He had flat-out refused Lute's offer to treat Sim. That should have been the end of it. But no, the sonofabitch snuck in anyway. *How could Lute think I wasn't going to find out about it?*

On the other hand, Kent felt relief like he'd never experienced before in his life. And, if he were to be honest with himself, he felt jealousy. That was because the moment that he had entered Sim's stall that morning, he could tell that the stallion was better. Emily's and Barry's tears of joy aside, it was obvious. Sim was on his feet and picking at his hay. It was the first the horse had eaten in a week. He had greeted Kent with tired equine eyes, but at least he was aware of his surroundings. His breathing was relaxed. He was not supporting weight on his injured leg but the swelling had come down a lot. It was a miracle. *How the hell had Lute done that?*

Lute was standing on the porch rolling through horrible thoughts of The Ferret being involved in Wren's disappearance when he heard tires crushing gravel in his driveway. The mobile veterinary unit appeared.

Kent saw Lute and made a beeline toward him, continuing beyond the driveway and lurching to a stop within inches of Lute's feet. Before he was all the way out, Kent was shouting. "Lute, you sonofabitch, I have a bone to pick with you!" He stepped onto the porch. "What the hell were you thinking, sneaking into the CVC? You know how I feel about…"

"Jodi's missing," Lute cut in, ignoring Kent's rant and lifted the note for him to see.

Lute's strange detachment and his words broke Kent's train of thought. "What?"

"Actually, it's Wren who's missing. Jodi's gone I don't know where searching for her. So, I guess they are both missing."

Kent took the note and read it for himself. After a second he said, "We should let Merrill know about this."

He stepped back to his truck, lifted the phone, and was punching in Merrill's number when Lute said, "You can't do that."

Kent brushed him off and kept dialing. "Merrill would want to know. And maybe he can help."

Lute's voice was more forceful. "Hang up the phone," he ordered.

Startled, Kent hung up the phone and turned to Lute. "Why the hell not? We have two missing persons."

Without answering, Lute turned and entered the cabin.

Kent shouted at his back. "What's your problem?"

Lute ignored him.

Kent grumbled under his breath and followed him. They ended up in Wren's room, and it only took Lute one quick survey to find the sliced window screen.

Silence held as both men worked through the situation.

Lute spoke first. "Feron took her."

"Feron? What would Feron want with Wren?"

Lute continued to search the room.

Kent decided that he'd held back what he suspected long enough. It was time to clear the air. "Wren isn't your niece, is she?"

Lute didn't reply for several breaths. Finally, he stopped his search, sighed heavily, and sat on the bed staring at his feet. "No. She's not our niece. We lied to you. Wren is not related to me or Jodi. She's not even Owahgena." He rubbed his face with his hands. Through them, he said, "I knew it wouldn't work."

Kent waited, hoping Lute would offer more.

"It's a long story."

Kent didn't push.

It was a full minute before Lute raised his head, his face folded with frustration. "We found her. Actually, Jodi found her. When she was out on a walk one morning. By the river. I guess she just saw this little girl wandering around the Northern Lights site and brought her home. Never reported anything to the police or anybody else. I tried to reason with her, finding a lost kid is not the same as finding a lost puppy, but she wouldn't listen." He picked at one of his bandaged palms. "Even when we figured out that she's the Korean kid that Feron and everyone else have been looking for, she wouldn't let go."

"The one that the smugglers 'misplaced.'"

"Right."

"I figured as much."

"But Jodi is convinced that Wren is a gift from The Creator, to replace the daughter she lost." He threw his hands up. "After a while, I just went along with it."

Even though Kent had suspected Wren was the Korean kid for some time, actually hearing Lute confirm it was a shocker. He ran his fingers down the slice Feron's knife had made in the screen. "You know we have to tell the police now."

"No. They'll take her away. That would kill Jodi."

"Feron might kill *both* of them. It's too big a risk. You'd never forgive yourself if anything happened to Jodi—and I'm with you on that."

The men's eyes met and held as Lute considered Kent's words. After several breaths, he nodded.

They moved to the kitchen phone and Kent dialed Merrill's number for a second time.

As he listened to it ring, his eyes drifted and stopped on Lute's bandages. "How did you hurt your hands?"

Lute growled. "In a dog fight."

Lute's bizarre answer was lost as Merrill's voice came over the phone.

Kent explained the situation to his brother but didn't mention their concern that Wren would have to be turned over to a child protective agency if they found her. When he was done, Merrill groused about how Lute should have made him aware of the whole thing a long time ago. Then he said, "Yeah, I agree with you, this is bad. But, there are two problems. One, a couple of hours ago, a drunk drove his car into Talbot's Five and Dime. He killed himself and his girlfriend who was with him, and the building is on fire as we speak. So we have our hands full right now. Number two, which you won't like, but I know you are aware of, is that what you are telling me is a reservation matter. It's in their jurisdiction, which means the Rez cops get it first and we can go in only after they officially ask us for help.

Kent remembered. "Sovereign Nation, blah, blah, blah."

"Sorry, but you're right. And, not to be too critical of fellow law enforcement personnel, but they probably aren't going to get too excited about a kid that's been missing for just a few hours. I'll make sure our guys keep an eye out for anything that looks suspicious, and I'll call the commander on the Rez myself, right now. I'll tell him we think it may be a kidnapping and see if I can light a fire under them."

Kent ended the call with a request that Merrill keep him posted. He turned back to Lute who had been listening. His face held the look of one who just had his world crash down around him.

"It's better this way," Kent reassured him. "The most important thing is that we get Jodi and Wren back safely."

Lute didn't look convinced.

Kent's thoughts shifted to the woman who meant so much to *him* and the girl who meant so much to *her*. He would not accept the loss of either.

CHAPTER 42

AS KENT STOOD WITH LUTE IN THE CABIN, AN image of Jodi, terrified by her child's abduction, flashed in Kent's mind, and it was agony. He had seen that fear before in many of the animals in his care. He ached to hold her. In frustration he turned to Lute. "Jodi's note said she is out searching, right? And her car's gone. But do you think she would really go after Feron by herself?"

"There's not a doubt in my mind. She wouldn't wait around for the police or anyone else."

"Yeah, you're right."

Lute's next words came from deep in his throat. "She hates Feron. Always has. I know they've got history, but I don't know exactly what it is. She would never talk to me about it."

Kent started to say that *he* knew their awful history, that Jodi had confided in him, but Lute would wonder why he hadn't been chosen. It was a cut he didn't want to inflict on his friend. Instead, he blocked Jodi's terrible story about the fire, murder, and the rape out of his head and lied. "I don't think Feron would hurt Jodi. He just wants the kid."

Lute glared at him. "He killed Pegger. I found the poison. He wouldn't think twice about killing Jodi."

An invisible blow forced the air from Kent's lungs.

Lute went back to assessing the situation. "So, The Ferret snuck in through the window and grabbed Wren. Then what?"

"But wouldn't Jodi have been home? Wouldn't she hear his truck? Wouldn't Max have barked?"

Lute crossed his arms across his chest, his shoulders rose then fell. "I want to check around outside."

"Good Idea."

Lute led the way and they stopped at the window of Wren's room. It was chest high, easy access for The Ferret. Lute pointed at the ground. "Tracks."

At first, Kent couldn't make them out. Lute squatted at the base of a yew growing along the footing. "Here."

In the soft soil, Kent saw a footprint. Its size was right for Feron's boot.

"Can you tell which way he went?"

Lute was already scanning the area. "No."

"He had to be on foot, right? If Jodi was home, Feron wouldn't have been able to just drive up the driveway. She'd have seen or heard him, for sure. I've got to believe he came and went on foot."

"Maybe."

They searched in the mowed grass and dry ground for more prints and came up with nothing. They were considering their options when, out of the blue, Kent said, "Wait here. I'll be right back." He retraced his steps through the cabin to Wren's room, looked around, then grabbed a pillow off the bed and a tiny pair of slippers beside it.

Back outside he whistled for Lucinda, who was in the shade chewing one end of a huge bone while Otsi chewed the other. She came on the run. Otsi, still limping, was close behind.

Standing at the window, Kent said, "Let's see what these guys can do." He held the pillow and slippers for the dogs to smell. He goaded them. "Where's Wren? Go find Wren."

Lucinda caught on first. Her eyes lit up, her tail wagged. She began circling, her nose to the ground, huffing loudly. Within seconds, Otsi was doing the same, happy to be part of the game.

Kent and Lute stood still, careful not to distract the dogs. A few seconds later, Lucinda let out her trailing bay and took off down Jodi's path to the river.

"They've picked up the scent," Kent shouted, his pride causing more jubilation than was in order for the situation.

"Yep, they got it," Lute agreed, more sullen. "And they're moving fast."

Kent chased after the dogs at a run. "Come on, or we'll lose them."

When he was close to the dogs, he slowed, letting them work while he caught his breath. Instinctively, he turned, expecting to see Lute charging up behind him, like he'd done on so many coon hunts over the years. But Lute was nowhere in sight. He was wondering what happened to him when off in the distance, back toward the cabin, he heard a shrill whistle—a series of short blasts. He'd heard that sound a hundred times before. It was Lute whistling through his fingers, calling Otsi.

Both dogs heard it, too. They stopped trailing, raised their heads, perked their ears. Lucinda froze. Otsi took off back up the trail toward the cabin as fast as his three good legs would carry him.

Then Kent heard another familiar noise come from the same direction. It was the sound of an engine starting—Lute's old pickup.

It took him a minute to figure out what was happening, then it struck him. "Sonofabitch!" He kicked at a bush. Lute had double-crossed him. He was going to let Kent and Lucinda follow the trail, just in case Feron was still on it, but *he* was going to drive straight to Feron's houseboat. He was making sure *he'd* get the first crack at The Ferret.

CHAPTER 43

AFTER JODI SCRIBBLED THE NOTE TO LUTE AND tacked it on the front door, she grabbed Max and her favorite little Beretta pistol, then climbed into her beat-up bug. She headed for Feron's houseboat because she was sure that's where she would find Wren. The road was slippery from the night air, her vision blurred by tears, but she pushed the little car as hard as it would go. Her brain sagged under the weight of what was happening. One moment she was nearly overcome with fear, the next she was spitting mad.

She pounded the wheel with her fists. "He's not getting Wren, goddamnit. I swear I'll kill him. I should have done it a long time ago."

She rounded corners on two wheels. At most, The Ferret had two hours on her. If he hurt that little girl…She didn't let herself finish the thought.

She doused the headlights and slowed to a crawl as she approached the houseboat. For once, she was thankful for the weathered dullness of the old car's black paint.

She noticed movement a hundred yards ahead and stopped—a flashlight waving, shadows moving in the dark, and people. She couldn't tell how many exactly, but at least half a dozen.

It looked like they were filing out of a small barn and milling around a shiny new pickup truck, a big one—Feron's.

"Where is Wren?" Jodi said to Max, who was on the seat beside her. She strained her eyes searching the group and didn't see her.

At the sound of the girl's name, Max let out a single yip. Instantly, Jodi had her fingers around the little dog's muzzle. "No, Max! Quiet," she told him with a squeeze. He got the message. When she let him free, he stood on his hind legs, front feet on the handle of the passenger door, staring out at the people in the dark. But he didn't make a sound.

Jodi watched. As her eyes adjusted, she could tell the people were being loaded into Feron's truck. In a few minutes they'd be gone. Maybe Wren with them. Then what?

She began to shake. She had to do *something*. She wished Kent and Lute were with her.

She drew a breath and released it through her mouth, trying to steady her nerves, then grabbed the Beretta she had placed on the seat.

Leaning her face close to Max's, she ordered the little dog to stay put. "Don't make a sound," she told him. He seemed to recognize the urgency and obeyed. But, when Jodi eased out of the car, Max couldn't help himself. He whined softly.

In a strong whisper, Jodi again warned him to be quiet, then closed the door with the lightest of touch. Max watched through the window as Jodi disappeared into the darkness.

Feron paused as he secured the last corner of the tarp. His woodsman's senses were on high alert. Was that a dog he just heard? He waited for it again. But there was only silence. He was refocusing on the tarp when LipLip turned to stare down the lane, ears pricked. He let out a deep growl. *Yep, there's something out there.*

Jodi crept closer to Feron's truck, staying in the shadows. She could make it out well now, but she no longer saw any people. She was sure that they were under the tarp. Instinctively, she pointed her gun away from the truck as she considered that Wren may be in it with the others. Where was Feron?

She stepped out of the shadows when she was within a few feet of the truck, gun raised and ready if she needed it. With her free hand, she reached for a corner of the tarp.

That's when she felt a crashing blow to the back of her head. The night lit up with fireworks and she felt herself melt to the ground. For a moment, she lost consciousness. Then, as blurry awareness returned, she felt a hot, foul-smelling breath in her face. It made a huffing noise as it moved down her neck. Through the roaring static in her head, she heard The Ferret's voice. "Get back, LipLip. I've got her now."

Helpless, she felt her gun being pulled away. Rough hands rolled her over and a knee pressed hard into her back as her hands were yanked behind her and tied.

CHAPTER 44

FERON HEAVED JODI UP SO THAT SHE WAS SIT-ting with her back against a wheel of his truck, then stood over her. She blinked to clear her head. LipLip drooled at her from just beyond her feet.

"You are one big pain in my ass, lady."

"Where's Wren?"

Feron smiled with his mouth but not his eyes. "Your daughter?"

"My little girl."

Feron blew a chilling laugh. "Your girl? That kid is *my* girl, Jodi."

"She's mine now."

"No, she is not." Feron pointed at his chest with his thumb. "I brought her down from Canada, just like I was hired to do. She got separated from her mother in the shuffle. That's all there is to it."

"I found her."

"That don't mean shit. She ain't even Indian, she's Korean."

"I don't care."

Feron gave a dismissive wave. "Well, it don't make any difference. She's going out with the load tonight."

He stared out into the darkness, trying to figure out what to do with Jodi for now. He was cutting it mighty close for his rendezvous with the semi. He couldn't take her along.

"The police are coming. I called them," she lied.

"Yeah, right. Like the Rez cops are going to come running right over here for a kid missing a couple hours."

"I called the Jefferson cops."

"They got no say on the reservation. They'll have to work through the Rez cops."

"That shit won't bother Merrill, and you know it."

She saw Feron squirm. He knew she was right.

"Whatever," he said, and went silent.

"Is she in there?" She gestured to his truck by tapping her head against it, and the movement instantly made her feel nauseous. "I know you've got people in there. Under that tarp. I saw you loading them. Where are you taking them?"

Feron didn't answer right away. When he did, his voice was maudlin, apologetic. "I never really wanted to hurt you, Jodi," he whined. "Even back in Canada when I…" he swallowed hard. "We just went there, to your place, looking for Dewey. We was just getting paid to collect a debt. We didn't mean to kill him."

"Fuck you, Feron. You shot him."

"The fella with me said you guys had run out of the house. I wouldn't have torched it if I knew you were still in it. For Chrisake, I knew you since you were a kid. Me, Doc, Merrill, Jimmy, we all watched you grow up behind Lute."

"Fuck you, Feron."

He was almost in tears as the memories seeped back into his mind. "And your baby. I'd never kill a baby on purpose."

"You raped me!"

"I didn't mean to do that either."

"Feron, you are so full of bullshit! You can't *accidentally* rape someone."

He had no reply. He drew a deep breath, and his thoughts shifted. In a pitiful voice, he said, "I'm Owahgena, too. You know that."

"*Part* Owahgena, maybe," Jodi sneered.

"Okay. But I grew up with all that Indian shit. I respect the earth, the woods, and the river, and crap. I know what those Northern Lights guys have planned for the river, and I'm against it, just like the rest of you. I had no idea it was going to come to this when I sold them the land."

"Liar. You don't give a shit about the river. You knew exactly what would happen. You just wanted the money."

"No," Feron said firmly. "When they first came to me, they made it sound like they were just going to put up something small, and that's all I agreed to. Something just big enough that I could use it as a place to move stuff I brought down from the north was all I was interested in."

"For your goddamn Canadian Express."

"That's right," Feron defended himself. "My Canadian Express, as all of you call it. For years I done it. No problem. Cigarettes mostly. Once in a while some weed or some guns." His voice trailed off, remembering the good times. Then, as if a switch turned, he said, "And then that fucking son of yours came along."

The mention of her son startled her. "Pegger?"

"Yeah, Pegger. It was all his idea to build my business."

"There goes your bullshit again, Feron. No way Pegger would work a deal with you."

"Oh yeah, he would, and he did. I took his bait hook, line, and sinker. 'Get big', he told me. 'The money's in hard drugs. Screw the marijuana.' He…"

Jodi cut him off. "You are a fucking liar!"

"I'm not. He told me he was sick and tired of being poor and working for Indian causes all the time. He wanted to make some money, real money. Me and him, we'd be partners. He sold me on the whole thing." Feron made a grunting, disgusted sound. "So things were going pretty good, and then this guy asks me if I could help him get some people across. I decided, why not ratchet it up even a little more? That's what Pegger wants, right? We could make some real easy money smuggling people. So, without running it by Pegger, I brought a couple loads down in my boat and everything went fine. The people got in, the guys paid, everybody's happy—until the mix-up with the kid. Pegger had a shit fit when he found out about that."

Jodi strained at the ropes on her wrists. She wanted to strangle Feron. "Pegger would never do anything like that."

"If you don't believe that, you won't believe this. *He* shot Jimmy Silverheel."

"I hate you! You fucking bastard. You'd say anything to hurt me." She spit the words at him.

Feron ignored her venom, his mind locked in the memories. In a voice that was disturbingly calm, he said, "Jimmy was in on the smuggling with us. He's been helping me with my little operation for years. But I don't know, somehow the cops must have gotten something on him. They turned him. Pegger found out he was working with the cops and," Feron pointed an imaginary rifle into the darkness and jerked his shoulder back feigning a recoil. "Pow! No more Jimmy."

"I fucking swear I'm going to kill you, Feron."

Feron shrugged. "He shot him with that weird caliber rifle he liked so much, and now, every cop in the county is looking for it. What, .264, right? Another dumbass move on his part."

That Feron actually knew about Pegger's rifle disturbed Jodi. And she knew, deep down, that Feron was right. Pegger had been discontent with his lot in life. He had confided in her. They'd talked about career options for him, ways for him to escape the Indian world. It scared her to think that Feron knew about Pegger's discontent—and the .264. He had two pieces of the puzzle *that fit*. No, she could never let herself believe that Pegger would kill someone, or that anything else Feron said was true.

"I want Wren!" she shouted.

He smiled. "She's not five feet from you right now." He tapped his knuckle on the truck.

"So, she *is* in there?"

"Yep. Happy as a clam. She's with *her* people again. And this time she's going to go where she was supposed to go in the first place. As a matter of fact, you are making me late for my connection." He squatted next to her, his face so close she could smell his breath and it was worse than Lip-Lip's. He ran his hand along her thigh, then across her breast, and pinched her nipple hard. She winced but bit her lip so he would not get the satisfaction of a scream.

His face turned lecherous, all remorse vanished. "I'm thinking that maybe, when I get back, I'll have some fun with you again. Like before." He worked his arms under her then heaved her up over his shoulder like a rolled rug. "For now, I'm going to stash you on my boat."

As he stepped toward his houseboat, he felt a pain shoot up his leg so sharp it made his knee buckle. He gasped and almost went down under Jodi's weight, but he managed to keep his feet. When he looked, he saw Jodi's little dog latched on his leg just above his boot, driving tiny teeth into his calf like a pit bull going for the kill.

Feron swore and shook his leg, but Max clung. He kicked his leg waist high, almost toppling, and nearly dropping Jodi. Still Max held on.

Enamel razors ripped into the back of Feron's leg making his breath catch in his throat. For a second he thought the damn little dog might actually take him down—except he knew what to do. He whistled to LipLip, who had wandered off. "*Kill*," he commanded, and gestured toward Max. "Kill that little sonofabitch."

It was as if a smile broke onto LipLip's face. His eyes said, "Gladly." With a ferocious growl he lunged at Max, teeth bared.

From her spot on Feron's shoulder, Jodi saw what was happening. "Run, Max!" she shouted.

With LipLip only inches away, Max released his hold and, in one quick bound, ducked under Feron's truck.

The truck was higher than most pickups, but not high enough for a mammoth beast like LipLip. In full chase, he lunged for Max, but his shoulders struck the running board hard enough to make the whole vehicle shake. The impact knocked him back and stunned him for a second. He braced on spraddled legs.

A black and tan blur circled the tire from under the truck and came up behind the dazed monster. Max sank his teeth into Lip-Lip's hind leg where thin skin covers bone just above the hock. They grated against the bone.

LipLip let out a primal roar. The pain caused him to rear his head, which smashed into the truck with a sickening thud. By the time LipLip recovered, Max was out of reach back under the truck. This time he stayed there, as LipLip circled and strained to grab him from all directions, his teeth snapping.

Feron carried Jodi to his houseboat. LipLip would get the little bastard eventually, he was sure of that. Jodi twisted on his shoulder, trying to get a glimpse of Max. She sent up an Owahgena prayer for her little protector.

Feron dropped her onto a bench in the stowaway's room and made sure she was bound tight.

"I'll be back," he said. "And then we're going to have a little fun, you and me. You'll think what I did to you in Canada was a picnic."

She spit at him and struggled against the ropes.

He cursed and wiped his face, then slapped her with a force that spun her head. "Just think," he said with a smile, "I'm gonna go out there and drive my truck away. That's gonna leave your little mutt in the wide open and ol' LipLip's gonna be right there ready to eat him up." He tied an oily rag across her mouth that made her gag, then he turned and left the room. She heard the rattle of the lock when he closed the door.

CHAPTER 45

SOUR EMOTIONS ROLLED IN LUTE'S MIND LIKE turned compost as he and Otsi drove toward Feron's boat. Guilt and cowardice because he had deceived Kent—twice. First sneaking into his hospital and second just now, duping him on the trail so that he, Lute, would get the first shot at The Ferret. These were not the acts of a friend—and Kent was his best friend. There was regret for not having been more supportive of Jodi over the years and, especially now, with all this crap going on. He knew that wherever she was at the moment, she was distressed beyond words. And there was fear for Wren, who he had no doubt was in Feron's hands. But the emotion that superseded all the others was *hate*, burning, blinding, soulwithering hate for the man who had done so much damage to his family.

He reached behind the seat to make sure his deer rifle was there. When he ran his fingers along its steel and walnut, he thought, *Sorry Kent, but at this moment, my rifle is my best friend.*

He pushed his truck pitching and rumbling up Feron's driveway fast enough to remove any pretense of stealth. He didn't give a damn. He *hoped* Feron would hear him coming. A little farther and he came upon Jodi's old VW. That confirmed what he and Kent had suspected— she was going after Feron alone. He slowed just enough to inspect it. Empty. The passenger-side vent window was broken and sprung out on its hinges. What was that all about? He hit the gas again and blew

239

past Feron's truck, not even considering what might be in back under the tarp. He slammed the brakes within a few feet of the houseboat's gangplank at the same time Feron emerged from its cabin.

Feron froze—a big mistake. By the time he recovered, he was staring down the bore of Lute's deer rifle. His hands went up. In the most disarming tone he could muster, he said, "Hey, Lute. We need to talk."

Lute squinted at him down the barrel. "Where's Jodi?"

Feron feigned confusion. "Jodi? How would I know where she is?"

"Cut the bullshit, Feron. Remember who you're talking to?"

Feron's face folded into sadness. "I know that, Lute. We grew up together. We've been friends forever."

Lute pressed his cheek tighter to his rifle, lining up Feron in its scope. "We're not friends. Not anymore."

Feron forced a simpering smile, but the shine of sweat on his brow gave him away. He oozed more self-pity. "I know I done a lot of bad things. You know it, too. But you were the only guy I could always count on. You never turned me in for poaching and you always looked the other way about my… Canadian gig. You've been a better friend than I deserve."

Lute snapped, "You can bet I'm beyond done with you now."

A motion beyond Lute caught Feron's eye. It was LipLip circling his truck, still trying to catch Max.

"We can work this out, Lute," Feron pleaded.

"I know you killed Pegger."

Feron's back stiffened. "What?" he said, feigning innocence.

"You poisoned him with coyote poison. It was on Pegger's lips. And I smelled it on the pizza in his car."

"Now, Lute. Pegger crashed because he was drunk."

"Bullshit. You poisoned him with the same mix you and me and the others used to use to get rid of coyotes. You should have known I'd recognize it."

Feron was only half listening now. He was more interested in LipLip and watched him over Lute's shoulder. He pursed his lips and made a quick, high-pitched sucking sound. The big dog picked up on his signal. "You're wrong, Lute."

"Why did you kill him?"

Feron searched for something to say while LipLip figured out what his master wanted him to do. "I hate those Northern Lights guys as much as you do. I didn't think they'd hurt the river. They were going to build a small place, sell bait, tackle, and rent some boats. A delivery truck in once a week or so to help me with my business was all I was after."

"Bullshit. You knew all along what they want to do."

"Not at first. Once I agreed to sell my land to them, Balt and his buddies told me that they planned to get big. A hotel, restaurants, huge store! I don't want all that any more than you do."

Lute held the rifle firmly on Feron. "You could have stopped him. At least early on."

Feron could almost feel the crosshairs pressing on his chest, making it hard for him to breathe. Desperate now, he called Lip-Lip again with the sucking sound and wiped the back of his hand across his face hoping Lute wouldn't catch on. LipLip begin to slink their way. "I was gonna. Till Pegger came along with his bright idea."

Lute focused on Feron's words, letting his guard drop. The deer rifle's muzzle sank a fraction of an inch. "He was trying to get you to do the right thing. Pegger knew you had the power to stop the whole Northern Lights mess."

Feron shook his head. "No, Lute. That's where you're wrong. Pegger came to me because he wanted a piece of The Canadian Express."

"Pegger would never smuggle."

"He convinced me to go from cigarettes and pot to hard drugs—cocaine and heroin."

"Bullshit."

Frank Martorana

"He said he was sick of being poor."

Feron decided to take a risk to keep Lute's attention focused on him. "We had a big fight. Over me bringing in some illegals. He didn't agree with that. He thought it was too risky."

LipLip was moving faster now, his eyes narrowed into attack mode. Feron only needed to hold Lute's attention for a few more seconds. "Turns out I *had* to kill Pegger."

Those words were the confirmation that Lute needed to hear. He spit a curse in Owahgena, then raised the rife back up, re-centering the crosshairs on Feron. He was squeezing the trigger when LipLip crashed into his back. The big dog's weight drove Lute forward and together, they crashed to the ground. The rifle went flying.

Lute scrambled but LipLip was on him, tearing with his claws, biting, ripping through his shirt. He yelled to Feron. "Get this sonofa-bitch off me."

Feron's face was like stone—he didn't move. He only watched as Lip-Lip savaged Lute. For no reason except hatefulness, he yelled out, "Just so you know, I've got your sister in here."

Lute elbowed LipLip in the face. "If you touch her, I'll kill you."

"I'm sure your plan was to do that anyway."

Lute elbowed LipLip again and tried to free himself, but the monster dog continued to attack with vicious bites to his arms and shoulders. Then LipLip's huge jaws clamped on his neck, teeth driving toward the bone, and Lute thought this was the end. He curled into a ball and wedged his hands behind his neck forcing them into LipLip's mouth. *Better to have shredded hands than shredded neck.* He felt blood between his fingers and knew it was his. LipLip's teeth closed on his hands and Lute screamed.

He began to chant in Owahgena. His eyes were closing. "Call him off," he heard himself say to Feron. He was spinning into unconsciousness when he heard Feron let out a loud curse.

A second later, he was jarred by the collision of bodies above him. LipLip's jaws released and his weight lifted off.

As Lute lay on the ground thanking the spirits, he heard dogs fighting and opened his eyes to see Otsi tearing at LipLip.

Otsi, his defender. Lute would have smiled but for the sight of his dog being destroyed by his colossal opponent.

Using his three legs as best he could, Otsi charged LipLip, but the big dog went up on his hind legs and pawed Otsi to the ground. He rolled Otsi over, opened his jaws like a bear and sank his teeth into Otsi's belly. Otsi let out a yelp and tried to regain his feet, but LipLip shook him in the air then slammed him to the ground.

Halfconscious, Lute searched. He had to find his rifle. His friend needed help. He couldn't let that beast kill Otsi.

Then his attention was drawn back to the fight by *another* loud roar that he knew was neither Otsi's nor LipLip's. The world exploded with snarls as the fight escalated into the mother of all dog fights.

Even in the heat of the moment, Lute allowed himself a flicker of a smile.

Lucinda had arrived.

CHAPTER 46

KENT HAD TO MOVE FAST TO KEEP LUCINDA within earshot as he followed her along the trail Feron had left. He was sure it would end up at the houseboat. Between heavy breaths, he cursed Lute for ditching him. Lute knew that Feron was unpredictable and dangerous. Now, if he was cornered, he would be vicious. He'd fight like a real ferret. *Dammit Lute, we should have stuck together.*

He pushed himself to move faster. Branches, heavy with pre-dawn dew, soaked him as he ran. It wouldn't be long now.

When he drew closer, he slowed, shifting into stalking mode. He couldn't see or hear Lucinda, but he knew she must be almost to the houseboat. He paused, listening—nothing but a night bird and droplets dripping off the trees.

He moved forward a few steps at a time, listening. He patted his pants pocket, wishing he had brought his revolver. If only he had known. He had gone to Lute's expecting to tell him about Sim. He hadn't expected to need a gun.

A noise came from the direction of the houseboat. The trees muffled it, but he could tell it was some sort of a ruckus. He took a few more steps. Dogs fighting—he knew that sound well—men shouting, an engine starting.

In a crouch, he moved forward, working to get a look. The growls and snarls became louder.

When he broke into the meadow at Feron's place, the first thing he saw was Feron's big pickup truck. Then he saw Lucinda fighting an animal twice her size—LipLip. Again, he wished he had his gun.

He could see Otsi was in the battle, too. And there was a man on the ground, not moving—Lute. The houseboat was pulling away from its mooring, engine roaring and blue smoke belching.

Lucinda was faster than LipLip. Like a prize fighter with a quick jab, she ducked in and out, each time sinking her teeth into him, but avoiding the big dog's jaws that grabbed for her like a *Tyrannosaurus rex*.

It didn't take Kent's veterinary-trained eye to see that Otsi was tiring. But even on three legs, wobbling and bleeding in several places, Otsi was giving it his all, distracting the monster dog from Lucinda as best he could.

He was desperate to help Lucinda, but there was Lute. *He* needed help, too, if it wasn't already too late. His heart was ripped as he made the decision he knew Lucinda would never make if their roles were reversed—he raced toward Lute.

Lucinda caught sight of Kent and hesitated. It was the chance that LipLip needed. He lunged at her and managed to grasp a mouthful of her neck. Otsi tried in vain to draw him off. Kent watched in horror as LipLip shook Lucinda, tossed her high, then slammed her to the ground. The sound of the air being forced from her lungs made him weak.

He fell on his knees next to Lute assessing his condition—multiple bite wounds covered in blood. He felt for a pulse—it was there. Then Lute drew a breath. He was pale, in shock, but alive. When Kent rolled him over, the movement brought Lute back to consciousness. He raised his arm and pointed to the dogs. His next words displayed the essence of their friendship. "Help the dogs," he said.

He waved his arm toward the tall grass. "My rifle is over there somewhere."

Shaking with fear for Lucinda, Kent pawed through the brush and grass, but he couldn't find the rifle. He was desperate to help her. Then, there was another roar, a growl that would have made a wolf proud, and it drew his attention back at the dogs.

At that second, a black and tan streak burst from under Feron's truck—Max. The other dogs didn't see him coming. He circled behind them, waiting for LipLip's tail to shift, then with perfect timing, he attacked. He grabbed LipLip's scrotum and crushed it in his teeth like a vice.

LipLip let out a cry of pain and spun off Lucinda. Max was whipped behind him like a kite, as the momentum magnified his body weight and stretching Lip-Lip's most tender skin even tighter. The big dog twisted one way, then the other, reaching back trying to get at Max. The more he tried, the more pain he inflicted on himself. The little dog was fearless. He held on and that gave Lucinda and Otsi the chance they needed. They attacked with a vengeance, gashing Lip-Lip with their teeth as the big dog struggled to free himself of Max.

For a moment Kent and Lute watched in awe as the trio wore the monster down. Then, Kent turned back to his search for the rifle and finally saw it at the water's edge. He grabbed it, threw off the safety, and brought the scope up to his eye. He was about to fire at Lip-Lip ending the fight once and for all when he realized there was no need.

LipLip, tail tucked, was running for the woods on unsteady legs. Lucinda, Otsi, and Max were sitting like the three wise monkeys watching him go.

Kent lowered the rifle and turned to Lute. "Where's Jodi?"

Lute worked himself onto his feet and braced himself with one hand on his knee. With the other he pointed to Feron's houseboat that was heading down the river. "The Ferret's got her."

CHAPTER 47

KENT AND LUTE STOOD ON THE BANK OF THE river and watched blue smoke billow from the engine of Feron's houseboat as it churned into the distance headed north at full speed.

"You know for sure that he's got her?"

Lute rolled his neck and shoulders trying to work through the pain and clear his head. "I didn't see her, but he told me he did."

"Headed to Canada."

"No doubt."

"Did he say anything else?"

The pain on Lute's face faded into a flush of anger. "Oh yeah, he said a whole lot."

Kent turned to him. "Meaning what?"

"Meaning, I'm going to kill that bastard."

Before Lute could say more, Kent heard a dog whine and turned toward it. How could he forget Lucinda? He was expecting to see her laid out on the ground, but she wasn't. He sent up a prayer when he saw that none of the three dogs had life-threatening wounds. Lucinda and Otsi were standing with their heads cocked, watching Max. It was Max, not Lucinda, he had heard. The Chihuahua was whining, spinning, and jumping at the tailgate of Feron's truck. *That little guy never stops! Why is he so interested in Feron's pickup?*

Kent stepped over, untied a corner of the tarp that covered the truck's bed, and cautiously lifted it. When he saw the people packed in, curled into shivering, terrified balls, he threw the tarp wide open. They stared at him through eyes rimmed in white. None moved or made a sound.

"Jesus," rolled up Kent's throat. He noticed the woman. She was shielding a young girl, the only child on board. He reached in and lifted the child from the woman's arms and held her for Lute to see.

Lute's eyes filled with tears as he ran them over the girl making sure that she was not injured. Then a smile pushed its way through the pain on his face, and he uttered something in Owahgena. He grabbed the child from Kent and hugged her. "Welcome back little one," he whispered to her.

She smiled her bright smile back at him and he hugged her tighter. Max went ballistic until Lute lowered her to where she could pet him. As if remembering what he had grasped in his mouth just moments ago, he withheld his kisses while she giggled and tugged his ears.

As Kent watched Lute and Wren, his joy faded back into distress as his thoughts returned to Jodi. "One down, one to go."

He pointed to the bedraggled illegals as they sat up, stretched, and breathed in fresh air. "Those people are in tough shape. They need help but we don't have time to give it to them right now." He hated himself for making a selfish decision at the expense of others so much in need. "I'd like to help them, but we can't. I guarantee that the Rez cops will be along soon. They'll see them and take over. That's the best we can do. We've got to get Jodi."

Lute's eyes were still on Wren as he forced himself to refocus on their mission. "Yep. I'm with you."

He lifted her, hugged her again, then passed her back to her Korean guardian. As he slowly released her, he told the woman, "Take care of her. We'll be back." The woman nodded.

Kent addressed the group, "Who speaks English?"

Their young leader raised his hand.

"Tell them to stay put. Stay in the truck. You are safe now. Help is coming."

The man translated and heads nodded.

Kent and Lute turned back to the houseboat. Thankfully, it wasn't built for speed, but even so, it was shrinking into the distance.

"If he makes it to Canada, we'll never find him, or Jodi," Lute said.

"The cops will get him."

Lute gave Kent a dubious look. "That's The Ferret out there, remember? He's well named. He knows every place to hide between here and the Hudson Bay. He'll be on the run for weeks, if they catch him at all."

Kent knew Lute was right. He stared out toward the houseboat and racked his brain for a plan. Suddenly, it was there. "The bridge," he said.

He was already running toward Lute's truck by the time the words registered with Lute. "I've got the rifle." He held it up for Lute to see. Are you okay to drive?"

"Not a problem."

Kent knew nothing short of a coma would have stopped Lute at that point.

As he passed Lucinda, Otsi, and Max he yelled, "Stay. We will be back for you," hoping they would obey.

All three dogs promptly flopped to the ground, exhausted, and injured, but accepted that they were responsible for the illegals.

Kent tossed the deer rifle into the truck and climbed in. Lute cranked the engine. The old truck's tires were spraying gravel as it climbed up onto the road along the river.

"If we're lucky," Kent said, "we can beat him to the bridge."

"Then what?"

He hadn't thought that far ahead. "We'll stop him." It was vague, but it was all he had.

"Good." Lute let the silence draw out for a moment. "How?"

"I don't know yet."

"You won't be able to get a shot at him if he's in the wheelhouse. If you do get him with a lucky shot, the boat will crash without anyone to steer it."

"You watch the road and get us there fast. I'll figure something out."

"Remember, that .30-06 will put a bullet right through the walls of that old boat. If you miss Feron, you could hit Jodi."

"Got it."

"Or, you could put a hole through the pontoons, maybe sink the boat."

Kent glared at Lute. "Will you shut up!"

Lute wrestled the old truck along the river road toward the bridge at top speed, both hands on the wheel. He glanced over and could see that they had come up even with the houseboat. It was fifty yards from shore, still belching smoke as Feron pushed it hard. Lute jammed his foot on the accelerator and shook the steering wheel with both hands as if that would goad the truck to a higher speed. Black smoke belched out of its exhaust matching that of the houseboat.

When Lute thought Kent had had enough time, he said, "So what's your plan?"

"You keep driving."

"No shit. Then what?"

Kent hesitated, then, "Turn onto the bridge."

Lute gave him an arched look and scoffed, "Pure genius."

Because he needed to give Lute something, he said, "Stop in the middle. See if we can get a shot at him."

Angrily Lute repeated what he said before. "If we shoot him, the boat's going to crash. Or, we could hit Jodi. We don't know where he's holding her."

"Jesus, Lute. Just say it's too risky."

"It's too risky."

They were on the bridge now. The boat was coming their way, only a few yards away.

When they reached the middle, Lute slammed the brakes. That's when he saw Kent exit the truck, leap like a cat to the top of the concrete guardrail, and disappear over the side.

"Shit! The crazy white man jumped," Lute said to Otsi before he remembered Otsi wasn't there.

CHAPTER 48

IT WAS HIS ONLY CHANCE, SO HE TOOK IT. HE aimed for the tin roof, twelve, maybe fifteen feet below—and jumped. He landed with a thud dead center and, as he had hoped, his weight was too much for the old roof. It caved in, breaking his fall and creating a depression that shielded him. He kept his body flat and did a quick check to see that all his body parts had survived the impact, then lifted his head just enough to glance over the edge.

Feron was in the wheelhouse. In a rage, he was trying to steer the boat with one hand, while glancing back over his shoulder with his gun in the other hand, trying to get a shot at Kent. When Kent's head rose up like a mechanical target at a carnival shooting gallery, Feron released the wheel, turned, and fired several quick shots. Kent ducked as bullets ripped through tin and whistled over his head.

The wheel, left unattended, began to spin and the boat drifted sideways. Both men were thrown as it struck one of the bridge piers then spun in the current. A surreal darkness fell over them as it hung up crossways under the bridge. The current raged against it, and the engine moaned trying to push the boat free.

Kent rolled to the deck. He was desperate to find Jodi. He needed to protect her from the stray bullets. And what if Feron had already done something to her? That thought drove the blood from his brain, and it took him several breaths to recover. *Find Jodi first, then deal with Feron.*

She had to be inside the cabin. He was crawling toward the door when he heard Feron's voice behind him. "You just never learn, do you, Doc?"

He turned. In the halflight, he saw Feron taking aim and knew that The Ferret's next shot would hit its mark. He pressed himself against the wall of the cabin. But the shot he heard next was not from Feron's gun. It came from above and was too loud for a handgun. There was a flash as a bullet ricocheted off the railing. Feron cursed and grabbed his thigh. There was a second shot and Feron dove for cover.

Kent could see Lute leaning over the bridge railing trying to get an angle on Feron. He was holding the deer rifle out at arm's length, aiming it under the bridge, shooting it one-handed like a handgun.

Another shot went wild. Kent thought of Jodi and prayed Lute remembered his own words about a rifle slug being able to penetrate the boat's thin walls. He pushed open the cabin door and slipped inside. He crawled under the buckled ceiling searching for Jodi. She wasn't in the kitchen. He called her name. No response. It felt like the air had been sucked out of the room.

There was only one other door—Jodi had to be behind it. He tried it, but it was jammed by the bent roof and wouldn't budge. He felt the boat shudder. It made a grating, creaking noise as the current pushed it free and it began moving under the bridge again.

He kicked the door with both feet. After several tries, he loosened it enough to squeeze through and saw Jodi bound on the floor. She was wild-eyed, struggling to breathe around the gag in her mouth, but she was alive.

More shots rang out, two different sounds—Lute and Feron were exchanging gunfire.

"Are you okay?" he asked as he pulled the gag away and started on the ropes around her wrists.

She nodded, working her jaw.

The ropes fell away just as the boat lurched again. "We've got to get out of here. Can you walk?"

"Yeah, I'm good."

"Stay as low as you can. That's Lute and Feron shooting."

"Where are we going? We're on a boat."

Kent had been running on instinct. He just wanted to get away. He hadn't thought it through. "Uh, over the side. Into the river."

Jodi gave him a worried look.

"Out the cabin door, three steps across the deck, then over the side into the water," he told her with more confidence than he felt. "You can do it."

She nodded again.

He signaled for her to go first. She scrambled, made it through the cabin door, across the deck, and was about to take the plunge, when she stopped dead and shouted, "Shit!" And Kent saw why.

The boat was scraping along the bridge pier. The pier formed a sliding, grating concrete wall right up against the railing. There was no space to jump.

Somewhere near, Feron lurked, gun in hand. Kent was trying to think of a new plan when the boat slid to a series of rebar brackets set a foot apart in the concrete wall, the rungs of a service ladder that ascended up to the bridge deck.

He grabbed Jodi's shoulder and pointed. "There's a ladder for the maintenance guys to use. Climb it."

Jodi didn't hesitate. Like a cat, she stepped onto an ice chest, then the railing, and onto the ladder.

Kent watched for Feron. That's when he saw blood on the deck.

CHAPTER 49

KENT SURMISED FROM THE BLOOD ON THE houseboat's deck that Feron was hit. But how badly? He had heard him exchange fire with Lute *after* he grabbed his leg, so he was probably still alive.

He looked up at Jodi, halfway to the top, moving fast hand over hand. Still, she was a sitting duck for Feron. He willed her to hurry.

"I'm coming for you, Feron," he shouted, hoping to draw The Ferret's attention. He looked around for something to use as a weapon.

"Be my guest," came from the bow.

He grabbed a pipe wrench lying on the deck and lobbed it over the cabin. It clattered onto the opposite deck.

"Nice try, Kent. I wasn't born yesterday. I know where you are."

If he could keep Feron focused on him, Jodi could climb.

"You make one move and Lute will nail you."

"I doubt it."

"He got you once already."

"Just a ricochet into my leg. I've had worse."

"I see a lot of blood."

"We're too far under the bridge. He can't get me from where he's at."

There was a pause. Then Feron said, "It looks like you're in a fix, ol' buddy."

"You don't say."

"Yep. Either you stay on this boat with me, and I'm the guy with the gun, or you follow Miss Jodi there up the ladder. I've got my eye on her right now. It would be an easy shot."

An electrical surge coursed through Kent's body. "She told me what you did to her family—and to her. You hurt her again and it will be the last thing you do."

"Sounds like you're kinda sweet on her."

Jodi was almost to the bridge deck now. It seemed like she was taking forever.

"That's none of your business."

"Yeah, well. I'd be lying if I told you screwing her wasn't fun."

Kent burned in silence. The only sound was the boat groaning as it scraped along under the bridge. Kent saw Jodi grab the top rung and Lute's arm reach out pulling her to safety.

Feron must have seen her, too. He shouted, "Okay, Kent, your turn. What you gonna do?"

Kent wasn't going to let himself be the easy target. He knew Feron wouldn't show him the same mercy he'd shown Jodi.

"I'm coming for you, Feron," he yelled for the second time, and he was still not sure how.

The boat lurched hard. Cargo shifted on the deck. As the boat rolled then righted itself, it broke free of the bridge. Instantly, its speed increased in the current.

Kent saw his chance. He grabbed the ladder and held on as the boat moved out from under him and his feet dropped into the water. He struggled to hold onto the iron rung. Thankfully, he was too low for Feron to get a shot.

He climbed as the boat sailed away. Out in the light, Feron knew enough not to show himself with Lute and his rifle overhead. When he reached the top, Lute grabbed his collar and pulled him on to the bridge.

As Kent sat on the bridge catching his breath, Jodi crawled over and hugged him. He'd never seen her cry before, and his eyes filled, too.

"Thank you," she said.

He squeezed her and searched for the right words, but none came.

He glanced at Lute now standing at the railing, rifle up, watching through the scope and hoping for a shot as the boat moved away. He ached with his friend's frustration.

"Let him go, Lute. The border patrol will get him. He's heading to Canada. We know that."

Lute's eyes remained fixed on the boat. "Like we've said before, The Ferret's got a dozen places to hide between here and there. He's good at disappearing when he needs to."

"It may take time, but they'll get him."

Kent and Jodi watched as Lute held his position, aching for a shot while mulling Kent's words. Finally, he cursed in Owahgena and lowered his rifle.

Just as Kent relaxed into Jodi's arms, she pulled away and moved to the railing.

"Nope. That doesn't work for me," she said, and snatched the rifle from Lute.

Kent watched a darkness move over her as cold as any winter night he could remember. She stared out at the boat then raised the rifle. She braced her elbows on the railing and squinted into the scope.

"Feron is in the wheelhouse at the bow," Kent pressed. "You haven't got a shot."

"Watch me," she hissed.

She took a long, careful aim.

Kent remembered how Jodi had hit the bullseye with that incredibly long shot on the target range and he knew that whatever it was she was aiming at, she would nail it.

Her upper body jerked back from the recoil as a shot exploded from the rifle. For a heartbeat, they kept their eyes on the boat as it escaped down the river. Then, as if struck by a missile, the boat exploded into flames. The inferno engulfed it before they heard the thunder, a hundred times louder than the rifle shot. A hot wind blew against their faces.

First the gas tanks, then the propane tanks, one explosion after another. Within seconds the only remains of Feron's houseboat were shreds smoking on the water. They watched without speaking, their minds casting about as they processed the knowledge that The Ferret was finally gone for good.

Jodi lowered the rifle slowly and slipped her arm around Kent's waist. In a tone that mixed satisfaction with disbelief, she said, "The damn fool stored his gas cans right close to the engine."

Lute stared out at the floating debris field. "The river will take care of the rest."

EPILOGUE

Fall, four months later

IT WAS A PERFECT MORNING. TO THE EAST THE
*sun was on the horizon sending an explosion of red and gold into the
sky. The air held the scent of a promising day.* Two canoes paddled near
the bridge that crossed the Chittenango River. Kent and Merrill were
in one, Lute and Barry were in the other.

Kent let the current ease their boat past the sandbar and Merrill
cast his line to it.

"I never really thanked you," Kent said.

"For what?"

"For hiding Wren."

Merrill shrugged. "Hey, what they don't know won't hurt them."
His mind rolled back to that day. "I got to Feron's truck first, recognized
the little girl among the others, and stuffed her in my car before any
other cops showed up. We just got lucky."

"You stuck your neck out—big time. I know that. If they'd found
out you did that, it would have ended your career."

"Ehh, that's what brothers are for."

"I owe you."

"I'll take a rain check."

"You made Jodi whole again. She's like a new person."

"I'm telling you, Jodi isn't the only one who is whole again. Look at you!" Merrill cast his eyes toward the heavens. "Saints be praised. The old Kent is back. Finally!"

Kent would never have said it in so many words, but it was true, he felt it, too. He was finally back. "It feels good."

"I bet it does. But as far as I'm concerned, the best part about the whole thing is that public records like birth and death certificates are so messed up on the Rez that the authorities will never figure it out. It's sad that Wren's real mother died, but we're the only ones who know that she was Wren's mother. Officially, nothing is known about the woman. The fellas in Atlanta and at the border reported that they weren't even able to find any family to claim her body. So, it's unlikely any relatives will come looking for Wren. The case of the missing Korean baby will go unsolved. Wren takes over Jodi's daughter's identity, and that's that, no one's the wiser. The risk was worth it."

They fished a while longer, until Kent said, "We've got enough fish. Let's head in."

They met up with Lute and Barry on the water.

"How did you guys do?" Barry asked.

"We got a few," Merrill replied, playing his cards close to his vest.

"Remember, we're going to need fish for the girls, too."

"We've got that covered."

"Ooh, sounds like you hit 'em pretty good."

They took a few strokes in silence. Then Barry rested his paddle across the gunwales. "Aren't you going to ask us how we did?"

Merrill chuckled to Kent. "I knew he'd crack."

"Skippy, I've got to teach you the fine art of being cagey," Lute grumbled.

Barry held up his creel and tipped it toward Kent and Merrill. "We caught a few, too.

"I don't see anything worth bragging about in there," Kent said, craning his neck in exaggerated inspection.

"Lute had a monster on," Barry said, "but…"

Lute cut him off sharply. "They don't need to hear about that."

"He decided to practice catch and release." That got the others' attention. They knew for sure that wasn't true.

Embellishing in true fisherman style, Barry said, "Oh, yeah. This big old trout rolled up behind Lute's fly and took it. Nearly broke his rod. I thought he was going to pull Lute out of the boat. Lute's playing the fish for all he's worth, saying stuff to me like, 'See kid, this is how it's done,' and 'We're going to need a bigger net.' All of the sudden I hear him say, 'Oh, shit!' I look over and his reel is in his lap. It fell off his rod!"

"It could happen to anybody," Lute deadpanned.

The others were laughing now.

"So he's trying to bring this fish in hand over hand—no reel. I wish I'd had a camera. He's all tangled up. The fish is on the line jumping and flopping."

Lute pulled off his hat and studied it like he'd never see it before. "It wasn't that funny."

More laughter.

"Then the fish makes a gigantic leap, I think just so Lute could see how big he was, dives and—snap—he's gone. He left Lute sitting there with his reel in his lap and his mouth open."

Three guys roared and a flicker of a smile even crossed Lute's face.

"I'm going to remember that look for a long time," Barry added.

"Good thing we caught a bunch," Merrill said, still laughing.

No one spoke for a while as they replayed Lute's moment with the big fish. After enough time, Barry drawled mysteriously, "He did eventually redeem himself."

Kent and Merrill looked over, confused.

Barry let them wonder a moment for dramatic effect, then reached down and, with two hands, raised up the biggest brown trout Kent had ever seen taken from the river. "He kept his rod and reel together for this one."

Lute smiled ear to ear. "I apologize, Skippy. I guess you *are* pretty cagey."

They were still batting around the fish stories when they got to shore. Jodi, standing in the sun, was there to meet them. Lucinda, Otsi, and Max circled at her feet. She was radiant even in her flannel shirt and capris.

"I'm hearing a lot of laughing going on out there for guys who were supposed to be catching our breakfast."

"Have no fear," Lute said, his voice like a revival preacher, "the river has provided."

"Good thing. Emily and I are starving. We've got coffee and corn muffins ready to go."

She tugged the bow of each canoe onto shore, then looked past Merrill and extended her hand to Kent, helping him out of the canoe. Their eyes met and held for a second. He squeezed her hand.

"He gets all of the attention," Merrill grumbled to Barry and Lute.

"Nope," Jodi said. She turned to Merrill and gave him a ferocious hug. "I will never be able to thank you enough for what you did."

Merrill, redfaced, hugged her back. "I know nothing about anything."

She hugged him harder.

"Where is Wren?" Kent asked when he noticed that she was not at Jodi's side.

Jodi thumbed over her shoulder toward their campfire. "Emily brought the pups."

The second Emily caught sight of Lute, she stopped her breakfast prep and charged to him. She threw her arms around him, just as Jodi had done to Merrill. "He's doing great."

Lute played dumb. "Who?"

"Sim, of course. I rode him over a few low rails yesterday. It looks like his leg will be one hundred percent."

"I know it will," Lute said with a dismissive wave.

Kent cleared his throat. "I'm going to say it again, Lute, I owe you an apology for how I acted when you offered to treat Sim. I know now that I was wrong. You saved his life."

Lute shrugged his big shoulders. "Friends are allowed to have differences."

He extended his hand and Kent grabbed it in a white-knuckle handshake.

For the nth time Kent asked, "Are you going to tell me how you did it?"

"Maybe. One of these days."

They cleaned the fish while the older dogs watched, and the four pups got in the way. Otsi was using his leg more and more every day. Lucinda looked like a tired mom, ready to be done with the little ones that nagged her constantly but really didn't need her anymore.

Barry gently pushed the pups out of the way as they worked. "I still can't believe it. We run every test possible, try every hormone known to man, and still, no luck—Lucinda doesn't come into heat. We figure it's hopeless and give up—out of the blue, she gets pregnant. Go figure."

Lute poked Kent in the ribs with his elbow. "Otsi is smarter than any veterinarian."

Kent suddenly got interested in *his* hat.

Barry cringed. "I'm not getting in the middle of that again. What I'm saying is four pups is a nice-size litter. Too bad that one's a runt." He pointed at the pup that was a quarter the size of the others.

Kent flashed Lute and Merrill a the-boy's-got-a-lot – to-learn look, and they nodded agreement. Over his shoulder, to Barry, he said, "Who says that one is a runt?"

Barry shrugged. "He's stunted."

"He's not stunted," Kent snapped. "He's small. There's a difference. He's strong and healthy."

Barry nodded agreement. "True."

"The three big ones are spitting images of Otsi, correct?"

"For sure."

Kent reached down and picked up the little pup in question—black and tan, oversize erect ears, fiery eyes.

Kent, Merrill, and Lute watched Barry waiting for the lightbulb to come on. When it did, Barry drew out the name, "Maaaax?"

All eyes turned to the Chihuahua. He was sitting between the two hounds, a sly smile on his face.

Barry pressed his palms to his forehead. "Oh my god, that pup is a Chi-bone!"

It took the others a moment.

"He's half Chihuahua and half redbone hound," Barry explained.

"You're weird" came from Emily. The others just laughed.

Lute nudged him. "Come on, Skippy. I'll show you how to cook fish over a fire before you start asking too many questions."

Lute grabbed a skillet and a tin from the cook box and moved to the fire. With a stick, he arranged a bed of coals and set the skillet over them. With his knife, he dug out a huge glob of soft white fat and dropped it into the skillet.

"Is that bear fat?" Barry asked, hoping to tap into Lute's primitive ways.

"Crisco," Lute said. "You can get it at Walmart."

Barry cursed himself. "When am I going to learn?"

Lute fried up fish after fish and handed them out to waiting plates. Before long, they were all feasting.

When he couldn't hold another bite, Kent leaned back against Jimmy Silverheel's tree stump. He took Jodi's hand. His voice reached back, recalling the events of the last few months. "It all started right here. Jimmy, Pegger, Feron—all gone."

Jodi's eyes drifted toward the river, and her shoulders sagged. "Pegger."

"We all miss him."

"I will always miss my son. But what really hurts is knowing that he was part of Feron's smuggling operation. How could he do that?" She choked on the words. "He actually killed a man."

"Life got away from him. He got tired of seeing everyone else with more than he had."

"That's no excuse."

"It's an explanation."

Jodi shook her head slowly. "I don't know that I'll live long enough to understand it."

Lute, who had been listening, said, "Pegger was more good than bad."

The lines on Jodi's brow creased, and she gave her brother a doubtful look.

"He was, Jodi. I knew him like a son. He had a good heart and he worked hard to protect the Owahgena."

"I don't know. I'll always love my son, but I don't know."

They sat quietly for a while reflecting and listening to the sounds of nature.

Otsi drifted over to Lute. Lute offered him a bit of fish and Otsi took it from his fingers. "Pegger was complicated. On the one hand, he wanted Northern Lights as a base for smuggling, and on the other, he fought their efforts to desecrate the river. He is a big part of the reason we have the river back. Pegger was on Northern Lights from the beginning. He was dead set on finding a way to stop them."

"Turns out he did," Merrill said. "Pegger figured out that Balt and his investors were so eager to get underway that they broke ground before they had clear title to the land. You have to love those fuzzy records. Feron's father got the land in the thirties in some sort of a hand-shake deal—the land for a truck, apparently, and some furs. Nobody is really sure. The Ferret got it when the old man died. Which nobody seemed to have noticed. No will, no record of probate, no nothing. That turned out to be just the roadblock we needed."

Lute scraped his plate into the fire. "They got what they deserved. They were so damn confident they could work out that little wrinkle. After all, they were just dealing with a bunch of dumb Indians. Pegger showed them. I just wish he could see how all his work came together and paid off. Plus, after all of the bad press—the shootings, the rumors of smuggling—the Northern Lights guys couldn't get out of town fast enough."

Merrill chuckled. "Balt and his boys were so eager to save face that *they* recommended that the land go over to the Rez."

"Let's hope it does," Jodi said.

There was another quiet moment, then Emily began collecting dishes. "Barry and I have cleanup."

Barry scowled at her. "Would you please not volunteer me?" But he began picking up, too. He looked over at Merrill and Lute, who were lounging like two snakes after a meal. "What about you guys?"

"We're supervising," Lute said. Merrill confirmed it with a wave.

Barry shook his head. "Must be nice."

"I'll help you guys," Jodi offered, but when she pushed herself up, Kent took her hand.

"They can handle it. Let's take a walk."

Kent and Jodi took the woods path. Lucinda, glad for a few minutes away from the pups, invited herself along. Hand-in-hand, they strolled to the center of the bridge. There was a mist on the water, but it was giving way to the morning sun.

"Black-fly season is finally over," Jodi said.

Kent automatically rubbed his neck, "That's a good thing."

"They'll be back next year."

"I'm sure of that."

His eyes settled on the Northern Lights site in the distance. It was abandoned now, the machinery and job trailers all gone. The weeds were already reclaiming the parking lot. The billboard announcing

The Future Home of Northern Lights Resort was peeling and looked strangely out of place.

As Kent stared at the googly-eyed fish, he could have sworn its expression was different—no longer embarrassed, it looked pleased. It may even have winked.

ABOUT THE AUTHOR

Frank Martorana writes the Kent Stephenson Thriller Series from his home in Cazenovia, New York.

For more information please visit frankmartorana.com.